DEATH
BY A
CORNISH COVE

BOOKS BY FLISS CHESTER

DEATH
BY A
CORNISH COVE

FLISS CHESTER

bookouture

Published by Bookouture in 2023

An imprint of Storyfire Ltd.
Carmelite House
50 Victoria Embankment
London EC4Y 0DZ

www.bookouture.com

ISBN: 978-1-83790-034-3
eBook ISBN: 978-1-83790-033-6

1

LORD AND LADY TREVELYAN INVITE YOU TO A
FANCY-DRESS BALL
AT PENBEAGLE HOUSE, TRELEW, CORNWALL
ON SATURDAY, 6 JUNE 1925, FROM 6 O'CLOCK
CARRIAGES AT MIDNIGHT

The Hon. Cressida Fawcett put her foot on the accelerator pedal of her little nail-polish-red Bugatti, while her best friend Dotty, or more properly Lady Dorothy Chatterton, read their invitation and gamely tried not to wince at the speed. 'Nowhere, and I repeat, nowhere, does it state that we have to come dressed as pirates.'

'Well, tough tootsies, I think we look smashing,' Cressida replied to her friend, taking her eye off the road just long enough to look over to Dotty, whose tricorn hat had now slipped down over her silky chestnut bobbed hair and come to rest on the top ridge of her tortoiseshell-framed spectacles. The invitation to the ball and Lady Trevelyan's letter were gripped in one hand, while the other was holding onto Cressida's little pug, Ruby, making it almost impossible for Dotty to adjust her headwear. Cressida chuckled. 'Those stripes suit you, Dot, and I must say Ruby makes quite the most perfect parrot in that green silk coat.'

'The silk coat isn't the bit she's been grumbling about,' Dotty said, clutching the small dog even tighter as Cressida jammed on the brakes while narrowly avoiding a seagull in the road, 'it's that feathered headdress Maurice made for her that's causing the most snorting and snuffling.'

'She's only looking missish as she can't see how fabulous she looks.' Cressida laughed and took one hand off the steering wheel to pat her pooch, but slightly regretted it as a bend came upon them most unexpectedly. Dotty, her eyes clenched shut, squealed as the car rounded the corner, but Cressida had it back under control in moments. 'There you go, chum, on the straight and narrow again!'

Dotty gulped and nodded, daring to open her eyes to the beautiful countryside of the west of England around them. The vast flat plains of Wiltshire and the gently undulating, gloriously green hillsides of Devon had been and gone and now it was the high-sided hedgerows of Cornwall that greeted them. Glimpses of glittering water teased the two of them every now and again as Cressida, to her mind at least, skilfully steered around the tight bends and narrow lanes that coursed their way along the coastline. The dusty road dipped down into valleys and rose high along ridges.

They were on their way to Penbeagle House in Cornwall, where, due to Cressida's mother being such a chum of Lady Trevelyan, they were invited to stay for a week after the fancy-dress ball. Lord Trevelyan had inherited the fine estate at Penbeagle and a substantial income, however he was also a shrewd businessman and had started a company that imported antiquities and fine arts and crafts from the Far East. With the level of imagination that the English upper classes were so often blessed with, he had named it the Far East Company. Despite the tenanted farmsteads, centuries-old cove-bound cottages and working tin mines that his estate covered, it was from this trade that most of the Trevelyans' wealth now came. And with wealth came parties... and an invitation to Lady Trevelyan's fancy-dress ball had been all that London society had spoken of for the last few weeks.

For Cressida and Dotty, the invitation had been a welcome respite from dwelling on the recent events at Dotty's own family home, Chatterton Court, where a murderer had struck at a party, killing one of their dear family friends before being outed by none other than Cressida herself. As if that hadn't been enough, dear Dotty had also suffered the ignominy of losing her fiancé to another woman. And, although Cressida worried for her heartbroken friend, to her mind, it was good riddance to Basil Bartleby and his philandering ways.

'I just wondered, Cressy, if perhaps I might not have looked more attractive as something like the Lady of Shallot or Guinevere...' Dotty, not blessed with Cressida's more sylphlike figure, pulled the striped tunic out a little to evaluate the stripes, '... not Red Beard the pirate.'

'You look a treat as always, Dotty. Sure to catch the eye of some brigand or braggart.'

Dotty sighed. 'That's the last thing I want right now, another b—'

'Well, quite. Good thing then that some proper corkers of husband potential are going to be there tonight.'

'Oh?' Dotty perked up, and Ruby, on her lap, snorted in anticipation. 'Who?'

'Patrick Trevelyan, of course, Lord and Lady T's son. He's a bit of a wet fish but set to inherit Penbeagle House and all that.'

'I've met him,' Dotty replied. 'Limpest handshake in London. He seemed awfully fond of horticulture, and I can't say he set my heart ablaze with his talk of hydrangeas and hyacinths.'

'Noted. So, if he's not your cup of lapsang souchong, then how about Sir Jolyon Westmoreland?'

'Isn't he about fifty?' Dotty looked disgusted and Ruby snorted in sympathy.

Cressida laughed again. She was uninterested in finding a husband for herself, though her dear mama was always on the lookout for her. 'I thought an older husband would be ideal, Dot?' She grinned. 'He'd die many years before you, leaving you disgustingly wealthy, not to mention his prized collection of saucy photographs, or whatever men his age collect...'

'If I wasn't holding your precious pooch, and you weren't driving, I'd fling this tricorn hat at you!' Dotty laughed.

'Ah, well don't you worry, there will be a whole ballroom of young men there tonight, some of whom may not be dressed as pirates even. I'm sure we'll find you someone to swoon over before the night is out.'

'And you, Cressy?' Dot knew Cressida's views on marriage but couldn't help ribbing her. 'Do you think one of those young men might actually turn your head? My brother Alfred will be there, and I know he's terribly fond of you...'

'Pfft.' Cressida kept her eyes on the road but shook her head. 'As much as I respect your dear brother, you know there's nothing I cherish more in this world than my independence. Except perhaps Ruby. And this car. And maybe you, Dotty dear.'

'Fourth... Not so bad.' Dotty giggled.

'And anyway, I've got quite a separate mission at Penbeagle. Lady T has heard about my love of interior decorating—'

'Love of?' Dotty interrupted her. 'You've got the best eye for colours and chintzes and whatnot of anyone I know.'

'That's awfully kind of you to say Dotty.' Cressida grinned, though she kept her eyes on the road. 'Anyway, Lady T wants me to have a nosey at something.'

'Oh yes, the boathouse...' Dotty found Lady Trevelyan's

letter that came with the invitation. '"Do come and stay and see if you can come up with some ideas for the old boathouse, dear girl, it's in dire need of some refurbishments and I'm at a loss..." Yes, sounds like you'll have more to do than sunbathe by the sea and catch the odd sardine.'

'Thank heavens for that!' Cressida laughed. And with that, and the knowledge setting in that they might be unforgivably late, Cressida gunned her red Bugatti faster down the ever-narrowing lanes towards Penbeagle House.

Penbeagle House stood glorious and elegant at the end of its long drive. It was a solid stone affair built in a classical style in the early 1700s. In front of it a long, sloping grassy lawn separated it from the jagged rocks that had been the nemesis of sailors and smugglers along that coastline for generations. But as Cressida had sped along the driveway she'd spied between those rough outcrops of dangerous rocks a gently curving cove with tantalising, sparkling water lapping at its sandy beach. A jetty and the boathouse sheltered there, looking idyllic in the golden glow of the early evening sun.

'What a spot,' Dotty exclaimed as she and Cressida hopped out of the car and stretched themselves, taking deep breaths of the fresh sea air.

Ruby, who was still unsure of her feathered headdress, gave herself a good shake and sat down to scratch behind her ear, releasing a flurry of little green feathers.

'Oh Rubes, you'll be a bald eagle rather than a parrot if you carry on like that.' Cressida shook her head.

A footman came forward and greeted them, and Cressida gave him the keys to the car.

'Just follow your nose around the pathway there, miss, and you'll see the way through.'

'Thank you.' Cressida smiled. 'Oh, and excuse me, but could you tell me how many pirates there are here?'

Without missing a beat, the footman replied, 'Plenty, miss. Of all persuasions. And smugglers, miss. As well as fishermen, mermaids and seahorses, miss.'

'Of course.' Cressida shook her head, laughing. 'What else would there be at an English country house party? Thank you!' Cressida turned to Dotty, who looked rather put out. 'What is it, chum?' Cressida asked, confused. 'Plenty of pirates here, you see. We'll fit in splendidly.'

Dotty sighed, running the toe of her buckled black shoe across the gravel of the drive. 'Mermaid. Now *that* would have been pretty.'

'Come on, Dot.' Cressida put her arm around her, careful to avoid dislodging the papier mâché parrot on her shoulder. 'Let's get inside. Where I promise you, you'll be the prettiest pirate that anyone ever saw.'

Dotty pushed her glasses up her nose and nodded her head. 'Heave-ho then, Cressy, lead on.' There were candle flares along the edge of the lawn, guiding partygoers down paths towards the water and across the gardens.

'Ready, Dot?' Cressida reached for her fellow pirate's hand.

'Ready, Cressy.' Dotty nodded, and with Ruby padding along, feathers floating off behind her in the light breeze of the evening, they headed for the orangery, from where the sounds of a hundred voices chattering, glasses clinking and a jazz band in full flow emanated.

Fun would be had tonight, that was for sure. Though she'd thought the same thing as she'd driven to Chatterton Court a few weeks ago... She shook her head. *There's no reason at all to think that this party will end in murder*, Cressida thought to herself sternly. But a few hairs prickled at the back of her neck, and she shivered the feeling off. *Why, that's just the sea breeze, surely?*

2

'Cressida Fawcett as I live and breathe!' Alfred, Viscount Delafield, Cressida's friend – and Dotty's brother – greeted them as they walked in. 'And hallo, Dot. Made it down in one piece?'

'Are you suggesting my driving leaves something to be desired, Alfred?' Cressida asked him, her hand resting against her papier mâché cutlass.

Alfred laughed and ran a hand through his chestnut hair. He leaned in and kissed his sister on the cheek and, much to Cressida's blushes, kissed her too. Despite her feelings on independence and marriage, she did have a soft spot for Alfred, with his dark, conker-brown eyes and kind demeanour. As the eldest son of Dotty's father, Lord Chatterton, who was an earl, he was a viscount and confusingly titled Lord Delafield, which was one of Lord Chatterton's subsidiary titles. To Cressida, though, he was just plain Alfred. And he looked astonishing.

'And what *are* you wearing, Alfred?'

'I'm an aardvark. Can't you tell?"

'An aardvark?' Cressida looked at him critically. He was

wearing grey tights and a similarly coloured woollen jumper that thankfully fell well below his waist, and on his back were crescent-shaped pieces of cardboard, each painted grey too.

'Yes. Ran out of inspiration and hit the encyclopaedia. First animal I got to that I recognised. Well, sort of recognised. Anyway, what are you two? Burglars?'

Cressida resisted the urge to kick him in the shin. 'We're pirates. This is Cornwall after all. Home of smugglers and marauders.'

Alfred chuckled. 'Speaking of marauders, I best stop hogging you here at the door. Algernon is shaking up some cocktails and the band are playing some cracking numbers.'

'Lead on then, Alfred!' Cressida scooped up Ruby and she and Dotty followed him.

Dainty lights were strung up all around the glass ceiling and they twinkled as the sun started to dip down over the horizon. The footman had been right, there were pirates aplenty, mingling with cats, harlequins, Tudor monarchs and racing drivers. Cleopatra danced with a medieval knight, both whipping their knees up and flinging their arms around as the muted trumpet gave a vigorous solo.

Cressida laughed as Alfred dragged his sister onto the dancefloor, glad that he too realised Dotty needed cheering up after the Basil fiasco. She waved them off, noticing that Lord and Lady Trevelyan's son Patrick was doing his best to Charleston while dressed as a tree. She chuckled to herself as she and Ruby found the bar. In a trice she'd been handed a strong-looking cocktail from a nice chap called Algernon Effingham-Gore, one of their social set, who had installed himself as bartender.

'What ho, Cressida,' Algernon said, pouring another exceptionally large measure for the guest next to her.

'What ho, Algie. Finally found a job?' Algernon was always complaining of his impecunity, due to his father having halved his allowance after a wild night that had ended with Algernon and the daughter of Lord Pirbright in the alpaca enclosure at the Regent's Park zoo.

'You know what they say, Cressy old thing, when life gives you lemons...'

'Make a darn fine lemon drop!' Cressida toasted her friend with his rather elegant concoction garnished with a curl of citrus peel.

'Exactly. Anyway, how are you? I haven't seen you since that night the chef at Claridge's chased us down Brook Street with his—'

Cressida was saved from Algernon's reminiscences of their exploits as a tall man dressed as a chicken asked for a rather complicated round of drinks and she merged back into the crowd, greeting old friends and meeting new ones. She was generally having an utterly blissful time when a familiar face caught her eye. Among the bright eyes and wide grins, she saw the curly red hair and horn-rimmed spectacles of Randolph, Lord Canterbury – and he was walking towards her.

'Ah,' Cressida said as she squeezed Ruby tight to her. Ruby, haloed by bright green feathers, her sequinned silk coat ripped slightly at the seams; Ruby, one of Cressida's many reasons for feeling like she didn't need a man in her life; Ruby... who had been a surprise gift from the very same Lord Canterbury who was now right in front of her, on the occasion of his proposal of marriage to her the previous year. The pair had been thrown together in society last summer and she'd attended a few exhibitions and lectures with him and gone to several dances. Then, out of the blue, he'd popped the question. She had declined the offer, but gleefully kept the pug.

'Evening, old thing,' Randolph said, and Cressida thought she could detect a slight slur to his words. She couldn't blame him; if Algernon had been doling out the drinks all night, it was surprising anyone was still standing at all. In a flash, however, all of her objections to marrying Randolph, objections that she'd had to repeat endlessly to her frustrated mother, came back. It wasn't just because this lauded Egyptologist would have whisked her off to Cairo, where her shingled bob would have frizzed up in no time at all, or that he had a violent dislike for lobster, absolutely no interest in motorcars, and an appalling lack of coordination on the dance floor. All of those things could have been outweighed by his brilliant brain and, of course, his ability to magic puppies out of seemingly nowhere. No, there just hadn't been enough reasons to entice her to abandon her independence, curtail her own freedom and give in to the holy state of matrimony. That and the fact that, whichever way you cut the mustard, as nice a man as he was, she just didn't fancy him.

'Hello, Randolph.' Cressida gulped as he stood there, tall and gangly, and far paler than a man who'd just spent several months in the blistering heat of an Egyptian archaeological dig should look. She tugged at her pirate tunic and composed herself.

'Is this Duchess Incarnadine Rose?' He reached out a hand to touch Ruby, who, at that very moment, sneezed as one of her feathers tickled her nose, and Randolph pulled back, using it as an excuse to take a handkerchief out of his pocket to dab the corners of his mouth. He was dressed tonight, as far as Cressida could see, as himself, being that he was in a khaki-coloured safari suit with a pith helmet on his head.

'Yes, she's called Ruby now. I could never have managed her full pedigree name every time I needed to tell her off.'

'Oh dear, bit of a feisty one?' Randolph asked, smiling and wiping his forehead with his handkerchief.

'Good as gold usually,' Cressida admitted. She paused before continuing. 'How are you, Randolph?'

'Oh you know, scarab here, scarab there. It's all been a bit quiet in the Valley of the Kings since Carnarvon died...'

Randolph paused to wipe his forehead again and was interrupted by the appearance of a beautiful blonde woman who suddenly appeared next to him, a silk turban swathed around her head in a matching colour to her cropped top and voluminous harem pants. She seemed even more worse for wear than Randolph as she stumbled slightly, catching his arm to balance herself.

'What ho, Selly,' Cressida grinned, and leaned over to kiss the cheek of Lord and Lady Trevelyan's daughter.

'Cressida,' she drawled in a languid tone, then took a deep inhale of her cigarette, which she smoked out of a long ivory handle. 'So wonderful to see you.' She paused and looked up into the piercing blue eyes of Randolph. 'Have you met my fiancé, Lord Canterbury?'

'F...fiancé?' Cressida stuttered, noticing for the first time the whopping emerald on Selina's ring finger. 'Y...es, we know each other.'

'From London,' Canterbury interjected. 'Royal Society meetings.'

Cressida nodded. She, Selina and Dotty had all been debutantes together in London a few seasons ago and were some of the only young ladies left of their acquaintance who hadn't married yet, much to all of their mamas' grumblings. Selina had been quite the hit during their debutante balls, but there had been rumours about her being caught in a clinch in a cloakroom at The Savoy with Percival Smythson-Fiennes and she'd been packed off back down here to Cornwall by her parents. How she'd had the chance to meet and be courted by someone so rarely in the country, while she was mostly down in this Cornish cove, and not even in London much anymore, was a mystery to Cressida.

'Oh, you're into the mummies and tombs thing too, are you?' Selina asked, then sucked on the long pipe of her cigarette holder, her eyes refocusing somewhere in the middle distance.

For the umpteenth time, Cressida wondered what Algernon was putting into the drinks tonight. Just as she was about to answer Selina, they were joined by their hostess, who, like her daughter, was swathed in lilac silk.

'Cressida, darling, how is your mother?' Lady Trevelyan leaned in and kissed Cressida, ignoring the snuffle from Ruby, who was momentarily pressed between them in a cloud of Moroccan Rose perfume.

'Same as ever, Lady Trevelyan. She asked the gardener to put my old iron bedstead in a herbaceous border and grow hollyhocks around it. She's calling it her *flower bed*.'

'Of course she is, mad as a badger your dear mother. But I'm so pleased she could spare you for a week. You must make yourself at home, dear... Then you must help me get some sort of design on paper for the boathouse. Something to celebrate our trade in the east. Something... Oh, ooops, let's talk about it later, it looks like a conga line has just started up!' Lady Trevelyan was nudged out of the way by a man dressed like a bunch of grapes, who Cressida briefly recognised as the Prime Minister, and laughingly merged into the hip-swaying, leg-kicking dance.

Cressida was tempted to join in, as it wasn't often, even in Cressida's elevated circles, that one got to conga with the Prime Minister, but she had rather a craving for another extraordinarily strong cocktail. Randolph Canterbury and Selina Trevelyan engaged! 'If there was a time when I needed a drink, Rubes...' she whispered, her words muffled by the remaining feathers of the small dog's costume.

Cressida found a space at the bar and, letting Ruby scarper off in the direction of a dropped cocktail sausage, waved a hand at Algernon who had an ice-cold Martini in front of her in no time at all. Taking a huge slurp, Cressida scanned across the party, trying to find Dotty or Alfred. She spotted the tricorn hat and strange scaled animal the other side of the room, so, with a precautionary extra sip to help prevent spillage, she started to weave her way through the crush to find them.

'I say...' 'Sorry, pardon me!' 'Excuse us!' Voices all around her moved through the crowd and like them, Cressida excused and pardoned herself as she weaved among them. She heard one voice in particular above the general melee and what he was saying caught her attention.

'Terrible blunder with the British Museum, don't you remember? Cost his client an arm and a leg with import duty and faffing around with hauliers.' Cressida recognised the deep resonance of Sir Jolyon Westmoreland, the very same fifty-year-old, complete with bald head and vast stomach, who Dotty had understandably turned her nose up at on the journey down. She listened as he continued. '... not to mention that mess in Egypt at the moment with the closure of Tutankhamun's tomb. Edgar, I do believe I'd be a better man for your ongoing projects. I've been importing antiquities since God was a boy.'

Edgar? Cressida, her interest already piqued by the conversation, subtly turned in order to confirm her suspicions. Sir Jolyon, dressed as a Roman emperor, was talking to Lord Trevelyan, himself dressed as a sultan. Without wanting to draw attention to the fact that she was eavesdropping, Cressida tilted her head and looked the other way, but listened as she nonchalantly sipped her cocktail.

'... all excellent points, Jo, but of course with the engagement...'

Another virtuoso saxophone solo drowned out their voices and Cressida, pondering what any of that meant, was nudged on by the crowd, thankfully in the direction of her friends.

'What ho, Cressy,' the aardvark formerly known as Alfred greeted her, while Dotty beamed up at her, her face flushed and her papier mâché parrot now quite askew. They were standing with two other people and Dotty was quick to introduce her.

'Cressy, have you met Sebastian Goodricke before?' Dotty gestured towards the rather handsome, blue-eyed, strawberry-blond man dressed as a Victorian industrialist, who was gulping down a glass of champagne.

'Hello, Sebastian, Cressida Fawcett.'

He nodded and then turned to what looked like a ladybird next to him. 'And this is Miss Catherine Bly.'

'Hello, Miss Bly.' Cressida smiled at the small bug, but her vermillion lips, as red as her cardboard carapace, stayed puckered and taut.

'Don't think this little distraction means we can change the subject,' the ladybird snapped. 'You can't ignore me now just because Miss Fawcett has turned up.'

Sebastian heaved a sigh. 'I'm not ignoring you, Catherine, I just can't see what I can do about it.'

Cressida was somewhat at a loss as to what they were talking about, though it seemed clear she had arrived in the middle of a squabble.

'You work in the Foreign Office, you can jolly well get the Foreign Secretary on to it.' Catherine continued. 'These digs need proper press coverage. How could Mrs Jones of Abergavenny find out about the wonders of Egypt if Lord Canterbury is only letting his cronies at *The Times* get the scoop? As a journalist, I find it intolerable that I'm barred from the site. Intolerable.' Her antennae wobbled furiously.

'Catherine, heaven knows I have no particular regard for Lord Canterbury, but I just don't think the Foreign Office has any sway over the matter.'

'Some of us have to work for a living,' Catherine continued. Cressida glanced across at Dotty, who had started to edge away. '... And the finds in the Valley of the Kings are the scoop of the century!'

Dotty, now stealthily far enough away to do so, beckoned Cressida and Alfred over and once the crowd had filled the gap, she shook her head and puffed out her cheeks.

'Blimey, she's quite a bluestocking.' Dotty reached over and took Cressida's Martini from her and gulped back a fortifying glug.

'Nothing wrong with being an intellectual, Dot, you of all people with your love of books should know that.' Cressida took her glass back and sipped from it too. Algernon really did make a darn fine Martini. 'But I know what you mean, she was het up about something all right.'

'Too right,' Alfred said, pulling his arm free from a stray cardboard scale. 'Seems Canterbury had had a word in Howard Carter's ear – you know that archaeologist chap who found the tomb of that pharaoh – and had her banned from all the digs last year. Not only that, he's apparently given some chap at *The Times* the exclusive rights to wire home about all of his finds, so that's what's really cooking her goose, I think.'

Cressida puffed out her cheeks. 'I can understand why. Anyway, as interesting as all that is, you'll never guess what I just found out.'

'Ooh, do tell?' Dotty leaned in.

Cressida was about to fill in her friends on Randolph Canterbury and Selina Trevelyan's engagement when the big band music stopped and the conversations and chatter around them faded out as the sound of a gong reverberated around the room. As its echoes disappeared, Lord Trevelyan appeared on the stage, with his wife, daughter and Lord Canterbury next to him, and cleared his throat.

'Friends, welcome to Penbeagle House and to our fancy-dress ball.' There was a cheer from the guests, followed by a good-humoured stamping of feet and applause. Lord Trevelyan looked gratifyingly out at the assembled guests and, with the bearing of a benevolent headmaster, shushed them all again.

'Thank you, thank you. There's always great debate around these parts as to what Penbeagle means, some say it's old Cornish for a big dog, but I say it's modern Cornish for a big party...' Another cheer went up from the crowd. 'And although society never needs an excuse for a party, it's my great pleasure to say that tonight we really do have one.'

Cressida sipped her Martini. Dotty was saying something about wanting to look up that old Cornish meaning in the library, but Cressida wasn't listening. She didn't care a jot for marriage itself, and Randolph had not persuaded her otherwise, but she still felt in some way slighted. Cressida was not a cruel woman and wouldn't have wanted Randolph to stay a bachelor forever, but a tiny part of her would have been gratified if he'd waited just a little longer and not already found his way into the affections of one her friends.

She took another sip and looked up at the man who by now could have been her husband, and she, at the grand old age of twenty-four, Lady Cressida Canterbury. He was mopping his brow again with his handkerchief and she could see that his hand was shaking. In fact, his whole arm was shaking and he looked decidedly green around the gills. Lord Trevelyan, however, was still talking.

'... A gentleman has to be very special for a man to give his only daughter over to him in marriage, and Randolph here is a man of honour, a man of integrity and intelligence...'

As Lord Trevelyan spoke, Cressida kept looking at Randolph. He was clutching his stomach now, his face grimacing in pain, and Cressida could hear murmurs all around her. A moment later, the guests gasped as one as Randolph Canterbury doubled over, then crumpled to the ground.

Lord Trevelyan, who'd been obliviously carrying on with his speech, stopped abruptly at the screams. Randolph was now lying on the floor of the orangery, his body spasming as he gulped for breath. The more able of the guests rushed to the ailing man, but within what felt like seconds, Cressida could see them shaking their heads.

A hush fell over the crowd, as Cressida saw a man dressed like Napoleon softly close Randolph's eyelids. Standing slowly, Napoleon's voice rose above the panic as he said the words Cressida dreaded most.

'He's dead.'

3

'Oh, Randolph!' Cressida's hand flew up to her mouth as she stood in shock at the scene before her. There were calls for any doctors at the party to come quickly and space was made around the stricken Egyptologist, but Cressida knew in the pit of her stomach that it was too late. Randolph was gone.

'Cressy.' Dotty was at her elbow, holding Ruby, who Cressida took one look at and burst into tears. She handed Dot her Martini glass, now drained of all its strength-giving liquor, and scooped her pup up and buried her head in the soft rolls of fur-covered podge. 'Oh, Cressy. I didn't realise you were so fond of him.'

'I'm not, I mean, I wasn't... It's just...' Cressida found it hard to put into words quite why she was feeling so upset, but Dotty, who had an unnerving knack at times of being able to read Cressida's mind, tried to comfort her.

'Sometimes things just are what they are, aren't they? You don't need to explain it to me.'

'I can't even explain it to myself, Dot.' Cressida wiped her eyes. 'I suppose it's the shock.'

'I'm glad I'm too short to have seen anything.' Dotty shuddered. 'I'm sorry you had to, Cressy. It must have been ghastly.'

Dotty rubbed Cressida's arm until her friendly aardvark of a brother was able to get close to them and ask how they were. He noticed Cressida's tears almost immediately.

'Cressida, old thing, I didn't realise...' Alfred said, his usual cheeriness nowhere in sight. 'Are you all right?'

It was all Cressida could do to both shake and nod her head simultaneously, trying to convince her friends that she would be quite fine.

At last, with a deep breath, she was able to collect her thoughts. 'Thank you both, I'm hunky-dory, I promise. It's just... he was a good man...' Ruby snorted and a green feather floated away from her nose. 'I would never have wanted to marry him, of course, but Lord Trevelyan was right, he was a good man and hugely intelligent. And I don't think it's fair that he's died so suddenly. I may not have found a place in my heart for him, but he certainly had a good one, and for it to give out like that...'

'Poor chap,' Alfred said, peering over some of the guests' heads to where the body lay on the ground, now covered by the purple cloak from Sir Jolyon Westmoreland's Roman emperor costume. 'To just keel over like that.' He shook his head.

'Serves him right.' The voice wafted past, and, as one, Cressida, Dotty and Alfred looked to see who it was. The ladybird was talking to Napoleon and his wife, a rather pinch-faced Josephine, who was nodding in agreement just a few yards away.

'How could they?' Alfred looked bemused and placed a hand on Cressida's arm as she made a move to go towards the disrespectful guests.

'It's all right, Alfred, I'm just going closer to listen. I won't thump them.' She brushed his hand away and passed Ruby back to Dotty, who took her turn to bury her face into the warm rolls of the pup's fur.

As Cressida inched closer, she could hear more of the conversation.

'He was bound to come a cropper with all his trades and deals. You know, Celia, I wouldn't be surprised if it was some curse of a pharaoh wrought upon him.' Catherine Bly wasn't holding back.

'Yes, Catherine, but to die here at Penbeagle House? To bring that sort of scandal to our perfectly nice village. It doesn't bear thinking about that those gentlemen of the press will be pushing their inky noses into our business,' Josephine, who was obviously called Celia in real life, replied.

Napoleon merely nodded as the ladybird, Catherine, loaded more insults onto the dead man. 'Egyptologist, my thorax. If he was in it purely for the academia, he'd have let me in to interview him and write about the dig. I bet he studied the ledgers more than the hieroglyphs and made a pretty penny on every antiquity he carted back, not to mention backhanders from his friends on Fleet Street. Hateful man.'

'Trevelyan obviously felt he'd be a good fit for the Far East Company,' Napoleon added.

'Oh, and I'm sure he'd make himself a pretty penny there too. Well, if Edgar wanted to bring a man who didn't believe in the freedom of the press into the company, the family even, then more fool him for it. Believe you me, Edgar knew my mind on it.'

'And I for one am surprised Edgar doesn't pay you higher regard, Catherine dear,' Celia replied. 'Top-notch brain like yours. It should be you the family are promoting. You could write some brilliant articles on all sorts of subjects.'

'Yes, if only I was given the chance...'

Worried she might end up doing something society might have talked about for many years to come, Cressida turned away and walked back to her friends. *So Randolph had been set to join the Far East Company,* she pondered. *Explains how he and Selina met, I suppose...* She was about to fill Dotty and Alfred in on it all, but as soon as she saw their faces, both drained of colour and pale beneath their chestnut hair, she knew there must have been a further development.

'What is it, you two? What's happened?' Cressida asked, looking from one to the other.

Alfred spoke for them both. 'Selina's collapsed now too, though they think it's just a faint. The doctor's with her.'

'Must have been the shock.' Cressida looked around her. The once jam-packed orangery was now almost devoid of all guests, with just a few still standing around the body of Randolph and those still left on other corners of the room putting on evening coats and capes. 'And where is everybody? The place is as empty as a hat shop on the first day of Ascot.'

'The Prime Minister didn't stick around either.' Dotty followed Cressida's train of thought. 'It must be most undignified, squeezing yourself into your car dressed as a bunch of grapes.'

The three of them stood in silence for a little while, watching the last of the guests leave. Lord Randolph Canterbury, famed Egyptologist, upstanding member of the Royal Society, giver of pugs, was dead, gone in his prime, finished at the peak of his success. As was the fancy-dress ball, with barely anyone left now in the pretty glass orangery, its dainty lights still twinkling but the big band no longer playing and instead packing their instruments away as silently and respectfully as possible only a few feet away from the cloak-covered dead body.

Cressida was relieved that obviously not everyone felt the same way as Catherine Bly did about Lord Canterbury and there were some genuine tears and shocked faces among the remaining guests. Lord and Lady Trevelyan must have been with Selina, as neither of them were still there. Napoleon and

Josephine were hovering by the door and Cressida saw how they shook hands with departing guests before waving to a man who looked like a chauffeur on the terrace and themselves slipping off into the night.

Cressida looked around the room, her arms now wrapped around her as a cool breeze came in through the open doors straight up from the cove. With so few people left in the glass-walled room, it had become quite chilly. And the temperature seemed to drop a degree or two more as mortuary assistants came with a stretcher.

'Come on, you two,' Alfred said protectively of his sister and Cressida. 'There's nothing we can do here. Let's find a stiff drink or three in the drawing room before you both catch cold.'

Cressida managed a thin smile, but as she watched the deft movements of the well-practised mortuary assistants lift the lifeless body of Randolph Canterbury onto the stretcher and bear him away, she felt those little hairs on the back of her neck prick once more and shivered as she silently bid goodbye to Lord Canterbury one last time.

4

Cressida stood quietly looking out of one of the vast sash windows in the drawing room. In daylight, one would be able to see across the lawns, where garden parties could be held, and down to the cove and boathouse, where paddling in the frothing shallows could be enjoyed and boating expeditions launched. But now, with only the moon to illuminate the landscape and the candle flares all but burnt out, there was nothing but a sea of blackness before the silvery reflections of the moon on the water.

Alfred touched her on the shoulder and offered her a glass of some deep amber-coloured spirit. She smiled and turned back into the room, attempting to ease her racing mind with a calm analysis of the decor. She cast her eyes up to the high ceiling with its gesso decoration creeping out from the cornicing. The walls were lined with rose-coloured damask silk, no doubt brought back by one of Lord Trevelyan's trading ships, while the fireplace, which was grand and made of stone, was flagged on each side by giant blue and white china vases. On the mantelpiece itself, there were two beautifully lustred bronze Foo dogs, their nostrils flared and their claws gripping the edge of their balls and pedestals. Other ornaments from the Far East filled the room, including screen-printed pastoral scenes and even a whole suit of Japanese Samurai armour. It was an impressive space, and one that reflected the tastes and trades of its owners perfectly. Cressida wondered if this was the look that Lady Trevelyan had been hoping to recreate in the boathouse, but she couldn't bear to dwell on that, not while the image of poor Randolph lying dead on the floor was so fresh in her mind.

She turned to Alfred and Dotty, who were perched on rattan-backed Bergère-style chairs by the fireplace.

'There's something not right about tonight.' She walked towards them, leaving her place by the window.

'There's nothing right about seeing one's friend die right in front of one's very eyes,' Dotty agreed, shivering across her shoulders as she said it.

'It's not just that, Dot. There's something not quite right in how, or why, he died.'

'What makes you say that?' Alfred looked intently at her. 'You're not suggesting he was... well, done away with, are you?'

Cressida sat down on the wicker-backed sofa opposite her friends. Ruby, who had been contentedly snoring on Dotty's lap, got up, plopped to the floor and demanded to be picked up, so Cressida put her tumbler down and pulled the parrotty pug onto her lap.

'I don't know what I'm suggesting, Alfred, but Randolph looked terrible earlier. He was sweaty and kept wiping his brow.'

'Dare I say it, but quite a few of us overexerted ourselves along with that amazing chap on the saxophone, Cressy,' Dotty suggested.

'No, Randolph was a horrendously bad, and therefore infrequent, dancer. He wouldn't have been doing that. And I know it was hot in there tonight, but he's used to the heat. He works in

Egypt, for heaven's sake. And he looked a darn sight paler than a man should who's been under the desert sun.'

'One might look a bit pale and wan if one was about to keel over?' Dotty suggested.

Cressida shook her head as she thought about it. 'I remember Mama chastising me last summer when I turned him down. "Excellent genes those Canterburys," she said, wagging a finger at me.' Cressida sighed at the memory. 'And only last week, Jonty Cunningham-Sloane said that he and Randolph were talking about an expedition to the Rub' al Khali desert in Oman... you wouldn't do that unless you were in peak physical fitness.'

The three of them sat in silence for a moment or two.

It was Alfred who broke the quietude. 'I don't know if you two could see what I could.'

'I couldn't, thank heavens.' Dotty shifted in her seat and pushed her glasses up her nose. 'Benefit of being five foot nothing.'

Cressida smiled at her, though wished she too had been spared the sight of... What was it that Alfred had seen? 'Alfred?' she asked, pulling Ruby closer to her.

'It's just I had quite the vantage, being that bit taller and, well, Randolph looked to be in pain.'

'A heart attack then?' Dotty all but whispered.

'I'm not sure that's how a heart attack goes down. I'm no doctor, but he was gripping his stomach and his face was contorted with pain.'

'Oh Alfred.' Dotty covered her ears, but Cressida looked at him encouragingly.

'No, go on, Alfred. What else did you see?'

'He was grimacing and gulping—'

'For breath?' Dotty asked.

'No,' Cressida answered for Alfred, remembering now what she had seen of those last few moments of Randolph Canterbury's life. 'At least not only for breath. Like he was trying to say something but nothing would come. He was shaking and his hands were trembling—'

'His whole body was too. Then the spasm happened.' Alfred completed Cressida's sentence.

She looked at him, and their eyes locked as they gauged each other's understanding. Alfred nodded and Cressida spoke their minds.

'He was poisoned, wasn't he?'

'Poisoned?' Dotty's voice quivered.

Alfred put a hand on his sister's arm. 'Possibly accidentally. Could have been an allergic reaction.'

Cressida picked her cut-glass tumbler up and swirled the dark brown liquid within it. She hoped that Alfred was right, and that the doctor who'd seen to Selina when she collapsed would confirm it. But the alternative – murder – gnawed at her thoughts. Was it too much of a coincidence that he'd died just moments before his engagement was to be announced? She took a sip and then almost spat the rum out over Ruby's head.

'Blimey.' She held the tumbler out in front of her as if examining it for the first time. 'You'd think the Trevelyans would have better-class stuff than this gut rot.'

'I think it's there for medicinal purposes only,' agreed Alfred, who had started to dismantle his aardvark costume and was placing his scales next to him on the floor.

'I spoke to Selina earlier this evening and she said there was an awful amount of rum smuggling going on round here,' Dotty said, putting her own glass down, having thought better of drinking it now too. Alfred shrugged. 'And rum is just the start of it. Perfume from Paris and cigarettes and whatnot too.'

'I suppose it's in Cornwall's blood. From those days hundreds of years ago when ships would be wrecked along the shoreline and the Crown's soldiers would demand huge taxes on things like spirits and tobacco,' Cressida mused, glad for just a moment to be talking of something other than Randolph's death.

'They still do.' Alfred sighed. 'And, actually, it was Suffolk and Norfolk that had more of a smuggling problem than Cornwall. Closer to France and all that. But the idea of the Cornish smuggler has stuck.'

The three of them fell into silence, the thoughts of the evening penetrating back into their consciousness, however much they tried to put them at bay with small talk.

'I suppose everyone who isn't staying here at Penbeagle has left?' Dotty tried another subject.

'I wonder if the Trevelyans will still want us to stay on?' Alfred looked across at his sister. The Chattertons were old friends with the Trevelyans, much like the Fawcetts were, and Lady Treveylan had insisted on all of them staying for the week, despite their parents being unable to attend. It was all part of the 'season', and despite the young people all having pieds-à-terre in London, no doubt Lord and Lady Chatterton, and Lord and Lady Fawcett, had been relieved to have a week off duty. Trying to marry off one's offspring was well known to be utterly exhausting.

'If Lady T doesn't mind, I'd like to. I can distract myself with ideas for her boathouse.' Cressida, who truly would seek solace in thinking about fabrics and paint colours, omitted the other reason she was keen to stay on; if Randolph had been poisoned, she wanted to find out who had done it, and why.

'I wonder what the locals will make of it?' Alfred asked, the last one of his cardboard scales now placed on the floor next to his chair.

'The boathouse? I shouldn't think they'd mind.' Cressida shrugged, then risked another sip of the burningly bad rum.

'No, Randolph's death.' Alfred replied, crossing his grey-stockinged legs and reclining back into his chair now he was free of scales.

'Oh.' Cressida thought about it for a bit, while noticing that Alfred could now pass as a Dickensian wraith if it weren't for his rosy cheeks and wavy chestnut hair. 'Speaking of locals, that Catherine Bly woman was talking to two of them earlier, Napoleon and Josephine, though I think Josephine is really called Celia.'

'Oh yes, what did she say?' Dotty asked, leaning forward.

Cressida took another throat-burning sip of the rum as she cast her mind back. 'Catherine was saying that she thought poor Randolph had it coming.'

'That's what we heard too, "serves him right" or something,' Dotty said, tentatively trying a sip for herself but very quickly putting her tumbler down, a look on her face as if she'd had to suck a lemon.

'She said she'd complained to Lord Trevelyan about Randolph's employment with them. She obviously isn't happy at all about the direction the Far East Company is taking.' Cressida got up from her perch on the sofa and moved back towards the window, Ruby snuffling at her heels. 'If Randolph *was* killed by someone, and I assume it's someone who was here tonight, top of my suspect list would be her.'

'Are you... are you going to look into it?' Dotty asked hesitantly. 'It's only that last time you did, you almost got yourself... well, that alabaster bust of Lady Adelaine smashed to smithereens from a great height right next to you.'

Before Cressida could reply, the door to the drawing room opened and a very solemn-faced Sebastian Goodricke, up-and-coming star of the Foreign Office, entered.

'Ah. Thought I might find you chaps here. Mind if I join you in that?' He gestured over to the decanter of rum and Cressida, Dotty and Alfred all nodded.

'Any news from the family?' Alfred asked. 'Is Selina all right?'

Sebastian carefully took the ball-shaped top off the heavy crystal decanter and poured himself a generous measure.

'You might want to try that before you commit too much further.' Cressida tried to lighten the mood, but Sebastian just shrugged. He looked like a man who'd seen a ghost.

'I'd drink paint stripper right now if it was all they had.' Sebastian sat himself down on the sofa and she circled back from the window and sat next to him.

'What is it, Sebastian? What's happened?'

He took a gulp of the rum and barely winced. 'It's the doctor. I overheard him talking to Lord Trevelyan.'

'And?' Cressida was agog.

'Is Selina all right?' asked Dotty again.

Sebastian looked at her for a moment, then nodded. 'Yes, Miss Trevelyan is all right. It's Lord Canterbury.'

Cressida caught Alfred and Dotty's eyes, each of them thinking that surely no worse fate could now be laid at Randolph's door.

'Poisoned.' Sebastian took another gulp of his rum and, once again, the other three all looked at each other.

Cressida was the first to speak.

'That's what we wondered. As far as we know, he was fit as a fiddle and the way he died...'

'But it could have been accidental?' Dotty looked almost hopeful. 'Or... or... perhaps a really bad dose of gastric 'flu?'

Sebastian shook his head. 'The doc was adamant it was poison. The post-mortem will show more in the next few days.' He sipped the rum and Cressida noticed the shadow of a thought cross his brow.

'Is the doctor suspicious?' Cressida asked him.

'He wouldn't be drawn, but the way he said it...' Sebastian took another sip.

'He made it sound like Randolph was murdered.' Cressida finished off his thought.

That onerous word hung heavily in the air between the four of them, and Cressida knocked back her own final shot of rum. Could someone in that orangery tonight, someone dressed as a tiger, a butcher, a miner or a flamingo, have been a murderer? What grotesque mask had been hiding a far more gruesome person? Cressida prided herself on her eye for detail... If she put her mind to it, could she unmask the killer?

5

Cressida awoke the next morning and pushed her silk eye mask up onto her forehead. She'd suffered terribly from nightmares, as her fitful sleep attested, and it was only the sight of her perfectly peerless pooch staring at her with her large, dark brown eyes, that made life seem any brighter. The sight of Ruby also brought back all the memories of Randolph Canterbury, however, and his proposal almost exactly a year ago. Not to mention his sudden death last night, which had plagued her dreams but was all too real.

Cressida lifted herself up onto her elbows, yawned, and then smiled as Ruby yawned too.

'Bad nights all round eh, Rubes?' Cressida asked her, stroking the folds of fur between her eyes, which elicited a satisfying grunting sound from the small dog. A stray green feather was gently floating up and down near Ruby's nose as she breathed in and out.

For the first time, Cressida looked around the bedroom she had been shown to in the early hours, when finally she, Dotty and Alfred had decided to call it a night. It was decorated, unsurprisingly, in the Chinoiserie style, with pretty willow pattern paper covering the walls and prints of ferns and exotic flowers hung upon it. The furniture was grand and brown, as was so often the case in these great houses, but there were also large bronze pots that held exotic fronded plants and a pretty mother-of-pearl inlaid cabinet, with a tasselled key that invited a nose. Cressida was about to throw her eiderdown off her and do just that when the bedroom door opened and a red-headed maid curtsied to her while bringing in a tray of tea.

'Good morning, miss,' the maid said, her West Country accent unmistakable.

'Good morning,' Cressida replied, then asked, 'What's your name?' She couldn't bear the anonymity of servants and made a conscious effort to try to remember the names of as many as she could. In some ways, it was easier than learning the names of her fellows in society, being that maids and footmen tended to have quite sensible names, such as Mary and John. Everyone she met in nightclubs and at parties these days had quite ridiculous names like Plumpy and Winko. Also, she was more often than not sober when she came across a housemaid for the first time, such as now. This, she felt, helped rather a lot when it came to remembering things.

'Morwenna, miss.' She bobbed a curtsy and Cressida thanked her again. 'It's Chinese tea, miss, and Mrs Dawkins says you prefer Indian, and I'm to pass on her apologies.'

'Gracious, don't you or Mrs Dawkins worry at all. You're more than kind to bring me anything. Thank you.' Cressida sat more upright and took a sip of the steaming hot tea. 'It's very good. Thank you, Morwenna.'

'Breakfast will be served in the dining room shortly, miss. I've left a plate of chicken livers outside your door, miss, for your dog.'

'Gosh, now that is kind of you. Ruby, did you hear that? You're being spoilt, you pampered pup. Go on then.' Cressida held her teacup up as Ruby scrambled over her and jumped off the high-sided bed, landing on the carpet with a satisfying thump.

Morwenna smiled and Cressida asked if she had any pets herself.

'No, miss,' Morwenna replied. 'Though it's always nice to see the ones that come to visit. We had a great bear of a thing here a few months ago. Twice the size of any normal dog it was.'

'Hmm. That sounds like Porthos, Mungo Stilton-Smith's dog.'

'That's right, miss, Porthos. He quite terrified the cat here, miss, though he was a big softie.'

Cressida smiled, glad of the distraction from the horrors of the evening before, but aware that everyone in the house must have been affected by it. 'Morwenna, how's the family today. And all of you below stairs?'

Morwenna shook her head. 'It's all been an awful shock, miss. I don't know... I mean to say, I'm not in a place to comment or nothing, but it's all a bit much, miss.' She bobbed a curtsy and disappeared out of the door before Cressida could ask her more.

'It is all a bit much, isn't it, Rubes,' Cressida told her pup as she enjoyed her breakfast, which was indeed a few perfectly cooked slices of chicken liver on a fine bone china plate.

Cressida, who, much to her mother's consternation, never took a lady's maid with her when she travelled, or indeed in her London pied-à-terre, got herself washed and dressed most ably. As she buttoned up her silk blouse, she couldn't help but think of poor Randolph once again. If only Morwenna hadn't rushed off so quickly, she would have loved to have asked her more about any rumours in the servants' quarters, being that maids and footmen in houses such as this were often privy to all the household's secrets.

'What secrets did you have, though, Randolph?' Cressida

mused as she straightened her cuffs. 'And did they get you killed...?'

'What ho, Cressy.' Alfred, dressed not as an aardvark but in seasonal light khaki twill trousers and a blazer with a rather snazzy cravat at his neck, greeted her as she came down the stairs.

'Morning, Alfred. How did you sleep?'

'Like a log,' he said rather triumphantly. 'You?'

'Like a log... if said log was being dashed about on the rapids of the Niagara Falls while being eaten from the inside by termites,' Cressida replied.

'Ah.' Alfred clasped his hands behind his back. 'Still, nothing a nice hot breakfast won't sort out.'

'I suppose it can't hurt. Ruby's had hers and I've left her snoring again in a sunbeam in our room. At least one of us should be able to get some shut-eye.'

Alfred led the way into the panelled dining room, where a breakfast buffet was laid out on a sideboard, each delicious dish covered by a silver dome, but labelled very precisely. Scrambled eggs, devilled kidneys, smoked back bacon and rounds of toast... Cressida could see Alfred's eyes light up, but before she helped herself, she took a moment to see who else was around the table.

Lord Trevelyan was seated at the head of the table, and Lady Trevelyan was next to him. Her Ladyship looked up and saw Cressida, and raised a hand in what was barely a wave. Cressida solemnly waved back, then with slightly more gusto waved to Dotty, who was sitting next to a handsome young man who Cressida didn't recognise. He had dark, almost black hair, and was deeply tanned, and even at this time in the morning, and after such a horrendous evening the night before, he had a twinkle in his eye and was making Dotty laugh.

Sebastian Goodricke, who'd been the bearer of such bad news the night before, was sitting the other side of Dotty, concentrating wholeheartedly on his breakfast, eating it quickly and barely chewing, it seemed. Cressida could see why, as next to him was Catherine Bly, now no longer wearing a ladybird costume, though something about how she was earnestly talking to Sebastian as he gulped down his scrambled eggs made Cressida wonder at what pace her antennae would have been bobbing around if she was.

The other familiar face was Sir Jolyon Westmoreland, dressed in a light country tweed three-piece suit and tucking into a plate full of eggs and sausages. If *he* was into trading antiquities, the size of his stomach told Cressida that he certainly wasn't squeezing into any pyramid antechambers to get them himself. Next to him, she recognised the Trevelyans' son, Patrick, now no longer a Charlestonning tree but dressed in a blazer like Alfred, his fair hair devoid of cardboard branches and crepe paper leaves... and much in the way of style.

But there was no sign of Selina. Her absence made Randolph's seem all the more acute, and Cressida shook off an irksome feeling of culpability. In the bright light of the morning, it seemed faintly ridiculous, but she had been writhing with guilt half the night. Guilt, because her dreams had had her marrying Lord Canterbury in his namesake cathedral, the train of her dress and veil stretching all the way from one end of the nave to the other, its champagne-coloured silk turning into the sands of the desert. Then, in an instant, they were away, in Egypt, she supposed, reading letters from home, reeling off the names of all the young men in England who had been poisoned, but they'd laughed because they were safe in this eastern paradise...

Cressida blinked the memory of the horrible dream away, but not so easily the feeling it left her with.

Guilt.

She couldn't help think, you see, that if only she had married Randolph last year, he'd still be alive now. And that guilt, gnawing at her still, made her all the more determined to find out who had done this to him.

She looked once again at the faces around the table, chewing and swallowing and talking to their neighbours... Could one of them be Randolph's killer?

6

'Cressida dear,' Lady Trevelyan called over to her and Cressida snapped out of her disagreeable reverie and went over to see her. As she did, she smiled at Dotty, who was beaming at the handsome man next to her over her boiled egg and toast soldiers.

'Good morning, Lady Trevelyan, Lord Trevelyan.' Cressida greeted her hosts and allowed a footman to pull a chair out for her next to them. 'I'm trying to think of the correct thing to say, be it to thank you for inviting me to stay, or immeasurable condolences on what happened to dear Lord Canterbury last night.'

'Thank you, dear.' Lady Trevelyan rested her hand on Cressida's for a moment, before pulling it away and picking up her cutlery again. She was a handsome woman, and reminded Cressida of a caryatid at the British Museum, especially with her hair swept up in a chignon. She had the same blue eyes as Selina, but a stronger jawline and a more expressive face. Those blue eyes were set deep, though, and dark circles showed through the light coating of powder she'd tried to conceal them with. 'Selina has taken it the worst, of course. Despite their tiffs, they were well suited, I think.'

'And how are you, Lady Trevelyan?'

Lady Trevelyan put her cutlery down again and sipped at her cup of tea. 'It's been a horrible, horrible shock, Cressida.' She sipped again, drawing strength from the warm brew. 'I just can't begin to think about it all really. You knew him, I believe?'

Cressida gulped and wished she'd been able to pick up a plate of breakfast before sitting down so that she could have had the excuse of chewing on something. Instead she managed to say, 'Royal Society things mostly,' and that was enough for her hostess, who nodded to herself.

'I assume you've heard what Dr May had to say about poor Randolph's death?' Lady Trevelyan had lowered her voice to a whisper.

'Yes. It's shocking, but I can see why he would think it.'

'Can you?' Lady Trevelyan looked askance at her guest. 'How so?'

'Randolph was a normal, healthy, young man. There's no reason he would keel over like that. This might seem like a foolish comparison, but I remember Mama last year got awfully upset when the sideboard collapsed. It had been doing perfectly well for the last couple of hundred years, then just as Stevens was serving lunch, the whole thing went over. Woodworm of course, riddled it from the inside and made what we thought was a perfectly sturdy piece of furniture as flimsy as a wig in the wind.'

Lady Trevelyan nodded and put her teacup down. 'So you're saying Randolph was like your mother's sideboard; perfectly solid left to his own devices...'

'But considerably weakened to the point of collapse by the introduction of outside influences.'

'I see.' Lady Trevelyan turned her teacup around in its saucer. 'Of course, we've had to inform the local police, but it's not often you get a poisoning here in this backwater. I fear they'll flounder, and if we don't get our best minds onto it, someone will get away with... with murder.' Lady Trevelyan spoke softly, but the other guests around the table fell quiet so that the end of her sentence hung heavy over all of them.

'I think I know someone who might be able to help.' The words were out of Cressida's mouth before she could think through what she was saying. But as she told Lord and Lady Trevelyan of the Scotland Yard detective who had been so discreet and useful at Chatterton Court, and who was a close personal acquaintance of her own family, she was only thinking one thing: *If Detective Chief Inspector Andrews is put in charge of this investigation, then there's a much bigger chance that I'll get to delve into it too without too much interference.* '... So, you see, he really would be the man for the job, if you think you can swing it with the local bobbies?'

'Edgar's a magistrate, so I'm sure we can,' Lady Trevelyan summoned a footman as she kept talking, '... and with the guests we had with us last night we'll need the utmost discretion from our investigating officer, so if you think he's the man for the job, then please, yes, let's telephone Scotland Yard straight away and request him.'

Cressida finally managed to get some marmalade and toast down her before breakfast was over, and after all the excitements of the night before, she and Dotty found themselves at a loose end. It was a beautiful early summer's day, one of those where the sun is all the more appreciated having been in hiding for a few months, and Alfred had thought to make the best of it and had joined the other chaps in going down to the cove. The tide was in and there was an admirable old red-sailed sailing boat moored at the jetty.

'I might let my breakfast settle before I go anywhere near

the water,' Dotty remarked. 'The idea of swaying backwards and forwards after those boiled eggs makes me feel a bit queasy. Mind if we sit in the drawing room for a little while?'

'Not at all, chum.' Cressida let Dotty lead the way and they entered the beautiful room in which they'd stayed up, perhaps unwisely, drinking rum into the early hours. Light was now streaming in through the sash windows and Cressida moved over to look through one of them, seeing the young men of the party saunter down the lawn.

'Penny for them?' Dotty came and stood next to her friend. 'You're unnaturally quiet, Cressy.'

'Just thinking about Randolph and why someone would want to kill him. Those young men down there, your brother excluded, of course... well, any one of them might have done it and yet they get to traipse down to that delightful little sailing boat and go and have a glorious June morning while poor Randolph...' Cressida shrugged. 'Oh, I don't know, Dot. It's not as if I've spared him much thought since I turned him down. But still, he was a lovely man and now he's dead, most likely murdered.'

'At least you've got Chief Inspector Andrews coming down. He was an awfully comforting presence when young Harry and... well, when we had our troubles at Chatterton Court.' Dotty looked up at her friend, who turned back towards the room.

'Yes, I do honestly think he's the man for the job. But, Dot, I have to admit something. As much as I admire Andrews and his detective skills, I asked for him to be called for, as I know after last time, he'll let me do some of the investigating. As long as he doesn't lecture me about—'

'Not getting yourself hurt.' Dotty all but wagged a finger at her friend. 'If there's a killer in this house, and I very much hope for all of our sakes that there isn't, then please be careful. I'll be very cross with you if you end up on the pointy end of a dagger or under some falling masonry, Cressy, as will Ruby. And Alfred. Not to mention all those poor bartenders in London who'd lose their—'

'Yes, quite.' Cressida raised an eyebrow at her friend before she could finish, but Dotty's joking had done its job and Cressida eased the tension in her shoulders and sat herself down on one of the Bergère-style wicker-backed sofas. The Foo dogs were looking more lustrous than ever in the morning light, changed from their dull bronze of the evening to a shimmering gold. Cressida was just about to remark on the stylish decorating in the room when the door opened and a pale-faced Selina Trevelyan walked in.

Dotty and Cressida quickly exchanged glances and Cressida stood up from the sofa and greeted her.

'Morning, old thing. We didn't expect you up. How are you feeling?' Cressida asked.

Selina looked at Cressida, her cheeks devoid of colour, dark circles under her puffy eyes. She blinked a few times and it looked like she was trying to focus on some distant object.

Cressida moved towards her, thinking that a steadying arm might be needed and instinctively Dotty did the same. But as they advanced, Selina took a step back.

'Sorry, sorry...' she murmured. 'Thought I'd left it in here.'

'Come on, Selly. There's really no need to apologise to us,' Dotty assured her. 'What are you looking for?'

Selina, swaying slightly from side to side, widened her eyes as if taking in Dotty for the first time. 'Oh hello, Dotty, Cressida. So sorry about last night. Poor Randolph.'

'Selina...' Cressida stepped closer, hoping she'd accept an arm and be led over to the sofa where she was in less danger of keeling over. 'Are you quite well?'

Selina just looked glassy-eyed at her, and Dotty whispered, 'I think she might have been sedated.'

Cressida nodded.

'Let's get you back upstairs, shall we? Dot,' she turned to her friend, 'I met a sensible-looking maid in my room earlier, Morwenna, could you find her and ask for her help?'

'Of course.' Dotty nodded and slipped out to the hallway in search of the maid.

Cressida put her arm gently around Selina's shoulders, but the young woman stood stiffly all of a sudden. Grief was a powerful emotion, and one could never tell how it could affect someone. Selina, it seemed, was catatonic, though Dotty could have been right and it might have been a heavy sedation that Dr May had administered last night. Cressida thought it might be best to keep her talking, worrying that if she were to completely conk out, it might be even harder for them to get her safely back up to bed.

'What was it you were looking for?' Cressida asked her again.

Selina scanned her eyes around the room before answering. 'Poppy.'

'Poppy? Is that the cat?' Cressida remembered Morwenna mentioning a cat who'd been scared by Mungo's giant dog a few weeks ago.

Selina just gazed back at Cressida, but, luckily, within moments, Dotty and Morwenna were back in the room, followed by another maid.

The two maids escorted the stricken Selina out of the drawing room and towards the stairs.

Dotty and Cressida looked at each other and sighed a deep exhale of relief.

'I'm not saying that was a crisis, but I'm glad it's averted.' Dotty said, crossing her arms.

'Indeed. It was strange; she said she was looking for Poppy. Who do you think Poppy is? One of the maids? The cat?'

'I saw that wild feline earlier and I don't think a name as delicate as Poppy suits it,' Dotty ventured, pushing her glasses back up the bridge of her nose. 'I think it's called Saracen, or Scimitar, or something quite frankly more appropriate like that.'

'Hmm.' Cressida nodded and looked back out towards the window where the young men of the party were doing something to the rigging of the red-sailed wooden boat down in the cove. The water in the bay was still, unbothered by the light breeze, sheltered as it was by the steep-sided cliffs. Opportunistic gulls circled overhead, the promise of a fish supper nabbed from the boat's nets on their minds. She could make out Alfred's dark brown hair and recognised Sebastian Goodricke among the others. Could there really be a killer in this house? Was it one of those young men enjoying the summer morning down by the water? Or perhaps someone who was at the fancy-dress ball and faded into the night as soon as their deadly mission was complete? She thought back to the terror she'd felt only a month or so ago at Chatterton Court when the bust of Lady Adelaine had smashed to the ground, barely missing her. She shivered, despite standing in a glorious sunbeam, remembering that near-fatal warning. *If I'm to start investigating this murder before the protection of DCI Andrews arrives, could the next victim be me?*

7

Cressida and Dotty were interrupted by the drawing-room door opening once again.

'Oh, Cressida, Dorothy. There you are.' Lady Trevelyan closed the door behind her and walked into the room. 'Thank you for being so kind to Selina. I just spoke to one of the maids in the hall and she said you'd noticed she wasn't terribly sparky. I think Dr May gave her something equivalent to a horse tranquilliser last night. Though one can't blame him, she was in a terrible state.'

'It must be a huge shock, seeing one's fiancé die like that, right in front of you.' Cressida raised her hand to her neck, remembering poor Randolph's lips moving in an exaggerated way, gasping for breath... or was it, as she had wondered earlier, that he had been trying to speak?

'Lady Trevelyan, you were standing next to him when he collapsed. Did you hear him say anything? I was a little far off, but I thought I saw his lips move.' Cressida realised, as she posed the question that what she was asking was macabre at best, hideously rude at worst, but she had to know.

Lady Trevelyan closed her eyes and shook her head as if both summoning and scattering the thoughts in her head. She opened her eyes again and spoke to Cressida with perfect clarity. 'Yes, I think he did say something. He said "food", which, of course, I presume to mean that he was affected by something that he ate.' She shook her head again. 'It's so very strange. Something must have been tampered with, as Dr May said it looked like poisoning, yet here we all are, fit as fiddles ourselves, having eaten the same things as Randolph throughout his stay.'

'How long had he been here, before last night, I mean?' Cressida asked, noticing a slightly raised eyebrow from Dotty. Yes, she was investigating before the safety net of DCI Andrews had arrived, but she couldn't help it.

'Randolph and Selina had been down here since Thursday. He'd proposed to her in St James's Park, I believe, on the Wednesday evening. Though, of course, her father and I knew it was coming as Randolph had asked Edgar's permission a few weeks ago.'

Cressida was good enough to show not a flicker of recognition or emotion over the fact that Randolph Canterbury had used the same place he'd proposed to her as the location for his latest down-on-one-knee moment, and instead nodded along with interest.

'And you'd eaten all of your meals together?' Cressida asked, hoping Lady Trevelyan wouldn't mind being asked these questions.

'No, not all of them.'

Cressida looked more intently at Lady Trevelyan as she continued.

'Randolph and Selina were out for the day on Friday, so we took luncheon here without them. We all had dinner together though, and most of us were around yesterday helping with the ball preparation, though I don't recall seeing Randolph during the day.' Lady Trevelyan sighed. 'Oh dear. I suppose that's the end of the annual fancy-dress ball.' She stepped over to the wicker-backed sofa and took a seat. 'I know it's nothing compared to poor Randolph dying. Still, can't have people coming to one's house and thinking they'll get poisoned as soon as they take a sip of the rum punch.'

Cressida and Dotty nodded sympathetically. The demise of the Penbeagle fancy-dress ball would be a huge loss to society. *But someone there last night thought that the demise of Randolph wouldn't be...* Cressida thought ruefully.

'Who else was here yesterday before the ball?' she asked, once again hoping she didn't push Lady Trevelyan too far.

'Oh, we had quite the houseful. Our children Selina and Patrick, of course, and Jago, our nephew popped by. Mr Parish arrived in the early afternoon—'

'Sorry, who's Mr Parish?' Cressida interrupted her hostess, but it was Dotty who answered.

'I think Her Ladyship is referring to George Parish. He was sitting next to me at breakfast, Cressy. He's...' she blushed, 'very charming.'

Lady Trevelyan raised an eyebrow but continued talking. 'Yes, he is, isn't he. A colleague of Randolph's from Egypt, another archaeologist, it seems. Randolph insisted we invite him to stay.' She paused. 'Then there was Sir Jolyon, who arrived by motor in the afternoon, and your brother Alfred, Dorothy, along with Sebastian Goodricke and Catherine, who came by train from London. Our chauffeur picked them up.'

Cressida had met all of the house guests then, except for the charming George Parish, who Dotty had clearly become acquainted with.

'While this is all horribly tragic, I find I can't just sit about all day waiting for things to be done about it.' Lady Trevelyan stood up from the sofa and straightened her skirt. 'Cressida, and

Dorothy you too of course, would you be so kind as to come down to the boathouse with me? I'd love your advice on how I can remodel it to show our vibrant trade in the Far East. Really jazz it up. At least it would be a good distraction for us, keep us busy, you know?'

'Of course. I couldn't agree more about the distraction. Just let me fetch Ruby from my room, as she needs a walk more than any of us after the breakfast she was treated to.' Cressida moved towards the door.

'I might go and join Alfred and the others, if you don't mind?' Dotty asked, and Cressida smiled, knowing that it wasn't her brother that Dotty was keen to see. 'I'm useless with colours, as Cressy will tell you.'

Cressida raised an eyebrow, knowing full well that heading down to the cove and messing about in a boat was far less likely to be her friend's thing than deciding on decorating schemes – Dotty being no fan of outdoor activities in general – but she let it go. For Dotty to be even vaguely interested in a nice young man after her heartbreak of a month or so ago, was a Very Good Thing.

'You do that, Dotty, and, Lady Trevelyan, I'll be with you in two ticks!'

As Lady Trevelyan and Dotty left the drawing room, Cressida paused to take another look around. If Lady Trevelyan wanted a scheme that celebrated their trade in the Far East, then this room would be a marvellous template for it. She took the decor in again, and as she glanced around she once more noticed the bronze Foo dogs on the mantelpiece gleaming a bright lustrous gold.

The sun teased an appearance from behind the most wispy of clouds as Cressida walked with Lady Trevelyan down towards the boathouse, Ruby trotting along at their heels and sniffing at the fresh, salty air. Dotty had waited for them while they'd gathered their notebooks and pens, but she now waved to them as they parted ways at the top of the lawn. Cressida watched as Dotty made her way down to the jetty beside the cove, where the young men were still entertaining themselves with the rigging of the old sailboat.

'It's a Cornish lugger,' Lady Trevelyan told Cressida. 'With the traditional red sail. You see the coastline at Falmouth teeming with them during the regatta and it looks rather wonderful, like the junks sailing out of Hong Kong harbour, or so I'm led to believe.'

'You've never been to the Far East yourself?' Cressida asked, assuming that Lady Trevelyan had her own adventurous spirit and might have taken the opportunity, veiled in mosquito-proof muslins and dressed in light cotton lawn gowns, to visit the far-off home of the silks and spices that had feathered her nest back here in England so finely.

'Dear me, no. All that humidity and spicy food – that's not for me. I let Edgar do the exploring. I find this house and garden has enough going on within its walls and bounds to keep me on my toes. Speaking of which...'

Lady Trevelyan waved at a young man who was kneeling down on the edge of a wide herbaceous border, and who had turned around at the sound of their voices. He was in brown corduroys and a red work shirt and was holding a heavy-duty trowel. He leaned back on his heels, one hand on his forehead, shielding his eyes from the sun, the knees of his trousers wet through with the damp from the lawn. In a moment, he stood up, dusting his hands together to rid them of loose soil and greeted them with a 'how do' and deferential nod.

'Good morning, Roscoe. All well in the garden today, I hope,' Lady Trevelyan enquired, but before he could answer, she introduced him. 'This is Miss Cressida Fawcett. Cressida, this is Roscoe Pearmain, our head gardener.'

'Good morning, Your Ladyship, Miss Fawcett.' He nodded at them both and Cressida said hello.

'Roscoe is very good at looking after our more exotic plants,' said Lady Trevelyan as Ruby started digging a patch of the fresh earth the gardener had just been turning over. Roscoe gently pulled her away from his work and placed her carefully back on the lawn. Cressida mouthed an apology as Lady Trevelyan continued. 'We have a small tropical garden and greenhouse as Edgar can't help but bring back an orchid or some such exotic thing from each trip.'

'Patrick's a great horticulturalist too, isn't he?' Cressida asked. 'I've heard him talk quite poetically about hyacinths.'

'Yes, he's forever pottering in the orangery with his bulbs and rhizomes. But Roscoe here is better with the ones Edgar brings back.' Roscoe nodded in appreciation to Her Ladyship.

'Does the Far East Company bring back garden ornaments at all? I can imagine some tremendous sphinx making itself at home among the rhododendrons,' Cressida said as she bent down and picked up her mucky-pawed pup.

'No, sadly not. Though I think it had been one of Randolph's aims, God bless him, to do just that sort of thing. But with Buddha statues and the like, you know the sort. Come, let's leave Roscoe to his azaleas.'

Lady Trevelyan dismissed the gardener and gestured for Cressida to lead the way back to the path towards the rickety and neglected boathouse. Cressida complied but turned to give a wave to the gardener. To her great surprise, instead of a friendly wave back, Roscoe Pearmain had a face like thunder. She could feel his eyes follow them as they walked down towards the shoreline.

After a few minutes, she chanced a glance back towards the azalea bed, and, sure enough, he was still staring at them, a scowl stamped across his face. As she kept pace with Lady Trevelyan, Cressida felt her spine tingle with the memory of that snarl. Whatever could be behind the animosity the gardener so clearly felt towards Lady Trevelyan, or indeed towards her? Perhaps he'd felt such rage towards Randolph, too? So much so, he'd decided to kill him?

8

'Allegra!' The voice screeched across the lawn, not unlike the calls of the bad-mannered gulls above them. It was accompanied by the body of the lady formerly known to Cressida as Josephine Bonaparte. 'Allegra!'

'Oh dear.' Lady Trevelyan sighed. 'Here we go.'

Cressida cocked her head on one side as Lady Trevelyan explained.

'Celia Nangower. Married to Monty. They live over at Peacehaven Gables.'

'They were dressed as Napoleon and Josephine last night, I think.' Cressida remembered all too well how the lady barrelling her way across the lawn towards them had agreed with Randolph-hating Catherine Bly the night before.

'How appropriate,' Lady Trevelyan said, and she exhaled a deep breath before putting on a large smile and waving enthusiastically. Between clenched teeth, she added, 'Though, if you ask me, she's the one who should have been dressed as Napoleon.'

Cressida caught her laugh just in time and turned it into a welcoming smile as Celia finally flustered her way over, pearl necklace swinging to and fro as she came within earshot of them.

'Allegra, there you are. I've been trying to find you all morning.' Celia Nangower was flushed pink with the exertion of crossing the lawns at speed, but Cressida noticed that the colour suited her, as otherwise she had a rather jaundiced complexion. She must have been in her fifties, Cressida thought, and well-preserved, thanks to a life of leisure, though there were now lines around the pinched-in creases of her lips, and her make-up sat heavy on her powdery skin.

'Celia, hello. Do you know Miss Cressida Fawcett?'

Cressida stretched out the hand that wasn't holding Ruby and Celia looked at it as if Cressida were presenting her with a three-day-old fish. After a moment she did accept it but shook it very limply, muttering something along the lines of 'how modern'.

'How can I help you, Celia?' Lady Trevelyan asked. 'It's been a trying morning after last night's tragedy and I—'

'That's what I want to speak to you about, Allegra. Last night. And my condolences to your family, of course.'

Lady Trevelyan accepted them with a nod, and after a short, mutually agreed, silence, Celia spoke again.

'You see, I heard from Parkins in the village that you'd telephoned Scotland Yard to invite some chief inspector to come and find out what happened.'

Lady Trevelyan looked at Cressida, who wondered if she should be the one to explain why it had been best for DCI Andrews to be called, but Lady Trevelyan answered instead.

'News travels fast in the village. But, yes. What with the delicacy of the situation, we thought Scotland Yard would be more appropriate than the local chaps. And we had a recommendation.'

'But Scotland Yard? The newspapers are sure to get wind of it! The scandal!' Celia Nangower gripped all three strings of pearls around her throat, as if the thought of a serious police presence was literally choking her.

'Celia,' Lady Trevelyan snapped at her. 'Our daughter's fiancé was killed, here at Penbeagle House, last night. What do you expect us to do, brush it under the carpet?'

'Killed?' Celia paled beneath the surface flush. 'I thought he'd suffered a stroke or heart attack?'

'Dr May has his suspicions. I can't say much more than that.' Lady Trevelyan sighed. 'It's all terribly, terribly upsetting.'

'I see. I see.' Celia nodded, a touch of colour returning to her cheeks. 'But, Allegra, this village, all of us who live here by the cove, will suffer if this becomes public.'

'Celia, calm yourself,' Lady Trevelyan shot back at her neighbour. 'Anyone would think you have something to hide.'

'I most certainly do not... I am just representing the village... it's the scandal...' Celia Nangower stumbled over her words and Cressida wondered if Lady Trevelyan had hit a nerve with this noxious woman.

'Scandal or no scandal,' Lady Trevelyan continued, 'Scotland Yard have been called and I hope you'll do your utmost, as our household will, in aiding the detectives. We must find out who did this to poor Randolph. We must.'

With that, Lady Trevelyan turned on her heel and headed into the boathouse. Celia Nangower, obviously not to be outdone, stalked away too, leaving Cressida and Ruby alone. Before she followed Lady Trevelyan into the boathouse, Cressida gazed out across the sparkling water of the creek, the rippling waves breaking over partially submerged rocks. Did Celia Nangower really have something to hide? Her rather spurious concerns about scandal aside, why else would she be so afraid of Scotland Yard arriving?

. . .

The boathouse smelt of tar and sodden old rope, wet timber and beeswax. It was chilly inside, with the constant sound of lapping water soothing Cressida's soul as much as the cool dampness soothed her pink cheeks after the sunshine outside. It was constructed entirely of timber, with struts criss-crossing each other, and a skeleton of beams with the thinnest skin of wooden boarding covering it.

From the outside, it had looked more solid, probably something to do with its square shape, but inside it felt fragile, vulnerable. The water came right up inside it and the decking floor ran around in a U shape so that anyone aboard the small rowing boat, which was moored up in the middle, could easily alight from either side. No wonder it smelt damp, as the water lapped and sloshed against the wooden jetty beams, each one home to countless molluscs and species of algae.

Cressida could hear the young men the other side of the cove, still playing with the Cornish lugger by the jetty, but their voices were muffled by the sounds of the water echoing around the inside of the boathouse. She let Ruby down and watched as the small dog snuffled around the decking boards, their moss-green covering obviously a library of delight for her nose.

Lady Trevelyan stood with her arms crossed looking out across the water from the balustraded decking. 'I'm sorry about Mrs Nangower. She's a bit of a local busybody and one of those exasperating people whose knickers are more often than not in a twist over something. Last summer, it was about the coastguard asking to use this boathouse to over-winter their boat and Celia said she thought it would lower the tone of the cove terribly. Silly woman. But they're our neighbours and Monty is a good sort. Very old family. Anyway,' she turned and looked around the shabby wooden structure, 'not much to work with, I know. But I saw your dear mother last month at the flower show in Chelsea and she said you were a wonder with interiors. Since you were coming down for the ball anyway, I...' she paused.

'You know, Cressida, it keeps hitting me in waves that poor Selina's fiancé died last night. More than that, most likely murdered.' She shivered. 'And Selina hasn't been herself lately. Away with the fairies, if you know what I mean.'

'She didn't seem that with it this morning, I must say, but like you said, we assumed she'd been given a heck of a sedative last night,' Cressida answered her, while sizing up the work that would be needed to convert this dank shell into something much more jazzy.

'Yes. Dr May said the normal dose barely affected her at all and he'd had to double it before she'd eventually slept.' Lady Trevelyan shook her head, her face pained with worry.

The light in the boathouse was poor, with the windows covered in a film of green algae, and the light that was there was refracted and rippled across the faces of the two women. Cressida wasn't sure if the green tinge that fell upon Lady Trevelyan's face was from the reflecting water or if she was about to faint. Her voice came out firm enough, however, for Cressida to no longer fear the latter.

'Cressida, could you keep an eye on her for me? Unlike you, she doesn't have more than a handful of friends and none of them as close as you and Dorothy are to each other. Not any more at any rate.'

'Of course I will. It's utterly beautiful here in Cornwall, but I suppose it's not as easy to keep in touch with one's London chums.' Cressida ran her palm over the rough grain of the handrail, thinking of all the times she'd counted on Dotty and all her other pals to get her through life's scrapes and adventures.

'Yes, perhaps that's the reason.' Lady Trevelyan looked out over the water again. 'We only did what we thought best for her after the incident at The Savoy with that Smythson-Fiennes boy, bringing her back here until she was no longer gossiped about. And it's not like she's a prisoner. Edgar took her to Egypt, which is where she met Randolph, of course. But she's been not quite herself for a few months now and despite her engagement to Randolph, which would have restored her reputation fully in society, she's seemed so withdrawn and vacuous. Like the spirit has gone from her.' She leaned on the wooden railing that ran around the decking. It creaked and Cressida stood ready to catch Lady Trevelyan by the arm if necessary. 'I know Randolph once proposed to you too, Cressida, and I hope that that hasn't made what I've asked of you awkward in any way, but I would so appreciate you looking in on Selina every once in a while. She's lost even more than she can appreciate at this moment.'

Cressida nodded. So, Lady Trevelyan did know about Randolph's proposal. She had, of course, recently viewed the flower tent at the Chelsea Spring Show with Cressida's own mother, Lady Fawcett, and indubitably the two of them would have talked about their daughters over jam-laden scones afterwards.

That must have been how Morwenna had known about my preference for Indian tea, Cressida thought to herself, while also remembering how Lady Trevelyan hadn't pushed her over breakfast at how she had known Randolph.

She looked back up at Lady Trevelyan and smiled. 'Of course I'll look out for her. Not just this week, or however long the police need us to stay here, but in London, too. We can be an exclusive club of two, those ladies who were honoured to have been proposed to by Randolph.' Cressida gave Lady Trevelyan's forearm a gentle squeeze. 'Now, let me have a think about this interior...'

After a blissful hour, Cressida and Lady Trevelyan, with an enthusiastic Ruby still snuffling at a gap in the floorboards, finished sizing up the boathouse. The time spent speaking of paint colours and sketching out ideas for a drinks terrace where the jetty U-shaped around the inside of the building had been a wonderful distraction from the horrors of the evening before. With thoughts of Kilim-covered furniture and bamboo lamps passing between them, they wrapped up their plans and prepared to head back out into the summer sunshine.

'I greatly appreciate your help, Cressida,' Lady Trevelyan said, resting a hand on Cressida's shoulder. 'I'd have never thought of taking away those last few feet of cladding, thus opening up the jetty to that glorious view. It'll be wonderful for me and Edgar to sit there with a rum punch on a summer's evening. You really do have such an eye for detail. As does Ruby, by the looks of it.'

Cressida followed her eyeline to where Ruby was scratching at one of the floorboards.

'Ruby, stop it! Oh, I am sorry, Lady Trevelyan, she does get a bee in her bonnet at times. Ruby, come here!' She went over to where the little pup was pawing the ground and scooped her up. 'You better not do that when these have been whitewashed, you naughty houndlette.'

With Ruby safely under one arm, Cressida joined Lady Trevelyan outside. The sun was high in the sky and Cressida looked across the cove to where Dotty and the young men were looking intently at something to do with the rigging of the sailing boat.

'Shall we go and see what they're up to?' Lady Trevelyan asked. 'One more diversion before... well—'

'Excellent plan, Lady Trevelyan.' Cressida could quite understand her unwillingness to return to the house where her daughter's fiancé (and indeed her salvation in society's eyes) had been murdered.

Silver and gold flashes glinted off the water of the cove and the creek beyond it as they walked along the soft sand of the beach. Cressida was glad Ruby was small enough to only need one arm to carry her, so the other hand could shield her eyes from the glare of the sun. Despite this, when she turned back to appraise the boathouse one more time, she was sure she could see a figure hovering by one of its walls next to an algae-coated window. A now familiar figure belonging to that pinch-faced woman, Celia Nangower.

Why would she still be lurking around? Cressida thought to herself, turning her attention back to Lady Trevelyan, who was chattering about silks and imports coming into the Falmouth warehouse. But even as she joined in the conversation, her thoughts drifted back to Celia Nangower... *Was she lurking, or eavesdropping on our conversation? Curious, perhaps, about any speculation Lady Trevelyan and I might have had about last night? And could that curiosity be fuelled by the most guilty of consciences?*

9

Ruby, who had been born in Hampstead, gifted in St James's Park, spoilt rotten daily in Chelsea and who had barely left the comforts of the Home Counties in her whole short life, had certainly never seen a beach before. Cressida let her down once the soft sand of the gently curving cove was underfoot and the small dog happily bounded off towards the slowly lapping froth of the water's edge.

Lady Trevelyan began talking of local matters, how they suspected that smugglers were still working along the bays and the fact that a rare butterfly had been spotted in the inland pastures. While she was talking, Cressida nodded and *ummed* and *ahhed* as she watched Ruby bounce with great delight in and out of the shallow water. She kept half an ear on Lady Trevelyan's stories about the local vicar while remembering how she'd solved the case at Chatterton Court just a few weeks earlier. Her friend Maurice Sauvage, the head of fabrics at Liberty, was descended from French Huguenot silk weavers and although he now worked in the retail side of fabrics, he had his well-manicured fingers in all the different pies related to the 'rag trade'. He was her source of all the information she ever needed about the goings-on around London, from snippets of gossip he overheard in Mayfair drawing rooms as he held swatches of silk up against damask wallpaper, to proper chin-wags with the porters at Euston station and the East India docks as they hauled raw cotton from the ships or loaded it onto trains. He had also given her some excellent advice, and that was to treat the crime at Chatterton Court as you would when making a pair of curtains... *measure twice and cut once*... Cressida hadn't understood him at first, but he'd explained that before you can accuse anyone, or show your hand, you must have retraced the steps of the crime, over and over, measuring twice and then cutting, or in this case accusing, just the once. With this in mind, and when Lady Trevelyan had stopped telling her about the local fête and what the vicar had done with the jar of bonbons he'd won, Cressida started asking her some more questions.

'I'm sorry to bring up Randolph again, but I can't help thinking about him and how it could be that he was poisoned.'

'I can't stop thinking about it either,' Lady Trevelyan admit-ted, stopping short of the jetty and staring out to sea again. 'Despite wittering on about butterflies and fêtes, it really is all I can think of.'

Cressida nodded. She knew coping mechanisms came in all sorts of forms. But at least now the subject was broached. 'Lady Trevelyan, do you know what Randolph did yesterday? You said he wasn't here for luncheon, but do you know where he went and what he ate?'

Lady Trevelyan bent down to pick up a shell and Cressida noticed a shake to her hand as she showed it to Cressida in her palm. She dropped it again and replied. 'You mean because he said "food" as he was dying? Oh, it doesn't bear thinking about does it.'

'I know Dr May is yet to carry out any sort of tests, but it must have been something he ate, if poison was ingested,' Cressida surmised. 'I suppose that's what poor Randolph was trying to tell us.'

Lady Trevelyan sighed. 'Ghastly, isn't it? Poor Randolph indeed. I can't answer for every minute of his day, but, yes, roughly speaking, I think I know where he was.'

Cressida looked at her encouragingly and Lady Trevelyan continued.

'He and Selina breakfasted with us, I remember that because, despite their announcement looming, Selina and Randolph had had an argument over the pastries.'

'Oh dear.' Cressida remembered Lady Trevelyan mentioning their spats. 'Was it a real bust-up?'

'No, just a lovers' tiff,' Lady Trevelyan answered, somewhat indulgently. 'He said she looked as sleepy as a dormouse, which I thought was rather endearing, but it seemed to annoy her. Anyway, then he announced, quite out of the blue, that he intended to visit some of our local potteries.'

'Really? Did he say why?'

'No. You see, it hadn't been mentioned before and he's never shown much interest in the local life down here. It's hardly as exciting as the souks in Egypt, or as high-brow as the British Library or what have you.' Lady Trevelyan sighed, then turned away from the water and looked at Cressida more squarely. 'Finding Randolph for Selina was a catch and I was all for it. One's daughter being Lady Canterbury – absolutely smashing. But I was bracing myself for Selina to leave Cornwall for ever once she was married, bar the odd visit home, of course. I imagined they'd make their home in London once society had forgotten Selina's earlier misdemeanour. Or perhaps they'd travel around the world with the Far East Company.'

'She might have stayed here with you while he travelled, much like you've done while Lord Trevelyan has been away.'

Lady Trevelyan shrugged. 'Well, we'll not know now.'

After a respectful pause, Cressida carried on. 'And did he

seem pleased with his visit to the pottery, when he came back yesterday afternoon?'

Lady Trevelyan shook her head. 'I'm afraid I don't know; I was too busy with preparations for the ball and our costumes to find out.'

Cressida nodded, and watched as Ruby barrelled over a slick bit of seaweed, righted herself and then toddled off towards a rock pool to investigate its contents. It reminded her of Randolph and his Egyptian tomb exploring. 'Do you mind me asking what Randolph did for the Far East Company? His expertise lay in Egyptology, not importing furniture from the Far East.'

'To be honest with you, Cressida dear, I don't know the ins and outs of Edgar's business dealings, but I believe Randolph had connections and could find antiquities for the company to import; Ming dynasty vases and jade lions, you know the type of thing. He specialised in finding top-quality genuine artefacts that could either be shipped to order for clients or sold to dealers once back here.'

Cressida looked over the shimmering water to the opposite shore of the cove, where nesting birds called to each other from the craggy rocks. Cornwall was a wild and wonderful county known for mining, fishing and, beyond that, good solid, rustic ceramics.

'Don't you think it strange,' said Cressida, forming her thoughts as she spoke, 'for a man obsessed by genuine antiques to be interested in modern, dare I say, artisan ceramics?'

'Yes... and no. It's not terribly far removed from his area of expertise, is it? But, as I say, he'd never expressed an interest in such local matters before and he would have been awfully useful here the day of the ball to help, but he insisted he had to go to Pencarrick Pottery.'

Cressida noted the name, determined that a visit there would be on the cards for her too today.

Lady Trevelyan carried on. 'Then, of course, he missed luncheon with us all as he was still out, but when he returned, he said he'd eaten in Falmouth. Jago, our nephew, who is very much in with Randolph and Edgar about business things, came by and they did their tea thing.'

'Their tea thing?' Cressida was intrigued by Lady Trevelyan's turn of phrase.

'Yes, they take tea, the three of them, when there's something to be celebrated. It's a Chinese ceremony, I believe, and the tea is some horrible green colour and quite off-putting to smell, but they've all travelled to those parts, so it means something to them. I think they let Patrick join in this time, which was sporting of them as he's not really very business-minded, the poor lamb. He's weak in his lungs, you know, has been ever since he was a child.'

'What were they celebrating?' Cressida was keen to stay on point, not discuss Lady Trevelyan's disappointing eldest child.

'Well, the engagement, I suppose.' As Lady Trevelyan said it, Cressida cringed. *Of course they would be celebrating that...* 'And a new shipment of antiques had just landed at Falmouth and it's one of those merchants' superstitions to celebrate once a ship is safely home. Like those balloonists who always insist on champagne once the basket is safely landed.' Lady Trevelyan smiled to herself.

'Could the tea have been poisoned?' Cressida asked, thinking about the time it had taken for whatever the poison was to take effect.

'I don't think so, as Edgar, Patrick and Jago drank from the same teapot. Morwenna, one of our maids, could vouch for that as she brewed the tea for them. Jago always says she's the only one who gets it right.'

Cressida paused, deep in thought, while Ruby chewed on something that looked quite disgusting but was obviously giving the small dog joy beyond words. As she watched her, she thought of Randolph drinking the grim-flavoured green tea. An odd sort of celebration was it not? She, like those balloonists, would have much preferred champagne. But, of course, it could not have been the tea that poisoned him, given that Lord Trevelyan and his son Patrick and nephew Jago were unaffected by it. Her mission now was to find out what else he'd eaten, and with whom. Someone among the remaining guests was sure to know. Whether they wanted her to find out was another question altogether...

10

'How did the sailing go, chum?' Cressida had bid goodbye to Lady Trevelyan, who'd gone back up to the house, and had wandered over to join the little crowd at the jetty. Ruby, still licking her muzzle after eating whatever it was she'd found on the beach, had been told to stay well away, lest she bring that odd smell of rotting fish and moulding vegetation with her. They had found Dotty, along with Alfred and the other young people, looking in some confusion at the state of the rigging.

'I don't think you could class it as sailing, Cressy.' Dotty stood with her hands on her hips, looking rather sporting in her khaki knickerbockers, neat-fitting cashmere jumper and natty silk neck scarf. 'I would say bobbing, or perhaps swaying, might be a better description.'

'Did the boat even leave the jetty?' Cressida asked, raising her eyebrows at her friend.

'It did not,' sighed Dotty. 'And you wonder why I prefer the library to outdoorsy things. There is far less faff required to sit down with a good book.'

'Be that as it may, my library-loving chum, I've got an

outdoorsy thing that I think you might enjoy doing. Fancy coming for a drive with me to Pencarrick Pottery?' Cressida ignored the expression on Dotty's face when the word 'drive' was mentioned and carried on. 'It's not far and apparently Randolph went there yesterday morning before heading into Falmouth for lunch.'

Dotty bit the inside of her lip, obviously torn. 'Cressy... are you really sure about doing all this sleuthing before the inspector arrives? It's just I'm worried that you might end up—'

'I know, but I'll watch out for any falling alabaster busts this time, I promise. I have my eyes peeled.'

'Maybe Alfred could come too. A sort of chaperone or... or bodyguard?'

'Pish posh, Dotty, we don't need a bodyguard to go to a pottery. Anyway, the Bugatti only has two seats, plus we have Rubes to look after us, don't we... Oh Ruby!' Cressida was suddenly distracted as Ruby, at quite some pace for a little dog, had set off across the beach in pursuit of an exceedingly handsome Siamese cat, who in turn on seeing Ruby was now chasing her down, straight back towards the vile-smelling seaweed. 'Dotty, see you in the garage in five mins, I better rescue this idiot pup... and give her a thorough hose down!'

With that, Cressida ran off down the beach to save her dog, if not from the claws, then at least from the indignity of being done over by the family cat.

'I don't know why you don't like me driving you places, Dot,' Cressida said, her hair fastened into her cloche hat so that stray strands wouldn't get in her face now the roof was down on the Bugatti.

Dotty, who had forgotten to bring a hat, was trying to keep her hair in place with one hand, while holding onto Ruby with the other. She was losing the battle with one, but luckily doing very well with the other, with Ruby contentedly snoring in the crook of her arm.

'It's very invigorating, I'll give you that!' Dotty exclaimed, letting go of her hair in order to grab the door during a turn that was worthy of the drivers in the recent Le Mans race.

'And there's nothing better than motoring around with the roof off.' Cressida beamed at her friend, who had managed to stabilise herself and Ruby and was once again fighting a losing battle with her flyaway hair in the wind. 'Look, you can see the sea through the gaps in the cow parsley, and look at those birds — Oops yes, well, I'll watch out for them in future.' Cressida had narrowly avoided a pheasant who had skedaddled down from one of the high-sided banks and all but dropped into Dotty's lap.

'I'm sure it's all lovely, Cressy,' Dotty practically whimpered. 'If I could only bring myself to open my eyes.'

Cressida laughed, knowing Dotty was only teasing, or at least hoping that was the case.

Without too many more incidents, they arrived at Pencarrick Pottery and drove into the flagstoned forecourt in front of the low-slung one-storey buildings. They were made of brick with white-framed windows and had curved corrugated-iron roofs. Bill posters were stuck up in one or two of the panes of glass, advertising open studio days and pottery tours in the coming weeks, but the place looked deserted today.

'Sunday,' Cressida sighed. 'Still, always worth a nosey. Coming?'

'I better, just in case you get into trouble,' Dotty replied, getting out of the car in a fashion that suggested she'd be happy never to set her bottom inside it again. She put the little dog down and Ruby snuffled around, sniffing the flagstones and snorting away to herself.

Cressida strode off towards one of the buildings, leaving Dotty to take a deep breath of the salt-tinged air. Cressida was peering in through a dusty windowpane, her hands cupped around her eyes, by the time Dotty had quite recovered from the drive and joined her.

'What sort of pottery do they make?' Dotty asked, making Cressida jump as she sidled up next to her.

Cressida pulled back from the window and straightened her blouse. 'I'm not sure. All I can see are some very artisanal-looking potter's wheels in this building. Splattered with clay and the like. So I assume they're throwing pots or vases. What does that poster say?' She pointed to another of the windows, where a bright yellow flyer was pinned onto the wooden transom between the panes of glass.

'Exhibition of works, Tuesday next. Blue slipware pottery, local earthenware, lustreware, studio seconds available at a discount...' Dotty read out the poster. 'Looks fun. Maybe we could pick up some souvenirs?'

'Hmm,' Cressida agreed in a noncommittal sort of way, her attention elsewhere. 'Look at this, Dotty, one of the buildings is locked like a bullion depository, whereas the others don't have any chains and padlocks at all.' Cressida pointed over to one of the sheds that stood on its own away from the courtyard. 'Don't you think that's odd?'

Before Dotty could agree, Cressida had set off over to the securely locked building and was rattling the chains and testing the padlocks.

'Don't you think you should... Cressy, I don't think it's—' Dotty's protestations fell on deaf ears. Or at least ears that were full of the sound of clanking chains. Eventually, Cressida gave up of her own accord and shrugged as she walked back to Dotty.

'Locked as a nun's knickers,' Cressida said, and they headed back towards the car. Suddenly, they heard a smash and Ruby started yapping and Cressida and Dotty turned towards the sound, and a movement the other side of the courtyard caught Cressida's eye. There! She saw it again, a figure disappearing behind the padlocked shed.

'Hello there!' Cressida called out, walking quickly back towards where she'd been rattling the chains only moments ago. 'Hello!'

She reached the shed and peered around it, but there was nothing there but smashed and broken old pieces of pottery, a waste heap of cracked ceramics and shards of lustreware.

Cressida turned back and shook her head at Dotty, who raised her eyebrows at her.

'I'm sure I saw someone, Dot,' Cressida said, walking back towards the car. 'A woman, I think.'

Just then, the figure darted back out from behind the shed and ran across the far side of the courtyard. Cressida was right, it was a woman, and she was wearing a maid's uniform. Before Cressida could call out again, she was gone and Cressida turned to Dotty, a look of confusion on her face.

'Gosh, do you know who that was?'

She told Dotty before her even more confused friend could attempt an answer.

'That was Morwenna, one of the maids from Penbeagle House. She brought me my tea this morning.'

'How odd. I wonder why she didn't stop and say hello when you called out?' Dotty pondered.

'And, more interestingly, why she's beaten such a hasty retreat. And, indeed, what she was doing here in the first place?'

'I suppose it's Sunday, and she may have a few hours off. She might have come on a day trip or a drive out like we have?' Dotty speculated.

Cressida shook her head. 'She lives here, she wouldn't need to come sightseeing, and being local, I'm sure she'd know it was closed today. But you might be right in a way though, Dotty. Maybe she did come here for the same *reason* we have. Maybe she wonders if the pottery has something to do with Randolph's death. Maybe, Dot,' Cressida clicked her fingers, then tapped her cheek as the connection came to her, '*she* knows something about his death, too.'

11

On their drive back to Penbeagle House, Cressida took a different route through the village of Pencarrick. An excited Ruby stretched her head out as far as little pug heads could stretch over the side of the car, no doubt catching all sorts of flies in her mouth, much to her abject joy. Whitewashed and thatched cottages lined the lanes, with pretty gardens spilling over their stone walls. A brick-edged bridge bearing the name of a Victorian engineer carried them over a stream, and then the lane widened as they found themselves in what looked like the centre of the village. The postman wobbled along on his bicycle and risked his stability to doff his cap at the ladies in the car. Cressida tooted her horn and waved at some boys playing hoop in the road and they obligingly got out of the way, their eyes staring at the smart little motor from under their caps.

Cressida slowed the car when the sixteenth-century coaching inn, the Bootlegger's Arms, came into view and, to their pleasant surprise, they spied Alfred and George Parish sitting on one of the old wooden tables outside the front of the thatched and solid-looking old inn. Cressida sounded her horn again and she and Dotty waved enthusiastically at the two young men, who waved back. Cressida was also very aware of the eyes of several other pint-drinking men and caught-mid-gossip-over-the-wall women watching her as she expertly swept the Bugatti into a space between someone's bicycle and an old dray cart outside the public house.

'What luck, Dotty,' Cressida whispered as she cut the engine and removed her cloche hat. 'You seemed quite happy in George's company earlier. Shall we see if they'll shout us lunch. I'm famished, aren't you?'

'Oh rather. Worrying if you'll die around the next bend does rather take it out of you,' Dotty said, but laughed as Cressida playfully hit her on the arm.

'Come on, you. We might find out a bit more about Randolph's movements yesterday from your friend George, or Alfred might have an update from the house. And yes, Rubes,' she took the small dog so Dotty could salvage what she could of her usually sleekly bobbed hairstyle while looking in the car's wing mirror, 'I'm sure a stray sausage will find its way off my plate for you.'

In fact it was a stray piece of pastry oozing with delicious gravy that found its way to Ruby while Cressida and Dotty sat down to a proper Cornish pasty with Alfred and George Parish, who had just been about to order when the ladies had arrived. Explaining how they'd thought it best to leave the family to grieve, the two of them had wandered down to the village and enjoyed a pint in the midday sunshine before feeling peckish themselves.

'So it's all worked out rather well that you two have shown up.' Alfred grinned at Cressida. 'Rather like that time you arrived at The Ritz just as dinner was starting at Toppy's birthday, having already eaten at Simpson's with Beefy, and Toppy said—'

'Yes, quite. Thank you, Alfred.' Cressida shot him a look. 'Anyway, thank you both for standing us lunch. We've just been down to Pencarrick Pottery.'

'What took you over there? Closed on a Sunday, I should think?' George said, and Cressida nodded.

Now she had a chance to meet George properly she could see why Dotty had been so happy to sit and have breakfast with him this morning, and, despite her usual abhorrence of it, go and do something 'outdoorsy' just because *he* was. Cressida could imagine Dotty putting up with rather a lot of damp rigging to get lost in his twinkling hazel eyes. His hair was dark and wavy, and his face square, with a good, strong jawline. He was tanned too, no doubt from working out in Cairo with Randolph. *Yes*, thought Cressida to herself, *this could be just the chap to help mend Dotty's broken heart.*

'To be frightfully honest with you both, I was looking for clues,' she managed to say, having snapped out of her reverie regarding Dotty's love life.

'Oh Cressida...' Alfred exchanged a worried look with his sister, who merely shrugged, but George looked more intrigued.

To save her friends from having to explain all about the murders at their family home, Cressida carried on. 'You see, it's clear from what Dr May said that Randolph was poisoned. Now we don't know for sure yet if it was accidental or... well, something more nefarious, but I thought a run-through of how he spent his day yesterday up to the ball wouldn't hurt. Who he saw, and especially what he ate and all that.'

'A good way to open the batting,' Alfred agreed, then turned to George. 'Cressida recommended Lady Trevelyan use the same chap from Scotland Yard who came to Chatterton Court a few weeks ago after we had, well, a spot of bother.'

'Yes, and though he's a good sort, he can be a bit gruff, so I thought I better have something to tell him when he gets here. Something about this poisoning.'

George put his pasty down and gawped at Cressida. 'I say, are you thinking that Lord Canterbury was murdered?'

They all looked at each other, before Cressida sighed and nodded. 'Yes. That's what I'm assuming anyway. Of course, he could have swallowed a bottle of pills by mistake, or absent-mindedly eaten the wrong sort of mushroom... that's why I wanted to track down his movements the day of his death, see what he might have eaten and with whom he might have eaten it.'

'Could he have been poisoned another way?' Alfred asked. 'Injected with a serum or touched something caustic?'

'Lady Trevelyan said his dying word was "food", hence I'm assuming he ate whatever killed him and was trying to raise the alarm as he collapsed. But you're right, Alfred,' Cressida smiled at him and he blushed just a little. 'We shouldn't rule out anything until the doc's done the post-mortem examination, which I suppose we won't know much about until DCI Andrews gets here.'

George, who had snuck a mouthful of rich, meaty pasty in while the others spoke, swallowed and chipped in again. 'So, are you thinking Lord Canterbury knew who killed him? If he sat down and ate with them, that is.' His tone became more serious.

'Yes, perhaps,' Cressida replied, thinking about it. 'I think he knew in those last dreadful moments what was happening to him, and maybe even why. I just wish rather than telling us the method, he'd tried to say a name instead.' She sighed. 'George, Lady Trevelyan said you worked together. You must know him the best out of all of us. Do you know who might hate him enough to kill him?'

George wiped his fingers on his napkin and leaned back on the bench seat of the pub table. Like Alfred, he was wearing a blazer and had done his cravat up around his neck, which he loosened a bit as he exhaled, deep in thought. 'Now there's a question. And yes, I did know him. I first met him in Egypt in the Valley of the Kings dig last year. He'd just been jilted by some young lady.' Cressida blushed, realising that must have been her, but didn't say anything. 'It was about then that he started receiving rather aggressive letters from a certain Catherine Bly. They became more and more frequent and more and more vociferous in her annoyance regarding his dealings with one of her rival journalists from *The Times*. It came to a head when the telegrams were being delivered to the camp on an almost hourly basis.'

'Did she threaten him?' Cressida asked.

'Yes. Though we all laughed it off. You know what telegrams are like; *I'm telling you you must stop. STOP. Or If you think I'm going to stop, I won't. STOP.* So many stops...' He huffed out a laugh.

'So how come she was invited here if she was such a pain in the backside to him?' Dotty followed up, and Cressida saw a look of mirth passing between her and George. He quickly became more sombre again as he continued.

'That's the interesting thing. Catherine Bly is a cousin of the Trevelyans, I think, and it was through her that Randolph met Selina. It was all rather juicy actually, with Catherine accompanying the Trevelyans to Cairo, where Lord Trevelyan had a meeting set up with Randolph to discuss importing some of the finds. Catherine got overexcited and started telling everyone that she'd have the scoop of the century, what with the tomb of King Tut being old news and Randolph's new dig being all very hush-hush, to the extent that it got quite embarrassing. It was when Selina told her cousin what a fool she was making of herself, assuming she'd have the exclusive rights to report on the dig, while they were all drinking cocktails on the terrace of the Cataract Hotel, that Randolph started looking at her all dewy-eyed. He'd heard the rumours of the scandal Selina had been involved in, but I suppose in his mind that faded away compared to being saved from the constant nagging of

Catherine Bly, not to mention there being excellent prospects in marrying Trevelyan's daughter.'

Cressida sighed. It made sense that he should fall for someone so soon after being turned down by her, especially if that person had done him such a service. 'And Selina felt the same? Catherine hadn't, well, for want of a better word, poisoned her against him?'

'From what I could see, there was no instant attraction, I'll give you that. But Randolph pursued her, and her parents thought it a good match.'

'A good match, but not a love match?' Dotty said quietly, but loud enough that the rest of them nodded.

'Exactly. I won't say she didn't love him, but she certainly didn't fall for him in Egypt, and those were heady, hot nights full of promise and all that.'

George pushed his plate away and took a silver case full of cigarettes out of his pocket. Alfred accepted one from him, but Cressida and Dotty demurred. Once lit, George took a deep puff of his cigarette.

'Then, of course, the other person who had very good reason to dislike Lord Canterbury was Roscoe Pearmain.'

'Roscoe? The gardener? I met him just this morning.' If the other information hadn't been interesting enough, this really intrigued Cressida, especially after the dirty look he'd given both her and Lady Trevelyan as they'd left him by the azaleas. 'What could he have against Randolph?'

'Roscoe's not your common or garden gardener, as it were. He started life set to inherit his father's business, Pearmain & Co. They were antiques dealers here in Cornwall, with plans to take on a London flagship store. I don't know the ins and outs, but I heard that there was something Randolph did that jeopardised the move and set wheels in motion that brought down the whole company. Cash flow, creditors, you know the sorts of things. I saw them having a rather heated tête-à-tête yesterday morning by the dahlias.'

'Gosh.' Cressida thought back to the strapping gardener she'd been introduced to earlier. 'I don't know, though, you'd think a fit, strong, young man like that would use his strength to kill someone, not some complicated potion.'

Alfred raised an eyebrow at Cressida. 'Strong he may be, but there are plenty of nasty things in garden sheds.'

'Yes, like hatchets and sharp, pointed gardening tools.' Dotty shivered and pushed her glasses back up the bridge of her nose.

'No, Dot, I mean like rat poison.' Alfred stubbed out his cigarette, picked up his pint glass and took a sip of the lightly frothing ale. 'I suppose we don't know which poison was used yet, do we?'

'No,' confirmed Cressida. 'I'm hoping I'll be able to wangle that from DCI Andrews along with the rest of the post-mortem results. Lady Trevelyan did mention that Roscoe was a dab hand with her "exotic plants", and I suppose some of them can be dangerous.'

'Oh yes, and not just exotic plants. I read that there's hundreds of poisons in your average herbaceous border. Foxgloves for digitalis and laburnum and all that,' agreed Dotty.

'Homegrown poisons or not, there's one more person up at the house that you might want to consider.' George picked up his pint glass too, but paused before taking a sip. 'Or at least, he was at the house yesterday, even if he doesn't live there. And judging by the argument I saw them having, he could well have motive to kill Randolph...'

12

'Who's that?' Cressida asked, wholly intrigued and wishing she'd brought a notebook with her.

'Jago Trengrouse,' George answered, stubbing out his cigarette. 'Cousin to the Trevelyans.'

'Another cousin... interesting. Do you know what they were arguing about?'

'No.' George sucked his teeth. 'But it looked heated. Real finger-stabbing going on.'

'When was this?' Cressida asked.

'Late afternoon, I suppose. Four-ish perhaps,' George replied.

Cressida thought for a moment while a waitress came over for their plates and took their order for another round of the local golden ale. She'd have to thank Dotty later for saving a piece of beef from Alfred's plate and sneaking it under the table to Ruby, but she was too engrossed in her thoughts to do it now.

Once the four of them were alone again, she spoke up. 'And then they had tea together. Lady Trevelyan said they were celebrating, with Lord Trevelyan too, of course.'

'Were you thinking the tea might have been poisoned?' Dotty asked.

'As soon as Lady Trevelyan mentioned it, I did, yes, but then she pointed out that Lord Trevelyan, Patrick and Jago all drank cups of tea from the same teapot, so it can't have been that. But,' she picked up a snuffling Ruby from under the table and lifted her onto her lap, 'it's clear that Randolph had at least two arguments yesterday, not to mention a tiff with Selina over breakfast, plus Catherine Bly was there, who we now know had cause to dislike him, plus we overheard her saying some terribly cruel things about Randolph to the Nangowers last night.'

'The Nangowers.' George said their name with quite some contempt. 'Now they're the worst sort of small-minded snobs. Which is a shame, as this pub serves a rather good toddy called a Nangower Cup. It's rum-based, but what else is in it I couldn't tell you—'

'Sounds like most of the cocktails you drink in London, Cressida old thing.' Alfred raised an eyebrow at her.

'Touché, Alfred, touché.'

'Why's it named after them?' Dotty leaned in, resting her chin in her hand as she pointedly asked George the question.

'Oh, they're a local family who go way back. Randolph brought me down here on one of his visits a few months ago and we had the dubious pleasure of meeting them. I got the story from Patrick about how it's rumoured Monty Nangower's ancestors turned a blind eye to the smuggling around here and helped the locals sell tax-free rum around this whole cove. Landed his family in hot water with the Customs chaps, huge fines to pay to the Crown and all that, hence them not living anywhere quite so grand as Penbeagle, though they count themselves among the gentry class around here. Sadly, without the *oblige* that goes with the *noblesse*, it seems, or indeed the pounds and shillings that go with the pence.'

'Celia Nangower had a sort of pinched look about her,'

Cressida agreed. 'I met her properly this morning down by the boathouse and she was terribly upset about the police being called to investigate poor Randolph's death. Took it as almost a personal affront on the village.'

'I suppose when you're clinging onto your family pile by a thread, the last thing you need is the bank's attention being drawn to the area and threatening to foreclose before the price of land tumbles,' George suggested.

'Or... perhaps you don't want the police called as you had something to do with a recent murder.' Cressida let the thought hang, remembering how Celia Nangower had been loitering by the boathouse to eavesdrop on her and Lady Trevelyan's conversation. 'I don't suppose Celia Nangower has a motive, but she was definitely acting fishy, if you ask me.'

'I'll tell you what's looking fishy.' Alfred jerked his head over to where a Wolseley had pulled up over the other side of the village green. 'Don't all look at once, but isn't that Selina Trevelyan in a headscarf and hiding behind a ginormous pair of sunglasses?'

Cressida, risking being seen, craned her neck to look past Dotty. A recently erected war memorial stood in the middle of the small patch of grass that served as a village green and its obelisk form was obstructing the view of the car and its occupant somewhat, but she saw that Alfred was right. She bobbed her head back down when both doors of the car opened.

'That's Selina all right, and it's a rather lovely Hermès scarf actually,' she agreed with Alfred, then raised an eyebrow as she saw who she was with. 'And look, Sebastian Goodricke's with her.'

The four of them pretended to find the top of their wooden table very interesting so as not to draw attention to themselves. Risking being noticed, Cressida looked over to where the couple had left the car and were now walking off towards the post office. They stopped and Cressida saw Selina lay a hand, palm flat, on Sebastian's chest. He grasped it with his own hands, but then she pushed him away, and although Cressida couldn't make out any of the words, she could see they were fighting.

'What's happening now, Cressy?' Dotty whispered, still keeping her head low.

'I can't see so well, they're back behind the war memorial.' Cressida arched her back, holding onto the tabletop with one hand to stop herself from falling off her bench seat. 'Oh hang on, yes, they're heading back towards the car now. She's taken those huge glasses off.'

'How odd, to come out for a drive, park up for two minutes, have a row, and then go back,' Dotty stated, much to the muttered agreement of the others.

They fell silent as the barmaid brought out their tray of drinks, and once she was thanked, they started their conversation up again.

'Makes sense, I suppose, if you wanted to have your row in private, or at least away from the house. At least it looks like Selina is feeling better, though. She's definitely got more oomph to her than she did this morning,' Cressida said.

'Sedative wearing off then?' Alfred asked as Cressida leaned back in her seat again to try to glimpse the car and its passengers once more.

'Seems to have done. Oh, gosh!' Cressida couldn't quite believe her eyes.

'What is it? What's happening?' Dotty asked.

'She's crying now, I think,' Cressida provided a running commentary for the others. 'And Sebastian is shaking his head. Oh gosh, hang on, now he's pulled her towards him and she's in his arms... Crikey, he's kissing her now! Full on the lips... By Jove.' She sat back, as did the others. 'Well, that's interesting, isn't it. Her fiancé has just been murdered and she's just been kissed by another man.'

'Sebastian and Selina?' Dotty asked. 'But that's... well, poor Randolph.'

'I suppose they met in Egypt too,' George mused, and Cressida looked at him.

'Really? When Catherine Bly was introducing Selina to Randolph? Was Sebastian there too?'

'Yes, as a matter of fact, he was. Working with the embassy on the trade mission. Caught some flak from that Bly woman too on the whole "reporting from the dig" thing. I remember them having a bit of a set-to about it.'

'All this fighting!' Dotty exclaimed. 'It seems everyone's at it!'

'Gives us another motive, though,' Cressida replied to her thoughtfully.

'Who for?' Alfred asked, now the one to crane his neck to watch as the Wolseley pulled out of the village and headed back down the lane towards Penbeagle House, Selina and Sebastian within it.

'Both of them,' Cressida replied chillingly. 'Selina can't have loved Randolph if she's kissing another man just one day after his death, in public no less. And Sebastian might well have done anything to see off his love rival. Either way, they've both just been added to my list of suspects.'

13

Cressida drove Dotty, with a perfectly content Ruby on her lap, back along the lanes to Penbeagle House. They'd left the village on the same road that they'd seen Selina and Sebastian take, and discussion about the pair occupied them as Cressida dodged more pheasants and accelerated and braked accordingly past hedgerows full of cow parsley waving gently in the breeze. Dotty had bravely opened her eyes as Cressida had pointed out the sea again, though regretted it when it meant Cressida had failed to avoid a particularly bumpy pothole.

'I'm surprised you didn't want to take the car back with the handsome George, chum,' Cressida playfully teased her friend. 'I saw he had a four-seater.'

'And leave Ruby here with no cushioning beneath her?' Dotty retaliated. 'She needs my thighs as padding against the bumps... taken at speed!'

Cressida laughed. 'Straight up though, Dot, he seems awfully nice. Very handsome. And amidst all the food for thought he was giving me, did I detect quite a frisson between you two?' Cressida risked taking her eyes off the road and glanced over to where Dotty had blushed a very pretty shade of rose.

'I didn't think I'd find anyone I liked quite so much, so soon. And, of course, I don't know how he feels about me...' Dotty tailed off.

Cressida knew she'd been heartbroken by her ex-fiancé Basil cheating on her, and it had been Cressida's mission to find her a new beau before the summer season was out. That it had happened so quickly was better than she hoped, although it was a bit of a worry that it was a man she'd met at a party where almost anyone could be a murderer. Cressida knew she'd have to find out some more about George Parish. In the meantime, keeping Dotty's spirits up was paramount.

'Pish, there's no doubting in my mind, Dotty, that he's got the absolute hots for you. Did you see how he looked at you as he loosened his cravat? Positively sizzling! But what do you know of him? Did you meet at the ball last night or just over breakfast this morning?'

'Last night. He was dressed as an Egyptian mummy and I accidentally stepped on one of his bandages.' Dotty giggled. 'He said he was "quite undone" by me, and we were then talking for most of the evening, well, before "you know what" happened.'

Cressida frowned as she drove, the shock hitting her once again that poor Randolph was dead. Dotty, however, and her love life, were very much alive, and deserved Cressida's attention right now. Avenging Randolph by finding out who killed him could wait for another mile or two.

'And... tell me, Dot, pirate to pirate... is he a gentleman of means or an adventurer on the high seas?'

Dotty laughed again, and despite this weekend's sadness, Cressida was thrilled to see her dearest friend so happy. 'Well, he's a bit of both. His father's in the army, I believe. They're Northamptonshire people, I think. But George is a favourite of a rich uncle who's starting to be very generous.'

'Always useful. Carry on.'

'Well, he didn't grow up in a house like Mydenhurst Place or Chatterton Court like you and me, and unlike Alfred, he didn't know if there would be one to inherit. The uncle was abroad then, you see, so he studied hard and then went to university and came out with all sorts of honours. He read Classics and is now doing his doctorate in archaeology, which was how he met Randolph.'

'Randolph wasn't that much older than us.' Cressida shook her head as she thought once again of his untimely death. 'But I suppose he was born into the sort of contacts that got him seats at the Royal Society and introduced to Lord Carnarvon. Does... I mean did, George see him as a sort of mentor?'

'Yes, exactly that. Randolph was a great help to him throughout his time in Egypt and I think George was invited to stay this week at Penbeagle as Randolph was meant to be introducing him to Lord Trevelyan and Jago Trengrouse. Something about a new business venture, but I'm afraid I rather got lost in his dreamy hazel eyes when he was telling me. Well, that was after he'd unbandaged his head a bit. He is awfully handsome, isn't he? And so clued up on everyone.' Dotty pulled a dozing Ruby up to her chin and nuzzled the small dog dreamily.

Cressida nodded. 'Yes. He's been a veritable gold mine of information. And yes,' she reached a hand over to Dotty and briefly clasped one of hers, 'he is terribly handsome.'

The two of them were in high spirits indeed when they rolled up the gravel driveway to Penbeagle House. Their girlish giggles subsided, though, as the house loomed into view and the events of the night before hit them afresh. How Randolph had clutched at his stomach and throat, how he'd gasped for breath. How he'd collapsed on the floor in front of them all, unable even to call out for help. Cressida shivered.

'Dotty, do you mind if I leave you to your own devices for two ticks? I rather fancy I saw Roscoe Pearmain, the gardener, down by those long grasses in that bend in the driveway and after what the gorgeous George told us about him, I'd like to ask him a few questions. Just to get all my ducks in a row before Andrews arrives.'

'Of course, Cressy. I've been meaning to raid the library and I'd be rather pleased of a quiet moment to oneself.' She pushed her glasses back up her nose as they had a habit of falling down. 'Be careful, though, I'd far rather you waited until DCI Andrews was here before you started putting yourself in danger.' Dotty had paled.

'Don't you worry, Dot,' Cressida reassured her. 'I've got the finest guard dog in the country with me – isn't that right, Rubes?'

Ruby opened an eye from where she'd curled up on the seat left behind by Dotty, who was now shaking her head in dismay.

'Fine, but if you're not back up at the house by teatime, I'm going to come and find you.' Dotty crossed her arms and tried her very best to look stern.

'Thank you, Dot.' Cressida blew her a kiss. 'Now, come on, Rubes, we've got a gardener to quiz.'

Cressida found Roscoe easily enough down by the edge of the lawn, scything tall white flowers in what looked like a rather wonderful piece of natural meadow.

'Oi!' he called over to her, a scowl on his face, and Cressida, remembering the filthy look he'd given her and Lady Trevelyan just a few hours earlier, wondered if she should have heeded Dotty's warning. Perhaps it had not been wise to come down to the bottom of the garden to ask awkward questions of the man – the very athletically built man – wielding a sharp and deadly-looking scythe, with only her wits and a terribly small dog for protection.

'Mr Pearmain! Roscoe... we met earlier. I'm Cressida Faw—'

'Get away! Get on with you, miss!' He shooed her off and she noticed that he was wearing a bandana around his face and had long gauntlets up his arms.

'I don't mean any harm, I'm—'

'It's not *you* that'll cause the harm, miss!' He flung down his scythe and pulled down the bandana. He really did look as cross as two sticks as he strode across the meadow-like ground to meet her.

Cressida started to tremble slightly, relieved that the scythe wasn't accompanying him at this velocity towards her. She glanced down to where Ruby was cowering behind her legs and picked up her trembling pup.

As the gardener closed in, his face like thunder, she all but winced as he spoke again. 'These plants are poisonous!'

'P... poisonous?' Cressida faltered in her steadfastness. Perhaps trying to find out what had happened to Randolph really was best left to the police? But the link to Randolph's death... She took a deep breath and carried on. 'What do you mean, poisonous?'

'Giant hogweed. One of the most poisonous plants hereabouts.' Roscoe's voice had lost its harshness. 'I'm sorry if I scared you, miss, I didn't mean to cause alarm, but if you'd come any closer, you might have been sprayed with the sap and it's as caustic as quicklime. Makes your skin burn for years. Hence these gloves and this.' He indicated the bandana he'd pulled down from his face.

'Oh. I see. Thank you. I had no idea. I thought... Oh never mind.' Cressida felt a bit foolish, blundering down to the gardener and expecting suddenly to find all the answers. Her hot-headedness had landed her, and Ruby, in the soup before.

So what he said next surprised her, and put her right back on her guard again.

'You thought I'd poisoned Lord Canterbury?' He looked at her, his blue eyes piercing hers.

Cressida, unsettled, unnerved and thoroughly unprepared, nevertheless held her ground. Returning his stare with an inquisitive one all of her own, she asked the simple question: 'Did you?'

14

'No, miss. I did not,' Roscoe said, taking the bandana off from around his neck and using it to mop his brow. He wasn't scowling anymore, but there was a look of disappointment on his face. 'I'm used to the likes of you going back on your word and destroying my business, but I didn't think I'd be collared for a murder just because I'm not as hoity-toity as you all up at that house.'

Cressida crossed her arms. She knew she held no distinction between a marquess and a manservant when it came to suspects, but she relented, wanting to keep the gardener on side while she questioned him. 'I'm sorry, Mr Pearmain. I shouldn't have been so blunt. And, actually, it's your old business that I came to ask you about.'

He looked up at her. 'Pearmain & Son? Why do you want to know about it? We sold all the stock to pay the creditors. There's nothing left.'

'That's what I want to know. Someone told me that Lord Canterbury had been the reason it had folded. How so?'

Roscoe looked at her, caution and suspicion clearly showing in his eyes. He stayed like this for a moment or two, before his face relaxed. 'I may as well tell you,' he said, sounding resigned. 'It doesn't paint me in the best of lights, but hear me out and I hope you'll agree that I had no recourse to hurt his lordship.'

'Please, do tell me. I promise I won't leap to any conclusions,' Cressida said, uncrossing her arms, and tried not to be taken aback when Roscoe laughed at that.

'Very well. You see, Father knew Lord Canterbury through the antiques trade and they struck some sort of deal wherein our warehouse, down in Falmouth, could be the receiving post for these new antiquities he was bringing into the country. Father assured our creditors, who were by then calling in the debts we owed on rent and the like, that new business was on its way. He pulled every favour he could to secure our tenancy there for one more year with the promise of increased business and all that. Even spoke of taking on a London showroom. Then, with no word of warning, not even an explanation, Lord Canterbury reneged on the deal. Said he'd found a preferable agent in London who could deal with the onward sales to museums and the like around the country. Made it sound like we were a little Cornish backwater with nothing.' He kicked a particularly sturdy tuft of grass. 'Didn't even give us the chance to see if we could match what those fancy London dealers were offering.'

'I'm so sorry,' Cressida murmured. 'When was this?'

'A few years ago now – 1921 the company folded. I'd just left school and was about to join him, but all the creditors got wind of the deal falling through and were like piranhas. Stripped us of everything. If you could have seen my father's face when the lorry took his desk away from the office, nothing to show for twenty years of business except a receipt from the bailiffs. He died, of course, heart attack in '23.'

'I'm so sorry.' Cressida whispered it again, shaking her head. But despite promising Roscoe not to jump to conclusions, he had just given her a very convincing motive as to why he might want to seek revenge on Randolph Canterbury. 'Mr Pearmain, I truly am sorry for your loss. But you said your story would prove that you *wouldn't* want to hurt Lord Canterbury. I can't see how it does at the moment?'

Roscoe Pearmain sighed. 'Because you're right. I *did* want to hurt Lord Canterbury. I wanted him to know that his whim, his fancy, had destroyed our company. And most probably killed my father. But I knew a small-town antiques dealer couldn't make enough noise in the trade to ruin the reputation of society darling and famous Egyptologist Lord Canterbury with his membership of fancy clubs and articles in the broadsheets about his finds. I hoped an ancient pharaoh would curse him, and perhaps he finally has.' Roscoe chuckled at the thought, then composed himself. 'I knew I had to get close to him. And on reading one of those broadsheets, I saw he was starting to become connected to the Trevelyan family and the Far East Company.'

'I see,' Cressida was impressed at his ingenuity.

'So, having always been a bit green-fingered, I applied for a job here as a gardener. I think the Trevelyans had lost a good deal of their servants during the war, not all dead of course, but they hadn't wanted to come back to domestic service. So they snapped me up with barely a reference. I was ready to meet Lord Canterbury face to face and have it out with him whenever the chance came. I never wanted to hurt him physically, only give him a piece of my mind. And if it had been public and shamed him, more the better. I could have left here with my head held high. But then...' Roscoe trailed off.

'What is it, Mr Pearmain? What happened?' Cressida was hanging on his every word.

'Have you ever been so sure you want something that you forgo everything else?' he asked, taking Cressida by surprise.

'I don't think so...' She thought of her hot-headedness in trying to solve the murders at Chatterton Court and how it had almost cost her her life. 'Well, perhaps yes.'

'You see, that was how I felt about giving Lord Canterbury a good roasting. Maybe even a punch on the nose. Then it all fell to the wayside.'

'Why?' Cressida asked, wondering what on earth could have diminished his resolve.

'Morwenna is what happened. I came to Penbeagle House for revenge, but I stayed because of love.'

'Oh.' Cressida was shocked.

'I met Morwenna within a few weeks of starting here and she stole my heart. We're engaged to be married now, you know, and it's made me realise that anger and resentment don't get you anywhere. But forgiveness and love, they're what make this crazy world make sense. Morwenna taught me that, what with what she's been through too. And after the war, what place was it of mine to bring more violence into being? And these gardens, oh these gardens. Polishing brown mahogany tables and trying to flog grandfather clocks to people with more money than time, pffft, you can keep that job. I've got fresh air, a good life here and the love of my beautiful Morwenna. I couldn't be happier.'

'And happy men don't poison people, is that what you mean?' Cressida asked.

'That's exactly it, Miss Fawcett. Why would I risk the noose when I have the most perfect life here now?'

'That's a fair point.' Cressida thought for a moment. 'You were seen having a fight with Lord Canterbury yesterday morning, though. Is there a limit to your forgiveness?'

Roscoe stubbed his toe against the grassy ground. 'Maybe that's so. I couldn't help myself and Morwenna says that although forgiveness and love will get you so far, you've also got to take opportunities when they come along. So, for Pa's sake, I had to tell him what damage he'd done. How he'd destroyed his business.' He clenched his fists open and shut.

'And how did it go, this set-to? What did Lord Canterbury say?'

'He hawed and hummed and all that posh way of not apologising, but it didn't matter. I'd said my piece and I realised that it was pointless to fight about it. Not now I've got my Morwenna.'

Cressida nodded. 'Can I ask you something about Morwenna?'

'Of course. There's nothing I don't know about her,' Roscoe said proudly.

'Do you know why she was at the Pencarrick Pottery this morning then?'

Roscoe paused. He looked confused. 'Pencarrick Pottery? Other side of Pencarrick village?'

'Yes, that's right. I took a drive out there this morning with my friend Dotty and we found it closed, all locked up. But I saw Morwenna there. Assuming your Morwenna is the same Morwenna who served me tea this morning.'

'Red hair, about so tall.' He stuck his hand out at about his shoulder height.

'That's right. I called out to her, but she ran away.'

'Well, I am sorry, miss, but I can't say for sure. I thought she was on duty up at the house all this week.' A flash of confusion rippled across his brow.

'No matter. And thank you for your time and for being so candid. I am sorry, once again, for your loss, but I'm also truly glad that you've found happiness here. It is a beautiful spot.' She cast her eyes beyond the giant hogweed across the meadow of long grasses that flowed down to the sandy cove.

'If you don't mind, miss, I better get back to work. Mind how you go, I'll not start cutting again till you're a way off.'

'Thank you, Mr Pearmain.' Cressida wished him farewell and, letting Ruby down to trot alongside her, walked back up towards the house.

Several things were going through her mind. Roscoe had spelt out exactly why he could very well be the prime suspect.

A business ruined and a beloved father so damaged by it that his heart gave out. But she wanted to believe him when he said he had forgiven Randolph for it all, now that he was so happy. He had a point; happy men do not kill people. And time was a healer too, or at least had taken the sting out of the hurt. But would Morwenna do anything for love? Would she avenge Roscoe for him? That sort of passion wasn't unheard of, and if she loved him with even half the fervour he so clearly had for her...? And seeing her at the pottery had cemented in Cressida's mind that there was something linking the maid to Randolph's movements yesterday. What was it Roscoe had just said? Morwenna was an advocate for taking opportunities when they came along?

'Ruby, we have to find out why Morwenna was at the pottery,' she said to the pup, who was bouncing along at her heels as they walked back up the driveway that curved its way towards the house.

As she cut across the lawn in front of the house, she saw Dotty waving to her from the terrace and she waved back. Dotty had made sure she was safe, and she appreciated it. Roscoe hadn't been a threat at all in the end, but if he didn't have vengeance on his mind and he wasn't the killer... who was?

She scooped up Ruby, who was now struggling after such a long walk on such short legs, and whispered into her ear, 'And until we know *why* Randolph was killed, Ruby, we also don't know if the killer is about to strike again.'

15

Ruby, obviously less worried about killers and motives and much more interested in cats, made an overexcited snuffling sound and suddenly leapt out of Cressida's arms.

'Oh, Rubes,' Cressida exhaled and, hitching up her skirt, caught up with the galloping dog in a few long strides. Picking her up, she scolded her. 'What would Andrews say if I turned you in for attempting to molest a pussy cat, eh?' Cressida looked around, but the Siamese cat had already scarpered at a pace that could always outrun a pug, so she deemed it safe to put Ruby back on the ground. 'Now, no more hounding the family pets... Oh! Ruby!'

This time, a squirrel was the cause of the excitement and Cressida, with a wave of apology to Dotty on the terrace, followed her little dog back down the lawn towards the cove and the boathouse. Just as she was thinking it was time to pick Ruby up again, saving her from the indignity of failing, once more, to catch her quarry, she noticed the boathouse door open and Patrick Trevelyan, Selina's older brother, appear from within.

'Hallo there, Patrick,' Cressida greeted him.

Patrick was one of those pale and sickly-looking types, with permanently clammy skin and a weak handshake. She could well imagine him as a feeble child with weak lungs, or whatever it was Lady Trevelyan had said. Where his sister Selina's blonde hair and blue eyes made her look ethereal, he just looked anaemic; his hair was lank and his eyes were watery. Cressida had heard that he was being passed over in favour of his cousin Jago when it came to inheriting the Far East Company, Jago being much more business-minded and on the ball, but Patrick would still stand to inherit Penbeagle House and the estate.

'Hello, Cressida.' Patrick closed the door of the boathouse and thrust his hands in his trouser pockets as he walked up the path towards her. 'Come to look over the boathouse again?'

'More squirrel saving than boathouse browsing, actually. Ruby has her eye on one.' She nodded over to where Ruby was excitedly panting at the base of an old beech tree.

'Old place does need a freshen-up.' He shrugged and made to walk on up to the house when Cressida remembered her manners.

'Patrick, I'm so sorry for your family's loss this weekend. Lord Canterbury would have made Selina a wonderful husband, I'm sure of it.'

Patrick turned and looked at her, his eyes narrowing. A flush had crept up his pale cheeks and he replied with an altogether unsavoury tone. 'Come on then, gloat if you will. Selina needed that marriage; we all know that. Save her precious reputation.' He thrust his hands back into his pockets and kicked a stone right off the pathway.

'Patrick, no, I'm not gloating, far from it. I'm sorry if you thought that. Genuinely, I just wanted to pass on my condolences.'

'Oh, I see.' He took his hands out of his pockets and crossed his arms instead. 'Thank you. It's just... well, it's put a real spanner in the works, Canterbury dying.'

Cressida thought the turn of phrase was a little odd. Surely dying had put the most fatal of spanners in Randolph's works.

'What do you mean?'

'Oh, company stuff. And family stuff. Canterbury had all the contacts, you see. And,' he uncrossed his arms and raised a finger to make his point, 'I was better connected to him than Jago.'

'Jago Trengrouse.' Cressida said the name out loud and Patrick nodded fervently.

'Yes. That's the blighter.'

'Blighter? He's your cousin?' Cressida asked, intrigued.

'Once or twice removed, I think.' Patrick scuffed his shoe along the path again.

'How did he become so integral to your father's company?' Cressida had assumed Jago was a very close relative, but perhaps not.

'Charmed his way in from the wrong side of the family when I wasn't looking,' Patrick said, and Cressida noticed him looking a bit sheepish. She wondered if she could push him for just a little bit more.

'I got terribly annoyed when my cousin Tabitha got Grandmama's best tiara.' This got Patrick's attention away from the stones on the path. 'I'm the eldest granddaughter and all that. But Papa made the excellent point that I'd spent every weekend doing something jolly and fun and Tabitha had spent a lot more time with Granny and it was my own fault if all I got was the... well, the other tiara. But you see what I mean.'

Patrick huffed out a mirthless laugh. 'Well, I dare say you might have deserved the second-rate tiara, Cressida, but that's not what's happened here. I've offered time and again to start at the bottom and work in the warehouse, but every time there's been a pat on the head and a "there, there" and I'm sent back off to the estate office to learn about running this place.' A strand of lank, blond hair fell over his forehead and he flicked it back.

'Well, that sounds like a rather large job in its own right. Running Penbeagle must—'

'But that's not the point.' Patrick all but stomped his foot. 'Father does both. But he obviously doesn't see that I can.' He crossed his arms again over his chest, his lower lip protruded slightly, and for all the world, he looked like a spoilt child released from the nursery. But his words weren't childish, they were full of passion...

Cressida let the thoughts fan through her mind like a spectrum of paint colours. Patrick had a bone to pick with his cousin Jago, and his father, but not with Randolph, it seemed. Randolph whom Patrick mourned, if not for himself, then at least for the opportunities he could have given him in the company. Patrick, it would seem, was not a fan of his cousin Jago, but did he know of the argument they'd had...

'Apparently Jago and Lord Canterbury had an argument yesterday. Did you know anything of it?'

'Yes, yes.' Patrick swept his hair away from his forehead, but was much more animated now. 'That's right, they did. A real brouhaha over the tea table.'

'The ceremonial tea?'

'No, no. A proper sandwiches tea. Dawkins, the cook here, makes a decent crab paste—'

'Sandwiches?' Cressida interrupted him. She remembered Lady Trevelyan's words... *Randolph had said food...* could one of those sandwiches have been poisoned? 'Did you see Jago eat one too?'

'Um... yes... well, maybe no. I can't remember. Anyway, important thing is I saw them having a real set-to. Angry as a September wasp, Jago was.' He chuckled. 'My money's on Jago poisoning Canterbury, don't you think?'

'If he has a motive, then maybe.' Like an annoying thread pulling through a piece of silk, Cressida felt that something about what Patrick was saying didn't sit right. 'Do you know why he'd want to kill Randolph?'

'Scheming chap, he is. As I said, not really a full cousin of ours, very distantly related. Father has polished him up, but his lack of class shows, if you know what I mean.'

Cressida, who was yet to properly meet Jago Trengrouse, did not know what Patrick meant, but for now just nodded and then partook in a few more pleasantries about the weather and such like before Patrick bowed a goodbye to her and scuttled off back to the house. She was getting the impression that despite him being his eldest child and only son, Lord Trevelyan was passing over wet fish Patrick for someone with a little more bite. But despite Patrick's obvious contempt for his cousin, it didn't mean he wasn't telling the truth. Whoever this Jago chap was, he might have been the last person to have eaten with Randolph – and he might just be the killer.

Cressida called Ruby back over to her, who, while Cressida and Patrick had been talking, had spent a happy few minutes excitedly looking up a tree where the squirrel had been nonchalantly preening itself, the attentions of Ruby obviously not bothering it a jot.

'Rubes, that was very interesting,' she whispered to her pup once she was in her arms. 'There's obviously no love lost between Patrick and his cousin Jago. No love lost at all. But Patrick seems to have no motive for killing Randolph. If anything, Randolph was about to help the Far East Company make more money, and Patrick thought having him on board would aid his cause with his father, so really no motive at all.' She murmured these words into Ruby's soft rolls of fur and absent-mindedly found herself right down by the water's edge, where, all of a sudden, voices and the sound of oars splashing through water broke her concentration.

She looked up and noticed Celia and Monty Nangower pulling themselves through the lightly choppy waters in a decent-sized rowing boat. A picnic rug covered one of the seats and a basket sat on another. Cressida raised a hand to wave to them out of politeness and Monty Nangower returned the greeting. She was about to turn around and head back to the terrace when, to her complete surprise, Catherine Bly let herself out of the boathouse.

'Oh, it's you and that dog. Hello,' Catherine said as she carefully closed the door behind her.

'Hello, Catherine.' Cressida had always been taught to be polite, but it was taking rather a lot for her to maintain her manners in the face of someone who may well have had quite some reason to kill Randolph. 'What have you been up to?'

'Wouldn't you like to know.' Catherine raised her eyebrows, creating an air of hauteur. 'Wouldn't you like to know, indeed.'

16

Cressida sighed. Yes, she did want to know, but she could see that if she asked outright, then Catherine Bly was the type of woman who, with her journalistic training, would toy with her and tease her and *she'd* then not get any sense out of her. Instead, Cressida, still with Ruby in her arms, forsook her usual excellent manners and turned her back on Catherine and started walking back up towards the house. She was pleased, and somewhat relieved, when, in a few moments, she heard Catherine's footsteps scampering up behind her.

'You were friendly with Lord Canterbury, weren't you?' Catherine said, catching up with Cressida and, to her relief, starting just the sort of conversation she'd wanted.

'I wouldn't say we were sit-down-to-a-cream-tea level of friends, but we did run into each other in London and the Royal Society and whatnot.' Cressida didn't think Catherine needed the full ins and outs of her past relationship with poor Randolph.

'Royal Society, pfft.' She mocked and pulled her thin cardigan around her slight frame. She was very slim, with the sort of thinness and pallor that made her always look – because she probably was – cold. Her pale skin was matched by auburn hair, and she wore a dramatic slick of bright red lipstick. Her pencil-thin skirt was inhibiting her from walking very fast and Cressida, naughtily, kept up a reasonable pace. Catherine was taking twice as many little steps to keep up as she talked. 'The Royal Society should have made an example of him, with this nepotism. Did you know he gave the full reporting rights on the discoveries in the Valley of the Kings to some old-school chum of his at *The Times*. Laurence Throckmorton is a hack of the direst order. It shouldn't be allowed and I'm aghast the Royal Society hasn't pushed for Canterbury's letter of resignation.'

As far as you're concerned, he's done one better than resign... Cressida thought to herself, but replied more politely.

'I'm sure Randolph wouldn't have done anything illegal...'

'Illegal? Morality, Miss Fawcett, that's what we're talking about here! Jobs for the boys! Where does talent get you these days? Nowhere if you're not brandishing a regimental tie or letters from someone's papa.'

'But you're quite well connected too, aren't you, Catherine? Couldn't Lord Trevelyan put a good word in for you at *The Times*?'

Catherine stopped in her tracks and this time Cressida halted too. Something she'd just said had obviously hit a nerve.

'I'm shocked that you'd suggest that, quite frankly.' Catherine pulled her cardigan around her again, and it empha-sised her birdlike frame. 'I won't stand for nepotism in any form, not even if it benefits me.'

Cressida understood her stance and although she still wasn't one of Catherine's biggest admirers, she notched her a little higher in her estimation. They'd strayed off topic though, and Cressida wanted to know more about Catherine and her possible motivations.

'Tell me about Egypt, Catherine. You went there with Selina and Lord Trevelyan did you not?'

'I did, yes.' Catherine closed her eyes. 'There's that smell, a mix of incense and animals, humans and spices, in such a crucible of heat that it can overwhelm one.' She inhaled as if breathing in the scents of the souk and then opened her eyes. 'And the sights. Those great pyramids at Giza, the Nile and the Cataract Hotel—'

'The Cataract. I'd love to visit. I heard you and Randolph had quite the set-to on the terrace there?'

Catherine glared at her. 'I don't much like your tone, Miss Fawcett. What are you driving at?'

Cressida took a deep breath. She knew she could get into trouble for this, aggravating suspects before DCI Andrews had even arrived, but she had to keep digging.

'Perhaps your letters and telegrams weren't getting through and you had to see Randolph in person? I don't suppose your cousin, Lord Trevelyan, looked too kindly on you causing a ruckus with his new recruit?' Cressida knew she was taking a chance revealing that she knew so much, but she wanted to catch Catherine out, see if she denied any of it. She did not.

'Those letters were honestly meant and purely professional and Cousin Edgar understands. He knows my views on journalistic integrity and I believe, deep down, he agrees that I have the moral high ground.'

'Randolph certainly knew your views, too, didn't he?'

'I don't care to think what you're insinuating, Miss Fawcett, but I too have heard the rumours of poison and I'll have you know, I had no cause to kill Lord Canterbury.' Catherine tugged at one of her sleeves and Cressida noticed how ill-fitting her cardigan was and slightly worn around the elbows and cuffs. Could it be that Catherine Bly was very much the poor relation in the Trevelyan family? It wasn't unheard of for hard-up cousins and aunts to accompany the rich young things as chaperones when it came to trips abroad like the one Selina had taken to Cairo. Perhaps, like Patrick and Jago, there was some cousinly simmering resentment going on between Catherine and Selina, and if her views on Randolph's nepotism wasn't enough, had Catherine killed him just to spite her younger, prettier and richer cousin? Catherine spoke again, filling the silence. 'It would be frightfully immoral, you see. To kill someone. And if – and I say again, *if* – I had wanted to do something as terrible as kill Randolph Canterbury, don't you think I would have done it in Egypt? When my blood was high? Away from the rigours of Scotland Yard, in a place where a few coins will buy you a pardon from the local bigwigs. Hmm?'

'I'm not sure that's a compelling argument, but I do see your point of view.'

'Point of view? It's the truth. And you'd be wise to remember it.'

'So,' Cressida changed the subject, realising that she had rubbed Catherine up the wrong way enough perhaps for now, 'what *were* you doing in the boathouse just now?'

'If you must know, the Nangowers had been generous enough to take me on a picnic with them. I may not have had much love for the deceased man, but I still didn't want to linger in a house of death and Celia and Monty gave me a smashing time with pilchard sandwiches and a tour of the creek and its history. They've just dropped me off in their boat.'

Cressida's stomach turned at the thought of pilchard sandwiches and almost remarked 'rather you than me', but kept her counsel. Instead, she thought that this might be a good time to ask about Catherine's whereabouts for the day before: the day of Randolph's murder.

'And were you with them yesterday too? They seem so generous with their time, and sandwiches,' Cressida asked, hoping it sounded innocent enough.

'Yes, as a matter of fact. Celia took me into Falmouth to try to find some glue for my costume and we had lunch by the harbour. It was a popular spot yesterday and we only managed to get a table as, believe it or not, Lord Canterbury was just leaving one.'

'Randolph?' Cressida asked, then remembered that Lady Trevelyan had said that Lord Canterbury had dined out in Falmouth for luncheon. 'Do you know who with?'

'No, I assumed he was on his own as he was paying the bill and got up and left, but now I think of it, the waiter was clearing away two plates from the table. I don't know who he had dined with. We didn't stop to chat.'

Catherine raised a well-plucked eyebrow at her and Cressida could sense that despite relishing showing off her journalistic eye for detail, the conversation was over. As they continued to walk back to the terrace in silence, Cressida thought about Randolph, dining in Falmouth mere hours before his death. His last, strained word... *'food'*. One thing was for sure, whoever had had lunch with him that day may well be suspect number one.

17

Cressida was pleased as punch that Dotty, Alfred and George were still sitting on the terrace, shielding their eyes from the sun as they pointed out circling sea birds to one another, and she was even more pleased that Catherine made her excuses and went into the house.

Dotty waved over to her and mimed pouring out a cup of tea. Cressida realised she was gasping, having not had anything since a couple of halves of warm, frothy ale with lunch in the Bootlegger's Arms a few hours ago, and enthusiastically gave Dotty a big thumbs up and mouthed 'yes please'. Ruby was obviously excited by the prospect of cream cakes and buns too and ran on ahead, taking up her position under the table, ready to pounce on any unsuspecting and unsupervised slice.

'Cressy, there you are,' Dotty said as Cressida approached with a smile, happy to be back among friends.

'We thought we'd lost you to the gardens, Cressida,' Alfred said, passing her a steaming cup of tea. 'Or worse, that boat.'

'Still smarting that you couldn't get that rigging up earlier, Alfred?' Cressida teased, accepting the cup and saucer with thanks.

Alfred raised an eyebrow at her and she laughed.

'Victoria sponge, Cressy?' Dotty asked. 'And apologies for playing mother, but Lady Trevelyan told us to help ourselves. I think she and the family are preparing somewhere for DCI Andrews.'

'Is he here?' Cressida asked, while encouraging Dotty to keep moving the knife so that she got a larger slice of cake, before Dotty made the plunge into the soft, cream and strawberry-filled confection.

'Not yet. Sunday service on the trains, I suppose,' Dotty said rather sensibly.

'Of course.' Cressida nodded. 'Any sign of Selina?'

'Not since we saw her and... well, we saw them at lunch,' George replied, his voice low.

'I'll pop in on her after tea.'

Cressida took her plate from Dotty and was just about to take a sumptuous bite of the light and fluffy cake when a handsome man in a well-fitting tuxedo walked across the terrace towards them. Dotty and Cressida instinctively met each other's eyes, brought up as they had been to recognise a single man at fifty paces (and possibly one in possession of a good fortune, as their forebear in society, Jane Austen, would have said).

'You two are like wolves,' Alfred said, putting his plate down. 'Shameless.' He shook his head, but he was smiling with it. 'Now, don't tell me, it'll be Jago Trengrouse, Cornish entrepreneur, who'll finally crack the Honourable Cressida Fawcett's resolution not to marry?' He winked at Cressida and she rolled her eyes at him. Cressida deplored winking, as it usually only happened late at night after far too many Gin Rickeys and from someone quite unsuitable, but she forgave Alfred this small misdemeanour. She did, however, ignore what he'd said and pose her own question to the group as the suave young man approached them.

'So this is Jago Trengrouse, is it? Interesting. Dotty, you

might want to put that book of old Cornish dialect down and pay attention to this one.' She flickered her eyes over to where George Parish was suddenly sitting up more upright and smiled to herself. *Yes he definitely has the hots for Dot,* she thought mischievously. She sat up more straight herself as the newcomer reached the wrought-iron table.

'Good afternoon, all,' he greeted them and Cressida heard the faintest touch of a Cornish accent still there behind his beautifully pronounced words. 'Do excuse my overdressing for tea, but I thought I'd not get a chance to change before dinner.'

'Not at all, Mr Trengrouse, it's nice to get to meet you properly,' Cressida said, stretching out a hand to him, having swallowed down her mouthful of cake.

'Please, call me Jago. And it's really very nice to meet you.' Jago's eyes glimmered with mischief as he took her hand in his and squeezed it gently.

Cressida, despite her best efforts, felt her heart beat a little faster. Jago was outrageously handsome, his dark hair set into a thick wave over his head, his eyes intelligent and dark... It was clear why he was preferred by Lord Trevelyan over his own son, as the person who could continue the family business one day. Jago didn't just look intelligent, he was obviously athletic and spry of body, as well as mind. He wore an expensive watch, and his smart tuxedo and pressed white shirt made her feel grubby and underdressed, being that she was still wearing the same clothes she'd been in since breakfast. Still, he couldn't have been more charming and a smile from him disarmed her totally.

'I hear you're pally with this Scotland Yard chap they've called for?' Jago sat down next to her and leaned in, giving Cressida his full attention. As he adjusted his cuffs, showing off his gold cufflinks and smart watch, she had to wonder why she was getting the full charm offensive.

For a moment, she looked up and saw Alfred watching her. She smiled at him, then turned back to Jago.

'Yes. Well, not pally exactly. There were several moments last time I saw him that I did wonder if it would be *me* being thrown into the cells for getting in his way.'

'But you were actually the awfully clever one who solved everything,' Dotty said, beaming with pride.

'Helped hugely by DCI Andrews, Dot. And Sergeant Kirby.' She turned back to Jago. 'Andrews was my father's batman in the Boer War. They became close, as men on the frontline often do, I suppose, and my father helped Andrews once he was back on Civvy Street. He's done well in the police force and Scotland Yard, though. He's a good man.'

'If a little gruff,' Dotty added, pushing her glasses back up the bridge of her nose. 'One sort of has to remind oneself that he has our best interests at heart when he tells one off.'

Jago sat back, nodding thoughtfully. Then he stood up, rather abruptly, and spoke to Cressida directly. 'Miss Fawcett, will you take a quick walk with me around the lawn. There's something of a delicate nature I'd like to discuss.'

Cressida, who had been rather enjoying sitting down and eating her cake, exchanged another glance with Alfred, but nodded. 'Of course, Jago. Dot, will you look after Rubes? I'm sure we won't be long.'

'Cressida...' Alfred said, but she gave her head an almost imperceptible shake in his direction and turned to Jago.

'Come on then, one more turn around the lawn won't kill me.'

'Thank you for humouring me,' Jago confided in her, leaning his head down and speaking quietly even though they had now wandered halfway down the lawn towards the cove, well out of earshot of those on the terrace. One glance back up to where Dotty, Alfred and George were sitting told Cressida that although they might be out of earshot, they were being keenly watched.

'What was it you wanted to tell me?' Cressida asked him, intrigued as to what could have required this private tête-à-tête.

'It's about Canterbury's death.'

'Oh yes?' She was definitely all ears now.

'Yes.' Jago stopped and turned to face Cressida, a look of clear consternation on his face.

'You know something?' Cressida asked, keen to know more.

'I don't know if it'll have any bearing on the case, but I thought, what with your connection to the Scotland Yard chap, you should know.' He paused. 'Selina and Canterbury weren't exactly love's young dream.'

Cressida narrowed her eyes. It wasn't hard to believe Jago, having witnessed the scene outside the Bootlegger's Arms. Sebastian Goodricke had kissed Selina just hours after her fiancé had died...

'Go on.' Cressida crossed her arms in front of her, looking squarely at Jago. His eyes had that intensity about them again as he looked right at her and spoke.

'I saw them having a fight yesterday morning. A filthy row. Hammer and tongs, they were.'

'A lovers' tiff?'

'If that's love then...' His eyes conveyed that he knew full well what love could be like.

Cressida sighed. He was flirting with her, that was for sure. But perhaps it was no bad thing to keep him on side, especially if it came with useful information.

'Passion can come in many forms, as I'm sure you know.' She looked up at him through her eyelashes coquettishly, playing him at his own game. 'Do you know what the fight was about?'

Jago's look intensified. His eyes really were quite mesmeric and a more romantically notioned female than Cressida would have to remind herself to focus on what he was actually saying.

After a moment or so, Jago replied and his answer chilled Cressida to the core. 'Yes, I do. And I hope it wasn't what got him killed...'

18

'Selina and Randolph's argument might have got him killed?' Cressida barely knew Jago and, although he didn't seem the type, she wasn't sure if he was prone to hyperbole or gross exaggeration. 'Tell me, what was it about?' Cressida pressed.

Jago looked at her, his eyes full of concern. 'Selina has... this is difficult to say, but she's been abusing opiates for a while now.'

'Oh.' Cressida was taken aback. This wasn't what she'd been expecting at all.

'Surely you can tell? She's a dope fiend.'

The image of Selina walking sleepily into the drawing room this morning made sense now. And, of course, what she'd asked for...

'Poppy...' she whispered. 'She was asking for Poppy this morning.'

'Yes.' Jago took a hand from his pocket and jabbed the air with a finger. 'That's what she calls it.'

'Because opiates come from poppies, that's correct, isn't it?'

'That's right. Opium poppies in central and Far Eastern Asia.'

'I thought since the end of the war, they've been illegal? I remember Mama complaining about it when she couldn't get any laudanum from the pharmacist. Not that she was a dope fiend, I hasten to add, but it wasn't uncommon to just buy it, I think.'

Jago shrugged. 'I wouldn't know. I don't touch the stuff. And neither, it seemed, did Randolph, as he hated the fact that Selina was so dependent on it.'

'But why would Selina being addicted to opiates, as unfortunate as that is, have anything to do with Randolph's death?' Cressida asked.

'Well, I overheard Selina warning Canterbury that if he mentioned anything to her parents—'

'They weren't aware?' Cressida thought back to how sedated Selina had looked this morning, and the way she had slurred slightly as she spoke last night, and Lady Trevelyan admitting to her that Selina hadn't been herself recently. 'I think her mother might have an inkling.'

'Perhaps.' Jago shrugged and stared off into the distance. 'From what I heard of the argument, Selina obviously thought that neither Lord or Lady Trevelyan knew how dependent she was. But Canterbury had noticed that her habit was getting worse and that seemed to be the catalyst for the frightful bust-up I overheard. Selina promised Canterbury that she wasn't getting anything through from us, the Far East Company, which is a huge relief.'

'I'd say!' Cressida rocked back on her heels. It had never crossed her mind how drugs were brought into the country, but she could, hand on heart, say she had never thought it would be through reputable trading companies.

Jago continued. 'Can you imagine how Cousin Edgar would feel if he found out that not only was his daughter addicted to drugs, but it was his company that was somehow supplying her? It's a relief to know we don't have to deal with a smuggling ring.'

'Quite. But Randolph was obviously upset enough about it to confront her? And she wasn't best pleased?'

'From what I overheard, she was livid. Threatening Canterbury with calling off the wedding and saying she'd feed lies about him to her father that would stop his employment in its tracks.'

'Hmm. Lovers' tiff, my derrière. Poor Randolph. But did she threaten to kill him?'

Jago paused. 'In a way,' he replied, adding, 'Selina said she'd stop at nothing to prevent her parents finding out. *Nothing.*'

'I see.' Cressida frowned. From what she understood, those high on opiates weren't prone to murderous outbursts, but if Jago was to be believed, and there was no reason to doubt him, Selina now had two possible motives for wanting Randolph Canterbury out of her life: her drug addiction, and Sebastian.

'Look, it was on my mind and I just thought you should know. If you have the ear of that detective, then perhaps you should tell him.'

'Thank you, Jago. You must tell him too, though.'

Jago nodded and was about to turn and walk back up to the terrace when Cressida stopped him.

'One other thing, before you go. I heard that you and Randolph had a fight. What was that about?'

'Us? I don't think so. Who said that?' Jago had the intensity back in his eyes.

'I heard it was just before your tea ceremony.' She stood, stalwart, awaiting an answer.

'Oh that.' Jago flicked a piece of fluff from his lapel. 'Not a fight so much as a minor disagreement.' He looked at her. 'I didn't kill him, if that's what you're driving at. We spoke a bit about some finer points of the contract as we took some air. He wanted more commission, I think, but I said we could discuss it with Cousin Edgar after tea. It wasn't anything I'd kill over.' His eyes were fervently searching hers now and, much to Cressida's surprise, she felt him take one of her hands in his. 'I swear to you, Miss Fawcett, I'm not a killer.'

'I see.' Cressida swallowed hard, aware of how this could look to those still sitting on the terrace. She blushed. 'Well, thank you for letting me know about Selina. And please, call me Cressida.' She saw him smile at this and as she modestly turned her head away, she glanced up towards the terrace, where Dotty and George were deep in conversation. Her senses had been right, though – Alfred was looking right at her. As their eyes met, Alfred looked at his watch and it broke the spell Cressida had momentarily been under.

She turned back to Jago and wondered how many other women he might have turned his charm on for, Selina Trevelyan for one. Might he have wanted to cement his position in the company by becoming more than just Lord Trevelyan's second cousin, or whatever he was?

'Jago, forgive my asking, but did you and Selina ever—'

'Selina? No.' He dropped Cressida's hand and examined his fingernails. 'I don't have time for people who ruin their lives with drugs.'

Cressida was about to answer when Dotty's flailing arms caught her eye. Her friend was waving frantically from the terrace. Cressida merely raised an eyebrow at Jago, still thinking about everything he'd just told her, and without another word walked back towards her friends.

'Cressy!' Dotty beckoned her back to where they were sitting. 'Cressy, he's here.'

'Andrews?'

Dotty nodded and Cressida was pleased of it. She was looking forward to filling in the genial policeman with everything she knew.

'Not long before the dinner gong though, I should imagine,'

Alfred chipped in, standing up and brushing some loose crumbs off his trousers, much to Ruby's delight. He hovered a hand near Cressida's arm, then seemed to think better of it. 'Don't play with Andrews for too long or you'll miss dinner.'

'Righto.' Cressida smiled at him, scooped up Ruby and said her goodbyes to her friends, and Jago, who had by now joined them, and headed inside. She had much to tell Andrews and country house dinner etiquette said she had to say it all before she swapped her sensible shoes for her silk slippers. Time, as ever, was of the essence.

19

'Good afternoon, Andrews, ah and Sergeant Kirby too! How splendid to see you both again.' Cressida, who had just entered the drawing room, greeted the Scotland Yard detective and his sergeant warmly, even putting Ruby down so she could stretch out a hand to them both.

'Good afternoon, Miss Fawcett,' Andrews replied, taking her hand and shaking it. Kirby, a generation younger than his colleague, and ruddier of cheek and stouter of frame, took her hand with great care too. Cressida noticed a blush grow over his cheeks. She patted his arm fondly and turned back to DCI Andrews. He looked in good health and Cressida smiled as she took in the well-polished shoes, neatly trimmed beard and smartly cropped hair of her father's former batman, who was now a senior detective in the London Metropolitan police force. She had helped him bag a killer at Chatterton Court only a few weeks back and although it had been kept out of the papers, he had been good enough to keep her appraised of how the case was progressing through the courts.

'You look well, Andrews,' Cressida told him, noticing that

he looked less dark around the eyes and the lines on his fore-head seemed less pronounced. 'Have you been sleeping better?'

Andrews nodded. 'Things have been a little easier since our success at Chatterton Court. Solving the case with yours truly and doing so with such discretion, without upsetting the high orders, has bolstered my standing somewhat.' He coughed and adjusted his already neat waistcoat that complemented his smart tweed suit.

'Oh good. I am glad. Gold stars all round, I hope.' Cressida also hoped it would mean he'd be more amenable this time round to her 'helping out', as at Chatterton Court he'd at times been terribly gruff. She knew now, of course, that it had only been due to his worry over her safety in a house where a murderer had been on the loose. She wondered if he'd be equally as protective, and therefore a hindrance to her, this time. She decided to head him off at the pass. 'Andrews, before you tell me not to go poking my nose in anywhere—'

'I believe your friend Mr Sauvage at Liberty called it your aristocratic nose, Miss Fawcett,' he cut in, barely containing his mirth.

'Yes, well, my aristocratic nose has already done some digging for you.'

'Shall I get the evidence bags from the motorcar, sir?' Sergeant Kirby asked. His cheeks had returned to a more normal colour and he was now standing ramrod straight to attention. Cressida wondered if he thrust out his chin so far merely so that his helmet strap didn't garrotte him.

'Not yet, Sergeant. Let's see what Miss Fawcett has to say. Please, go ahead.' He beckoned for her to sit down on one of the wicker-backed chairs by the fireplace.

Ruby looked up expectantly at her and Cressida pulled her up onto her lap. 'No need to hide behind a screen this time, Rubes, or put up with the whiff of fish paste sandwiches.'

'You're still lucky I didn't arrest you then, Miss Fawcett,

for spying on a police officer.' Andrews looked at her sternly and Cressida mimed pressing her lips shut, hoping she was right in thinking it was a fatherly telling-off, not an official one. Andrews sat down opposite her, pulling at the knees of his trousers, and spoke to Kirby. 'Notebook out please, Sergeant.'

Kirby fumbled in his pocket for his regulation notebook and pencil.

'Now then, Miss Fawcett, what can you tell me about this case so far?' Andrews asked.

'Well.' Cressida put Ruby back down, brushed dog hair off her skirt and then demurely crossed her legs. 'Welcome to Penbeagle House.' She raised her hands up, indicating the finery in the room in which they sat.

Andrews and Kirby both took a moment to admire their surroundings and Cressida could see the experienced policemen's eyes lingering on the tall fireside vases and bronze lustrous ornaments on the mantelpiece.

'It's certainly a fine house, and home to Lord and Lady Trevelyan, I understand.'

'Yes. Have they greeted you? Offered tea? Something stronger?'

'Indeed they have. Tea that is. And I'm sure a maid will be through with something soon. However, thanks to the Sunday trains, we took longer to get here than we planned, stopping off to borrow a motorcar from the Falmouth constabulary, and will take ourselves off to the... where was it, Kirby? Bootlegger's Arms, before long. Start afresh in the morning.'

'Well, you'll get a good dinner there if our lunch was anything to go by, and let me give you some more morsels to chew over while you're dining. Namely, that I knew the deceased man reasonably well. In fact, he proposed marriage to me about this time last year.'

There was an audible gasp from Kirby, though Cressida

supposed it could just be his chin strap strangling him, while Andrews just sighed and nodded.

'So you feel you owe this poor gentleman some justice then, I suppose?' He leaned forward in his chair. 'Remember what I said at Chatterton Court, Miss Fawcett. It's justice we're after, not vengeance.'

'Yes, Andrews, I remember. And I know justice was served there, too. As it will be here, I'm sure of it. And, before you ask, yes, I'm being terribly careful not to get myself firmly in the sights of any murderer.'

Andrews raised a sceptical eyebrow at her. 'So, what do you know so far then, Miss Fawcett?'

Kirby stood poised.

'Well, Lord Canterbury died last night in front of dozens of people at the Penbeagle fancy-dress ball. We were all there, everyone who's currently still in the house and, of course, plenty of other people who left after... the incident. Randolph collapsed at about ten o'clock, much to all of our horror. His fiancée, Lord and Lady Trevelyan's daughter Selina, fainted and several guests rushed over to help. It was Napoleon, who I later found out to be Monty Nangower, a neighbour of the Trevelyans, who closed Randolph's eyelids and it was then we knew he was dead.' Cressida looked at her hands resting in her lap. Saying it out loud did bring it all back, along with how adamant she'd been last night to seek justice for Randolph. 'Anyway, the local doctor was at the ball and he declared the time of death. He was also the one who suggested that Randolph had been poisoned.'

'I see.' Andrews sat back. 'And by poisoned, you took that to mean murdered, rather than poisoned by accident?'

'I'm keeping an open mind, Andrews. These people here are by and large my friends. But, you see, I've been working out what Randolph did yesterday, trying to track his movements, and at every turn I've found an argument or an intrigue, whether it was with his fiancée Selina over her apparent drug dependency or his cousin-in-law-to-be about the finer points of a business contract. Not to mention another cousin of the Trevelyans called Catherine Bly, who had been sending him threatening letters; Sir Jolyon Westmoreland, who I believe is angling for his lucrative contract with the Far East Company; Sebastian Goodricke from the Foreign Office, who is having some sort of dalliance with Selina; the gardener, Roscoe Pearmain, who held Randolph responsible for his father's early death; or, indeed, Roscoe's lover, Morwenna the maid, who I also saw creeping around the local pottery where Randolph had visited yesterday.'

'Hold on, hold on...' Andrews raised his palm to pause Cressida as Kirby wrote at a furious pace.

'I haven't found out anything about George Parish, though he gave me quite a bit of the information about the others and he seems a good sort. I'd say that Celia Nangower, who is a neighbour and married to Napoleon, I mean Monty, is a bit shifty, if you ask me. Always hanging around eavesdropping, though I can't see that she has a motive. Of course, then there's us, but you don't need to worry about me, Dotty and Alfred.'

Andrews and Kirby had gone from looking relatively calm and in control to being as flustered as feather dusters caught in a crosswind. Andrews was quick to regain his composure, however.

'I see. Thank you, Miss Fawcett. Leave us with that to ponder. We'll start interviews with the household and guests as soon as possible.' He looked at his watch. 'Hmm, not much time before dinner.'

'Oh lawks, dinner,' Cressida said, getting up. 'I'd better go and change before I'm cast out of society for being underdressed by the cocktail hour. Can I beg a favour from you though? Can we meet again tomorrow morning? I'd be awfully grateful if you'd fill me in on anything you discover and, of course, the findings of the post-mortem.'

Andrews looked at her sternly. 'This will be a police matter, Miss Fawcett. I can't go around giving you confidential information willy-nilly.'

'Of course, Andrews. I can see your predicament. I suppose, in that case, you won't want to know any more of what I find out from my chums here at the house. So much gossip... and that's just above stairs!' Cressida had been drawing a finger along the wooden arm of the wicker-backed chair, but now looked up at DCI Andrews, who had gone from looking stern to resigned.

He sighed and shook his head.

'You'll be pleased to know that a post-mortem was one of the first things I asked of the Falmouth constabulary. Along with full background checks on Lord Canterbury and the Trevelyans. We'll see what they come back with and if any of it matches up with your, shall we say, less orthodox form of research. And can I please ask you, Miss Fawcett—'

'Not to get myself into a pickle until then? Of course you can *ask*, DCI Andrews... Come on, Rubes. Toodle-oo, Andrews!' Cressida gave him and the exhausted-looking sergeant a wave and left them in peace in the drawing room, its large sash windows filling the elegant room with a glorious evening light.

20

Ruby, despite being as elegant a little snout-nosed hound as could be, had ideas other than those of what to wear for cocktails and pointed said snub nose in the direction of the kitchens.

'I suppose you've not eaten properly since that snaffled pasty at lunch, Rubes, as, of course, one never counts cake. Come on then, let's see if cook can spare you something, and while we're there, I'd like to see if I can talk to Morwenna.'

Ruby snorted and trotted happily along with her.

As with many large stately homes, there was a baize door that connected the servants' quarters with the smarter areas of the house, and Cressida easily found the one at Penbeagle House and pushed it open. It swung on two-way hinges and she and Ruby walked through. They were instantly greeted, much to both their satisfaction, with the smell of supper cooking.

'Gosh, that smells good. Seems like Mrs Dawkins can whip up more than just a decent crab paste. Now then, Rubes, we mustn't be long. Let's hope I can get Morwenna to corroborate what Roscoe said, as I'm inclined to agree that a happy man is not a murderous one.' She lowered her voice to a whisper as they neared the kitchen. 'But a woman so in love with someone might do anything for him... And I have to know what Morwenna was doing at Pencarrick Pottery earlier too, and why she pelted away from us with such haste.'

Ruby panted in agreement with all of Cressida's plans and Cressida praised her for being not only the prettiest pooch, but also the most wise, the rest of the length of the corridor.

Once at the door of the busy hive that was the kitchen, she popped her head around the doorway, calling out to the head cook. 'Hello? Mrs Dawkins?'

'Hello, miss, can I help?' A young scullery maid had noticed Cressida and had come up to the door, wiping her hands with the linen towel that was hanging from her waist.

'Yes, two things really. Firstly, is there anything going spare that might do for my dog? Morwenna was kind enough to bring up chicken livers for her breakfast, and I'm afraid the young pooch is pining for more.' Cressida looked down at Ruby, who did her very best impression of a starving dog for the maid.

'Of course, miss, there's some leftover beef from luncheon, I can plate some up for her.'

Ruby panted appreciatively and Cressida smiled at the helpful maid.

'Thank you. You're her new favourite.'

The maid blushed and was about to bob a curtsy and go off in search of the leftover beef when Cressida stopped her.

'Oh, the second thing, if I may... is Morwenna here?'

'Oh, sorry, miss. No, miss. And cook's in an awful tizz about it. No one's seen her for a bit.'

'But she's meant to be here?'

'Yes, miss, though she's had a few times when we thought she would be working, miss, but she didn't turn up.'

Cressida frowned and was about to ask the maid another question when Mrs Dawkins the cook bustled over and shooed the young scullery maid out of the way.

'I'll see about that beef, miss,' she said, and Cressida encouraged Ruby to follow her.

'Good evening, miss,' Mrs Dawkins said, herself now drying her hands on a similar linen cloth that was tucked in over her apron strings. 'What can I help you with?' The cook looked hassled, as well she might with a three-course dinner to prepare for a dozen people tonight, following on from the food for the ball last night... not to mention the unsettling matter of the death in the house. Cressida knew she should keep this quick.

'I was just wondering if Morwenna was here.'

'Morwenna? Curse the bairn.' Cook shook her head. 'I'd point you in her direction if I had any idea what direction that was.' Mrs Dawkins looked vexed. 'Though I'd wager it might involve that gardener she's taken a shine to.' She crossed her arms. 'Meant to be here, but now I've had to get Joanna there on the pots and Amy won't want to wash them all herself and—'

'Is she missing?' Cressida was suddenly worried about the maid.

'Missing?' Mrs Dawkins shook her head. 'I wouldn't go that far. Late is all. Tardy as ever these days. Like I said, she's got a distraction in the form of a certain green-fingered young man. Was she around when I needed her yesterday with the vol-au-vents? Was she ever!' She blew a stray few hairs that had crept out of her mobcap away from her eyes, then tucked the lock of hair back under her cap.

It was steamy in the kitchen and Cressida didn't want to wait long unless her shingled hair lost all its curls in the humid heat. Once again, she appreciated quite how hard life as a servant was, and how grateful she was for being born nibbling on the proverbial silver spoon. Perhaps Morwenna didn't like being in the kitchen either and was gearing up for life with Roscoe away from domestic service? From what Dawkins was saying, she was very much enamoured of him, which at least corroborated his version of events.

'Is she often late? Or skipping shifts?' Cressida wondered if the cook could tell her more about Morwenna's visit to the pottery, but also didn't want to land her in the soup.

'I'd send her packing with a flea in her ear if she weren't so... well, if she weren't so useful and we weren't so lacking in good staff,' Mrs Dawkins said, and Cressida nodded as the cook continued. 'And then, she fainted in the meadow the other day when she was picking the cow parsley for the flower arrangements in the orangery. Of course, Her Ladyship had florists in for the lovely displays last night, but one of them asked us for help gathering some more wild flowers and, what with the cow parsley all over, it was easy enough, you'd think, but Morwenna quite passed out down by the meadow and had to be revived by her Roscoe, so she did.'

'Poor thing. Did she say why she'd felt faint?'

'Well, it certainly wasn't from overworking.' Mrs Dawkins looked pointedly at the kitchen clock and shook her head. 'She's late as anything now and I've got ten plates spinning round me ears, I'm so busy. Excuse me, miss, but I really must get on. That parsley sauce won't stir itself. Joanna! Watch that pan!' The cook suddenly left Cressida's side and ran over to where a saucepan bubbled over on the stove.

Cressida moved back from the doorway, realising that the last thing these industrious women needed was someone watching over them as they worked, but while she waited for Ruby to wolf down some rather excellent-looking sliced beef, she could not stop thinking about Morwenna... Roscoe hadn't known about Morwenna's trip to the pottery, and Mrs Dawkins had noticed Morwenna's tardiness several times. Where was Morwenna now? And, most importantly, thought Cressida as Ruby licked the final scrap from the plate, what *was* Morwenna up to?

21

Ruby was more satisfied with her trip to the kitchens than Cressida, and while the small pup licked her chops as she walked along, Cressida wondered about the absent Morwenna. It made her all the more determined to find her and ask her about her visit to the pottery... and see if she had a good reason for not being around to help set up for the ball; the ball where Randolph had died. She was occupied by these thoughts as she came across Sir Jolyon Westmoreland in the hallway.

Sir Jolyon was a large man, tall and with a domed head completely devoid of hair. Where the follicles should have been, a light gloss instead occupied his forehead and Cressida wondered if his servants were a dab hand at the beeswax and polishing cloth.

'Miss Fawcett.' He bowed slightly as he greeted her, and Cressida immediately felt bad regarding her thoughts vis-à-vis his forehead.

'Sir Jolyon. I've been quite remiss at saying hello to you before now. Please do excuse my appalling manners.'

'Nothing to apologise for, Miss Fawcett. This has hardly

been what one might call a normal house party. How's your father, by the way?'

This took Cressida by surprise, though really it shouldn't have. After he'd been shipped home from the Boer War, injured, his life saved by dear DCI Andrews, her father had recovered well and he and Cressida's mother, Lady Rosamund, had been great ones for society. There had been many an evening when the young Cressida had hovered behind the ancient wooden banisters of the staircase at Mydenhurst Place, their ancestral home, listening to the chatter as her parents had played host to most of Edwardian society. That she couldn't recall a Sir Jolyon among the guests wasn't a big surprise; since she had been rather more interested in seeing what was being served in the family's crystal glasses and what the fashionable ladies were wearing than remembering everyone's names.

'He's well, thank you. And Mother. Both keeping their spirits and knees up in equal measure.'

Sir Jolyon chuckled, and Cressida felt more warmly disposed towards the older man now she knew there was a family connection. She hoped the feeling would be mutual as she decided to quiz him about his relationship with Randolph.

'Sir Jolyon, can I ask you something? I'm afraid it's about Lord Canterbury, who I believe you knew fairly well too?'

Jolyon Westmoreland took out a spotted handkerchief and, proving that no servants were needed, polished his own fore-head with it. 'Very sad affair, very sad,' he said, cramming his handkerchief back into the pocket of his tweed trousers.

'Were you upset at the advantage his marriage to Selina was giving him in his dealings with the Far East Company?'

'Well, that's... well, that's quite presumptuous, young lady.' He looked worried, Cressida thought, and although it strained against her good breeding and usually excellent manners, she believed she owed it to Randolph to push the older man further.

'I know, Sir Jolyon. But I know you were keen to work with Lord Trevelyan, and Lord Canterbury was standing in your way rather.' Cressida knew this was incendiary stuff, but she had to gauge Sir Jolyon's reaction. And gauge it she did, as she noticed his face flush and his hand reach once again for the spotted handkerchief.

'I'll have you know that Randolph and I had a gentleman's agreement in place. Recently, I was able to facilitate the sale of a superb mask of Agamemnon to a private collector. Randolph and I shared a whisky afterwards and he congratulated me on being the best man for that job. There was no cut-throat rivalry between us, dear girl.'

Cressida nodded, but hearing him speak of his 'gentleman's agreement' reminded her of something Randolph had said last year when he'd been courting her. 'I suppose it was all tit-for-tat as he'd managed to swing that mummy for the British Museum, hadn't he, when you'd been trying to organise the sale of it from the Egyptian authorities for months.'

'Well, yes, that was a blow to the portfolio.' Sir Jolyon coughed and said 'ahem' a few times too.

'So what with his new alliance with Lord Treveylan, wouldn't you say you were rather being squeezed out of the market?' She had to see how he'd react to this.

Sir Jolyon did indeed seem riled. The handkerchief was swiped across the sweaty brow another time and he looked to be very much on the back foot as he shoved it back into his pocket.

'Now, look here, young Fawcett, I don't much like what you're implying with all these questions and suppositions. You think I had something to do with Randolph's tragic death? Well, I can tell you that I did not. Were we rivals? Indeed we were.' He rummaged in his pocket and the handkerchief was brought out again. But instead of being wiped across his brow, it was kept bunched up in his pudgy fist as he jabbed a finger in the air at her. 'But I'll tell you who you should be asking about all this jiggery-pokery.'

'Who?' Cressida asked with great interest.

Sir Jolyon barely missed a beat in telling her. 'George Parish, that's who. That young man had a vendetta against Randolph if anyone did. Saw them having a filthy row in Falmouth yesterday. Over lunch it was, just hours before Canterbury fell down dead. So if you're looking for someone to blame,' the finger was still jabbing in the air towards her, 'then I recommend you go and talk to that Parish man.'

'George Parish?' Cressida was now very much the one on the back foot. George Parish, who had been so charming and given her some juicy background information on almost everyone else here at Penbeagle House... everyone, it seemed, except himself. So *he* had been the one who had lunched with Randolph! Cressida bit her lip and shook her head while Sir Jolyon, perhaps spotting an avenue to further distance himself from any accusations, carried on talking about Randolph in the most glowing, and non-murderous, terms.

'Parish was Canterbury's protégé. They worked in Egypt together for months, and I daresay Parish learned more from Randolph than from his academic studies beforehand.'

'George is a scholar, though, in his own right.'

'Undoubtably, but Randolph was the expedition lead. Head honcho. Took credit for all the finds and young Parish, a bright young scholar as you say, was not pleased with that. Thought his finds should be filed under *his* name. Misunderstanding perhaps, I'm not one to quiz about these academic niceties, but Parish was in a filthy mood about it. Threatened letters to the Royal Society and had no good word to say about his former mentor when the exhibits were brought back to the museum. I knew he and Randolph would be forced together this weekend, but I didn't realise it would end in the fisticuffs that I saw in Falmouth.'

'A real fight?' Cressida couldn't imagine it of the amiable young man she'd had lunch with. The amiable young man who'd said he'd been invited by Randolph. The amiable young man who she'd so hoped might be a match for darling Dotty... 'George, Mr Parish I mean, seems so nice. And Randolph, well, he never struck me as the type to resolve an issue with his fists. Pen is mightier than the sword and all that.'

Sir Jolyon shifted his weight and cleared his throat. 'Perhaps it wasn't so pugilistic as all that, the Marquess of Queensbury was not troubled for his rulebook, let's say, but scruffs of necks were taken, collars were ruffled. Two young bucks, antlers locked, you know the drill.'

'I see. And when you intervened?'

Sir Jolyon coughed and 'ahem'ed a few times before saying. 'Not my place, dear girl, not my place. Other side of the harbour and all that too. And Randolph seemed able to handle himself.'

Cressida frowned, deep in thought. 'So are you sure it was Mr Parish that you saw? If you were so far away from them both?'

'Positive, dear girl, positive. Seen him plenty of times at the Royal Society and would recognise him in a darkened tomb in a sandstorm, let alone across a harbour on an English summer's day.'

'Hmm,' Cressida paused and, noticing that Sir Jolyon was looking at a carriage clock on a side table, realised she really must get upstairs and change for dinner. 'That really is very interesting. Thank you, Sir Jolyon. I'll pass on your regards to my parents.'

Sir Jolyon nodded a brisk farewell and they parted ways.

Just a few hours ago, Cressida had been keen to find out who had had lunch with Randolph in Falmouth, suspecting that whoever it was could have been the one to poison him with something suitably slow-acting that would have resulted in his collapse hours later. Now, however, she wished she hadn't found out. Poor Dotty. Her heart had been broken once this summer already, and would Cressida have to tell her yet another beau was the wrong side of the moral compass?And, what was worse, could Dotty be in danger if George was the poisoner? What if he chose to strike again?

22

Suddenly, the thought of Dotty's life being in danger filled Cressida with horror and she beckoned Ruby to trot with considerably more purpose as she rushed up the stairs and towards her bedroom. She knew Dotty had a room very close to hers, so she headed for the same landing and glanced at each door, reading the names in the small brass frames at eye height on each one. On the other side of the landing from her own, she spied the name Lady Dorothy Chatterton and started hammering her fist on the door when she breathlessly reached it.

There was no answer.

'Dotty! Dotty!' Cressida rested her head against the gloss paint and called out to her friend between catching her breaths. 'Dotty!'

Ruby snuffled and pawed at the bottom of the door and it was a testament of how worried Cressida was about Dotty that she didn't spare more than a glancing thought for the poor paintwork. But Ruby was being more than just a pickle, and Cressida followed her lead.

'Of course, thanks Ruby.' She took a deep breath and

opened the door, the knob twisting with a catch. Ruby barrelled into the room before Cressida could even get the door fully open. 'Dotty!' she called out again, but there was no answer.

Cressida eyed the room, taking in the elegant Chinoiserie wallpaper and inlaid wood cabinets and wardrobe, where no doubt Dotty's clothes were neatly hanging. But there was no sign of Dotty at all. *Had she dressed for dinner and gone downstairs for cocktails already?*

Cressida glanced at a clock that was ticking gently on the mantelpiece. Dotty, being about one hundred times more punctual than Cressida herself, could well be perfectly fine, dressed and already sipping on the first dry sherry of the evening. She pulled open the wardrobe door and, sure enough, at least two of the hangers were empty, showing that an evening dress was most likely being worn. Dotty's knickerbockers and cashmere jumper, along with her blouse and neck scarf that she'd been wearing earlier were neatly draped over an upholstered bench at the end of the bed.

Cressida moved over to where a dressing table sat at an angle to one of the large sash windows. Dotty's silver-backed hairbrush and a few cut-glass and silver-topped bottles sat on the glass top of the pretty dressing table and Cressida absent-mindedly picked up Dotty's perfume bottle and smelt the reassuringly familiar scent.

The curtains at the large sash window, which were a damask silk like in her own room, but in a dusky rose colour, were not yet drawn and Cressida looked out over the lawn to the glistening waters of the cove in the distance. She gasped. There was Dotty, dressed for dinner in a pretty silver crêpe de Chine evening dress, her chestnut bob silkily swishing under a sequinned silver headband, walking down the lawn towards the boathouse with a champagne glass in her hand... with none other than George Parish.

Cressida pressed herself right up against the pane of glass to get a better look. Yes, that was George all right, she could see his wavy dark hair and occasionally he turned his head towards Dotty and laughed at something she was saying. He was also dressed for dinner in a smart black tuxedo, and as they picked their way over the lawn, Dotty was struggling slightly in her high-heeled shoes. George cupped one of her elbows in his hand, supporting her as she walked. Supporting... or coercing?

'Come on, Rubes, after what Sir Jolyon said about George, we mustn't take any chances...' Cressida scooped up her dog and hotfooted it out of Dotty's room, hoping with every step that Sir Jolyon had been wrong about George and that he wasn't the sort of man to slip a poisoned draught of something into someone's lunch... or champagne glass.

Cressida was down in the hallway in a matter of moments, and with Ruby still clasped in her arms, she headed for the terrace and the lawn beyond. The early-evening light was still good enough for her to see what she had spied only moments earlier from Dotty's bedroom window. Dotty and George were disappearing into the boathouse, their voices chattering, a giggle from Dotty carrying up with the breeze from the creek beneath them.

Oh Dotty... Cressida sent up a prayer, asking for her protection. She tried to placate herself with many a reasoned argument churning through her head as she picked up the pace towards the boathouse. She muttered them out loud to Ruby as she ran. 'George may have lunched with Randolph the day of his murder, but did he have the strongest motive? Surely Sebastian Goodricke who has the hots for Selina, or Catherine Bly who wanted the scoop of her life, had more passion, more reason to kill to get what they wanted? Roscoe Pearmain might still have harboured resentment for his father's death, despite being in love with Morwenna. Sir Jolyon himself admitted that they were rivals and Randolph couldn't say either way now if there had been a 'gentleman's agreement' between the two of them or not. Even Selina herself was heard saying she'd stop at nothing to prevent Randolph telling her parents about the opium... and Jago might have lied and in fact wanted to use his cousin to cement his place in the family business...'

Her rambling was interrupted when a scream pierced the air. A scream from the boathouse... a scream from Dotty.

23

'Dotty!' Cressida called out desperately as she ran the last few paces towards the boathouse, all reasoned arguments suddenly fallen by the wayside. The breeze had turned into more of a wind and with it rushing past her ears as she ran, she couldn't tell if there were any more screams or shouts coming from her friend. *If he's touched a hair on her head...*

Cressida cursed not running even faster as soon as she'd seen them walking ever so close together down to the dilapidated and deserted boathouse.

The perfect spot for a murder, her overactive imagination taunted her.

'Dotty!' Cressida called out again as she neared the door. Catching her breath, she leant on the door frame, the soft, rotting wood barely withstanding the pressure of her grip. She let a squirming Ruby down and the small pup darted in.

'Dotty?' Cressida peered around the door, the gloom inside the boathouse barely darker than the gloaming outside. The smell of brackish water and gently moulding timbers hit her as she cautiously stepped in, but then she noticed something else blending with the mould and saltwater... Alcohol?

'Cressy!' Dotty half shouted, half giggled at her friend. 'Oh Cressy, you have to see this!'

'Dotty, are you all right?' Cressida, accustomed now to the low light, moved swiftly over to where her friend was standing, holding the champagne glass in one hand and gripping her side with the other.

'Oh I'm all right, all right. Oh hello, Ruby.' Dotty laughed again, and then hiccoughed, taking a swig to try to curb the annoyances. 'Oops. Oh dear.'

'Dotty...' Cressida, whose heart was still thumping like that of a Grand National winner, could see that her friend was quite well... and quite tipsy to boot. 'You screamed, and I thought... well, I was worried and... Where's George by the way?'

A manly cough, followed by more giggles from Dotty, revealed to Cressida exactly where George was. He was about three feet beneath them, with his head on a level with an enthusiastically panting Ruby, and he was looking up at them from in between some broken floorboards.

'George! What on earth are you doing down there?' Cressida peered down at him. He must have fallen feet first through some rotting boards, but, luckily for him, not into the water itself, rather to a sunken, hidden floor beneath the normal one. As he moved, his feet made crunching sounds and Cressida realised where the aroma of alcohol was coming from.

'Looks like Dotty and I have made quite the discovery.' He disappeared from view for a second and then, to more giggles from Dotty, appeared again and produced a ceramic bottle. It was sheared off around the neck, but still sloshed with a healthy glug-glug as George shook it. It was at that moment that Cressida realised that although Dotty's champagne glass in her hand might be the same one that she had when she had seen her walking down the lawn, it was definitely not full of champagne.

Through her giggles, Dotty responded to Cressida's still-unanswered question. 'George and I came down here to... well, we came down here and almost as soon as we walked through the door, he crashed through those floorboards.'

'I can see that.' Cressida crossed her arms as Dotty tried her hardest to keep a straight face. She was pleased, of course, that Dotty was safe, and that George seemed no more of a threat than a nasty hangover, but she also felt foolish, and more than a little exhausted by the day's events. It obviously showed on her face.

'Fancy a sip?' Dotty proffered her glass to Cressida, who uncrossed her arms and accepted the glass with a twitch of a smile. She did sometimes wonder if her best friend could read her mind.

'Since you've gone to so much trouble to get it, go on then.' Cressida raised an eyebrow as she sipped from the champagne flute and Dotty giggled again.

'It's all right for you two up there,' George said. 'Think of a poor chap who finds himself knee-high to a grasshopper down here.'

'Oh George. You are getting a Ruby's eye view of the world.' Dotty laughed, and now her hands were free from glassware, she offered him one and did what she could to try to help pull him out, while not falling in herself. After a few false starts and plenty more giggles, she managed it, and George was left sitting with his legs dangling over the edge of the hole. The three of them, and Ruby, peered into it again.

'So what do you think this whole set-up is?' Cressida asked, risking another sip of the burningly good rum.

'I'm not sure,' George replied. 'But it looks like a secret stash. These boards are rotten,' he flicked off a piece of soft wood from one of the planks as he spoke, 'but I also think they were weakened from being prised up every so often.'

'Gosh,' Dotty said, peering further over, so much so, that Cressida stuck out her arm to catch her friend if necessary. 'It's like that time you found the secret bar at The Savoy, Cressy, with Guppy Catchpole and—'

'Yes, quite.' Cressida didn't think now was the time to relive one of her London exploits. 'But who's keeping a stash of rum under the floorboards here in the boathouse?'

'Unlabelled rum too,' George added, still holding the broken ceramic bottle and turning it around so that they could all see plain as day that it was, well, plain as day. 'Smuggled?'

'Gosh,' Dotty said again, reaching over to retrieve her glass from Cressida.

'Smuggled from where? And to where? And by whom?' Cressida mused and Dotty just shrugged.

'Hmm. Hang on...' George disappeared down the hole again to an accompanying gasp from Dotty, but surfaced a moment later brandishing a leather-bound notebook. He pulled himself back up, with a hand from Dotty, and then got up to standing. 'This might answer a few things.'

Cressida and Dotty peered over his shoulders to catch a glimpse too. Inside the notebook there was cursive script, written in fine, spidery writing, with details of transactions and receipts.

'Six bottles to the Bootlegger's Arms, paid, the nineteenth of May 1925,' Cressida read one line out loud. 'Clive says to deliver after midnight next time.'

'Two bottles to Pencarrick Hatch. Chase payment for previous. Maid in on it,' Dotty continued, pushing her glasses back up the bridge of her nose as she concentrated on reading.

'This is a ledger of some smuggling ring.' George flipped over a few more pages, then went back to the very start. 'This first entry is from 1923. It's been going on for a year or so at least then.'

'And look, it says PH Vol VI,' pointed out Dotty. 'So if that's a couple of years per volume, it's been going on for...' she paused as she calculated. 'A decade at least.'

'What does PH stand for? Public houses? Private houses?' Cressida wondered out loud, then asked George, 'How much is down there?'

'There must be a hundred or so bottles,' he replied. 'Less one or two perhaps.' He closed the book and bent down to pick up the ceramic bottle he'd been holding earlier. He poured some straight from the sheared-off neck into Dotty's glass. 'Best not to waste it, eh?'

'Oh, rather,' agreed Dotty, giggling as the rum sloshed over the rim of the elegant coupe glass. Cressida smiled at her as her mind raced over how and why the rum was down there, hidden beneath the floorboards of an ancient and rotting boathouse. A boathouse that was soon due to be redecorated and renovated.

'Lady Trevelyan never mentioned this, she must be completely unaware,' Cressida said to the others. 'Though, Ruby, you were scratching this exact spot this morning when Lady T was showing me around.' She bent down and gave Ruby a scratch between the ears. 'Clever pup. Lady T was talking about all sorts of jazzing up to the old place that she wanted to do and didn't once say, "Oh, by the way, there's a secret hidden floor under there."'

'Lord Trevelyan might know more, it's his ancestral home after all,' Dotty chipped in. 'There might be reference to it in the library. I could check.'

'Good idea chum. And didn't you say that Selina had mentioned smuggling still being rife along this coastline?'

'Oh yes, she did, didn't she. How exciting,' Dotty hiccoughed again.

'Lady Trevelyan mentioned it too, I think...'

A distant bell sounded the hour and Cressida looked at her watch.

'Oh bother it. Sorry, chaps, I better go and get my glad rags on. I'm going to need at least three glasses of that bootlegged rum to get me through supper tonight, I'm pooped!'

'I better change out of these rum-soaked trousers,' George added as they moved towards the door. 'Else the Trevelyans will think I've come straight from a distillery.'

'And whoever's stash it is will know you've rumbled them and might be hugely cross.' Dotty bit her lip and furrowed her brow.

The three of them left the boathouse and walked up the lawn towards the terrace, Ruby trotting along beside them. The light of the summer's day was just starting to think about fading, and the sun had disappeared behind the great facade of the house.

'And with Randolph killed for who-knows-what reason,' Cressida added sombrely, remembering all the motives she'd been thinking of as she'd dashed down to the boathouse, 'let's hope that whoever's stash that is doesn't find out that we're onto them and seek some sort of similar retribution.'

24

Cressida's ominous suggestion had made them all rather quiet, and Dotty was considerably less giggly as they marched back up towards the house. Dotty was finding the soft grass hard to navigate and had gratefully taken George's arm, and Cressida was about to leave them to their slower progress and dash upstairs to get dressed for dinner when Dotty asked: 'Cressy, why did you come running down to find us? How did you know we were there, down at the boathouse, I mean?' Dotty hiccoughed again and clasped her free hand over her mouth.

Cressida had no good answer except to explain everything to her dear friend, not to mention George, who was very much waiting for an explanation too. Dressing for dinner would have to wait a moment or two more. 'Well, this is a bit embarrassing really and, please don't take offence, George, but—'

'Don't tell me, I'm on your list of suspects?' George, whether he felt it or not, was putting on a good show of taking this all rather lightly.

Cressida had no option but to agree with him. 'Quite frankly, yes. But only because you left out the bit about you and Randolph having a filthy row in Falmouth yesterday lunchtime, when you were quite happy telling us all about everyone else's motives. A witness saw you having a real humdinger with him yesterday, shirts being rumpled and everything. Something to do with Randolph not crediting you for some finds you brought back from Egypt? It sounded like you were quite cross about it.'

George looked at the grass as they walked and Dotty looked at him, worry once more written across her face.

'George? Is this true?' Dotty pulled her arm ever so slightly away from his, though she still needed him for support.

He looked up at Cressida, and then to Dotty. 'Yes, it's true. And I'm sorry I didn't mention anything earlier. But, you see, I knew there wasn't anything in it and didn't want to muddy the waters, so to speak.' He eyed them, judging how his explanation had gone down, and something in Cressida's frown told him to continue. 'But you're right, it was remiss of me and, well, I had only just met you both and didn't want to make a bad impression.'

'Having a motive to kill someone who has just been murdered is, generally speaking, quite a bad introduction,' Cressida said, and George gave a hollow sort of laugh.

'True, true. You see, I didn't mention it because Lord Canterbury and I had resolved our differences. Yes, we had a tiff in Falmouth, I'm not denying that. Though I am ashamed that I let myself get quite so out of control, it was unforgivable, but it must have got my point across. Later yesterday afternoon, after he'd done his tea ceremony thing with Jago and Lord Trevelyan, he found me out and apologised and said he'd make sure I was credited completely for my finds. They were important ones, you see, and integral to my doctorate. If they'd gone into the museum under the Canterbury Collection, well, I couldn't then claim I had found them and use them to back up my assertion that the late-period Middle Kingdom in Egypt was as much about worshipping the sun god Ra as tomb-building for pharaohs.'

'I see,' Cressida said, and smiled to herself; she'd have to take what George said at face value, but it looked as if, with her love of reading, Dotty was more than happy with his explanation and had slipped her arm more fully into the crook of George's elbow. 'I'm sorry, George, that I leapt to the conclusion that you might have had something to do with Randolph's death before speaking with you.'

'Lord Canterbury said he'd send a message to the museum straight after we'd spoken. I hope he did, as it would prove what I'm saying is true. And it's hammering home my point somewhat, but can I just add one final thing?' George asked as they reached the terrace.

'Of course,' Cressida replied, mentally noting to ask DCI Andrews to look into this communication with the museum, while also itching to get upstairs to get changed, especially now she could see tuxedo-clad figures hovering on the terrace behind them.

'To put it frankly, Lord Canterbury was worth more to me alive than dead. He was a master of his subject, unrivalled for Egyptology and someone I'd do well to cleave to, professionally speaking, if I were to rise through the ranks myself. My doctorate relies on me being on his expeditions. Since Lord Carnarvon's death, his are the most well-funded and successful in the Nile delta and I'd be a fool to jeopardise the opportunity by, well, by killing him.'

Cressida nodded. 'But you were willing to risk it all by arguing with him, in public. Wouldn't that have riled him enough to never want to work with you again?'

George released Dotty from his arm and shook a damp leg out where his trouser was sticking to his calf. Ruby gruntled in shock as he almost accidentally kicked her. He exhaled slowly, then said, 'Yes. It was a risk. But all I'd worked for so far would have been ruined. I'm not a rich man, though I have expectations from an uncle.' He glanced at Dotty. 'So I had to make my point, and my only shame is how publicly I made it. We apologised to each other and, as I say, he made amends yesterday. He even asked me to join him next month on the dig in the Valley of the Kings. I have the paperwork upstairs to prove it. I can fetch it, if you like? I need to change these sodden trousers anyway.' He gave a dry laugh.

'That's all right, George. DCI Andrews will no doubt want to see them, but your word is good enough for me.'

Cressida gave Dotty's arm a squeeze and she and Ruby left them to it, Dotty no doubt to refresh her glass and George to refresh his trousers.

Cressida never travelled with a ladies' maid and it was times like this that she wished she did. She not only had to struggle into her satin evening dress, which she found far harder than her pirate costume the night before, and that had been done in a lay-by on the Great South West Road, but she had to do it at speed and fix her face and check her hair wasn't too haywire. In general, she hated being fussed over and on the whole didn't see the need to have someone at her beck and call. Now, however, as she craned her neck in one direction as an arm stretched down her back in order to find an elusive buttonhole, she wished she did. She had also forgotten to close her curtains and hoped that no one already out on the terrace could see her amateur gymnastics as she eventually found the button and slid it into place.

Straightening herself out, smoothing out the dark blue satin of her evening dress, she moved over to where her dressing table was positioned under the great sash window. As she chose bangles and found diamond drop earrings to match, a figure caught her eye out on the very edge of the lawn, where the sand of the cove almost came up to meet the longer grasses of that bit of wilderness.

'Morwenna?' Cressida could recognise the maid's long, wavy, red hair from here. She watched as the young woman walked onto the sand, closer to the lightly choppy water of the cove. 'What are you doing there?' Cressida asked herself. 'Mrs Dawkins will be going spare with dinner...'

As Cressida watched Morwenna down by the water's edge, another figure appeared to greet her. Cressida peered over her dressing table, looking intently from her window to where the two people were now talking. She stared as hard as she could through the glass, yet couldn't make out the figure next to Morwenna, save to observe that he was in black-tie evening wear.

'Who are you?' Cressida wondered aloud, narrowing her eyes, desperately trying to focus on the two figures in the distance. 'It can't be Roscoe... he wouldn't be in black tie.'

Ruby snorted out a sort of answer, but Cressida ignored her.

The man, whoever he was, suddenly pushed Morwenna, who stumbled back. Cressida gasped. Morwenna, though, seemed able to stand up for herself and Cressida saw her wagging a finger at him.

A flock of seagulls suddenly took up from the sand's edge and completely obscured her view with their slowly beating wings as they rose en masse into the sky. 'No, no, no...' Cressida muttered, straining to see through the flock of squawking birds. There was no hope of seeing what was going on by the cove now.

Cressida sighed, impatiently waiting for the birds to dissipate. She turned her silver bangle around her wrist until finally she could see the gently bobbing sailboats out on the water and the golden-tipped waves of the cove, reflecting the colour of the setting sun. But where she looked, there was no mysterious man in black tie, and more importantly, there was no Morwenna.

25

Cressida hitched up her full-length gown and held her high-heeled shoes in one hand as she ran down the main stairs of Penbeagle House, Ruby bouncing along at her side. Her alacrity had not so much to do with the sounding gong that was announcing the start of the cocktail hour, but with her wish to get to the kitchens again to try to find Morwenna.

She reached the baize door and swung it open just as a maid was coming in the other direction bearing a tray of glasses, narrowly missing her.

'Excuse me, miss,' the terrified maid said, steadying herself and her delicate tray of crystalware.

'I'm so terribly sorry!' Cressida gabbled, her heart still pounding.

'There's chicken liver for your dog again, miss,' the helpful maid said, and Cressida recognised her as the one who'd blushed at being called Ruby's favourite earlier.

'You're spoiling her now,' Cressida said, taking a breath and glancing at her dog, who had already had some delicious beef not an hour or so earlier.

'Morwenna said she was partial to it, miss.' The maid

bobbed and Cressida held the door for her as she went about her work, taking gleaming glasses out to the guests on the terrace.

'Looks like you made quite the impression,' Cressida whispered to Ruby. 'And you may have to perform the ultimate sacrifice and cope with two dinners as we go in search of her.'

Ruby gruntled in acceptance of her far from onerous task.

Cressida hovered by the kitchen door, aware that her presence there was the last thing that the hardworking Mrs Dawkins and her team needed as they buzzed around, adding the finishing touches and garnishes to the guests' dinner. Peering around the door frame as subtly as she could, to her great relief, Cressida saw the red of Morwenna's hair, tied up in a bun, across the other side of the room. Pans steamed with boiling water, undercooks chopped herbs on the wide central block in the middle of the kitchen and Mrs Dawkins barked out orders to maids who were carrying salvers and boards to and fro under her command.

Cressida knew she couldn't just waltz in and expect this well-coordinated dance to accommodate her, but she had an idea. She looked at Ruby, then leaned down and whispered in her ear. Much to her delight, Ruby seemed to understand her implicitly, though it might have had something to do with the fact that Morwenna had been the one person in the kitchen still dealing with a meat course. Still, the small dog darted in among the kitchen's swishing skirts and stockinged-legged footmen and yapped at Morwenna. The maid turned around, and Cressida could finally catch her eye. She waved and, thankfully, the maid put her knife down and moved through the clamour to where Cressida was standing, Ruby following her most diligently.

'Morwenna,' Cressida greeted her once they were in the corridor, away from the bustle and busyness of the stoves. 'Thank you. I just needed to see you about something.'

'Time's getting on, miss. I can't tarry.' Morwenna glanced

back towards the kitchen, where a wall clock dominated the chimney breast above the range cooker.

'I know, I'm sorry. I just wanted to check that you were all right. I saw you—'

'All's fine, miss. I've got it in hand, miss. Whatever you thought you saw,' she glanced back into the kitchen, 'it's not what you think, miss.'

'You don't know what I think, though,' Cressida said, desperate for the hassled maid not to disappear back into the steam of the kitchen before she'd asked her about the pottery and the fight she just saw her having. But Morwenna had other ideas.

'There'll be some livers by your door later, miss, for Miss Ruby here. I'll make sure of that. And don't worry, miss,' she looked Cressida straight in the eye, 'I'm fixing it all, miss.' With that, the maid darted back to the kitchen.

Ruby looked up at her mistress, who shrugged at her.

'She didn't want to talk, did she? And I'm afraid you'll have to wait for your second supper too, Rubes. All in all, not very satisfactory.'

But unsatisfactory though it was, Cressida knew she couldn't linger by the kitchen door any longer. Duty called, and with it drinks on the terrace.

'Cressida, there you are. Fashionably late as ever.' Alfred raised a cocktail glass to her, and she gave a sheepish smile as she emerged onto the terrace, hopping as she cocked one foot up so she could slip a shoe on while carrying Ruby. The rest of the house party were already drinking and gossiping on the terrace, no doubt discussing the terrible death of Lord Canterbury. She let Ruby down, hoping that the Penbeagle House Siamese cat wasn't around, and once her second shoe was on and she was upright again, accepted a glass of some concoction from Alfred.

'Thank you. And cheers,' Cressida sighed. 'Though I don't much feel like celebrating.'

'I know.' Alfred looked at her softly, and she smiled at him. He truly was, along with his sister, one of her favourite people. 'I spoke to DCI Andrews before he left for the Bootlegger's Arms.'

'He's gone for the night then?' Cressida asked.

'Yes, off for a decent supper, though I hope he sticks to the brown beer and doesn't take on one of those Nangower Cups.'

'Heavens, no.' Cressida shuddered, then sipped her cocktail, remembering the stash of rum they'd found down at the boathouse. She must tell Alfred all about that, but first she wanted to know what he'd said to the policeman. 'You said you'd spoken to him. What about?'

'It was more him talking to me, really. He asked whether we could all stay in place and he asked me to keep an eye on you, in case you started to poke your... what did he say...' Alfred looked up to the sky for inspiration. 'Oh yes, your aristocratic nose into things.'

'Oh pish posh.' Cressida rolled her eyes at him.

'Truly though, Cressy.' His use of her pet name filled her with the warmth that usually only a Martini could muster. 'You will be careful, won't you? I can't have you putting yourself in danger if there is a murderer around. We don't know who or how or why or whatever regarding Lord Canterbury, but I do know from watching far too many of those Hollywood flicks that bad guys don't like being hounded.'

Cressida looked up into his chestnut eyes and nodded. Then, so as not to disappoint Alfred, or risk falling out with him, she changed the subject. 'Lovely to see Dot so much like herself again. What's that she and George are looking at?'

Alfred looked over to where his sister was laughing at some-thing a now dry-trousered George Parish was pointing to in an old leather-bound book.

'Yes. He's a nice enough chap, though I'll be doing some digging, if you'll excuse the pun, to see what he's really like before any blessings are bestowed. After that rascal Basil broke her heart and turned out to be a real wrong 'un to boot, well, I think I rather failed in my brotherly duties on that one.'

'You can't be blamed, Alfred.' Cressida paused. There was no point dragging up all the pain and hurt from a few weeks ago now. Alfred did look forlorn, though, and so Cressida told him an anecdote or two from her last few nights out in London, and by the time she'd finished Alfred was all smiles again.

'So Rodney Figgis is secretly in love with his old nanny?'

'Seems so. And still very much enjoys large portions of her spotted dick.' She let Alfred chortle away as they moved over to where Dotty and George were still finding amusement in the pages of the old book. 'What ho, you two. What have you got there?'

'Oh, it's a blast, Cressy,' Dotty said gleefully. 'A lovely book full of old Cornish names. Look, the prefix Pen means "head-land", not "big" as Lord Trevelyan said last night.'

'I can see why this house is called Penbeagle then, what with it sitting right over the cove.' Alfred smiled at his younger sister.

Cressida looked over a few more of the translations. 'Oh look, Trengrouse means "farm at the crossing".'

'Thinking of a certain young man, are you?' Dotty raised an eyebrow at her, and Cressida blushed, aware of Alfred taking a very large gulp of his cocktail too. She decided to change the subject before it all got too utterly awkward.

'Recovered from your adventures earlier?'

'Oh yes!' Dotty exclaimed, and it occurred to Cressida, as she listened to Dotty and George fill Alfred in on their surprise find of cases of smuggled rum, that they would have been only minutes away from running into Morwenna and the mystery man in black tie. She was also pleased to note that it couldn't possibly have been George as he was now very much dry of trouser leg and no longer smelling like the slops of a jazz bar. He must have been in his bedroom changing when she spied the man in black tie down by the cove, a cove she could barely make out now that the sunlight was fading from the day.

Cressida was mulling all of this over when Lady Trevelyan ushered over Jago Trengrouse and the Nangowers.

'You've all met, haven't you? Yes? Wonderful.' Lady Trevelyan made efficiently elegant work of ensuring introductions, if needed, had all been made before returning to where Lord Trevelyan was deep in conversation with Sebastian Goodricke. Cressida watched her return to her husband's side, pausing on her way back to him to speak to her son Patrick and Catherine Bly, who were standing on the far edge of the terrace. Cressida was wondering if Lord Trevelyan had any inkling about Sebastian and Selina's tryst when Dotty, mind reading as usual, posed a question.

'I do hope Selina is all right,' Dotty said, sipping her cocktail. 'This all must have been an awful shock for her, even with —' Dotty stopped herself from saying anything untoward in front of the other guests by hiccoughing.

'I must pop in on her later.' Cressida exchanged a glance with Dotty. 'I promised Lady T that I would.'

Celia Nangower, who was tonight dressed quite normally and not at all like the wife of a despot, had obviously heard what Cressida and Dotty were saying, but rather than speak to them, snapped at Jago, 'How is your cousin?'

'She's resting still. Nasty shock,' Jago told them. 'Poor cuz.'

Most of those listening nodded, but Celia, ever brusque, continued on her own tangent. 'Cousins all over the place in this house.' She swept her eyes around, and Cressida saw them alight on almost everyone, including, to her surprise, Morwenna, who had appeared out on the terrace and was refilling a silver ice bucket. Celia clasped her pearls to her neck as she carried on. 'Trevelyans are like rabbits, family everywhere. And some of the burrows run lower than others.'

Cressida looked over to Morwenna, who, as she saw Cressida look at her, bobbed a curtsy and swiftly left the terrace.

Darn it... Cressida thought, as Celia's unguarded comment had just added another question to the list she wanted to ask the maid, but it would be terribly ungracious to leave her fellow guests and track the poor young girl down.

As she tuned back into the conversation, Jago was talking to Alfred, while Patrick Trevelyan had also sidled up to their little group.

'Cousin Edgar has done wonders for British industry abroad and it's a huge honour to be working alongside them. There are so many opportunities in the Far East, and I have some really good ideas on how to boost our revenues and keep things nice and efficient.' Jago sounded confident in his plans.

'I think British industry could do with more fellows like you,' Alfred said affably, before turning to Patrick, welcoming him into the conversation. 'And are you hoping to join the company too, Patrick?'

Cressida noticed how Patrick glared at Jago, especially when Jago spoke for him.

'Pat's got more than enough on his plate, what with being heir apparent to this place, isn't that right, Pat?' Jago raised an eyebrow at his cousin.

Cressida looked at Patrick, his face still pale despite the golden light of the now setting sun illuminating the terrace.

'I... I mean to say, I...' Patrick stammered over his words. 'I could do both, you know.'

Jago laughed. 'There, there, cuz, no need to get in a dither. I've got the company well under control.'

'You would have, wouldn't you?' sneered Celia, and Cressida wondered if she ever had a good word to say about anybody.

Jago shook his head dismissively, but Patrick stammered out a reply. 'Canterbury would have seen that I was involved. I knew him better than you, school and clubs and what have you.'

'Membership of some dining club, what is it, the Mutton Pie Club?' Jago snorted with derision. 'That does not mean you have the wherewithal to run a large company like your father's, Pat. Leave it to me, it's better this way.'

The conversation moved on, but Cressida wondered if Patrick had a point. Randolph may well have been a useful ally for Patrick in a bid to be more involved with the Far East Company. And if Jago Trengrouse wanted the Far East Company all to himself; then him getting rid of Randolph suddenly made a whole lot more sense. Jago Trengrouse, charming, flirtatious and confident as he was, had just been firmly added to her list of suspects.

26

Much to Cressida's disappointment, she wasn't seated next to either of her chums at dinner, but instead was placed next to Sebastian Goodricke. However, with hopes of having a subtle word with Morwenna dashed, quizzing Sebastian over his set-to with Selina at lunch was the next best thing, and easier with poor Selina still taken to her bed, too shocked or sedated for company.

For a man who worked in foreign embassies and had travelled extensively, Sebastian was being surprisingly reticent and not at all conversationally minded. *Might that have something to do with him carrying out an illicit affair with the fiancée of a recently murdered man,* wondered Cressida, *and not wanting to give anything away...* Still, she was struggling. She'd asked about Egypt, hoping it might lead on to her being able to question him about how he'd met Selina, but he'd failed to rise to the bait and only agreed that it was a very hot country and rather dusty. She'd asked him about the other places he'd been posted and he'd merely replied that Norway was both expensive and cold, while Muscat had been, surprise, surprise, much like Cairo and very hot and rather dusty, though with better dried dates. The words 'old toast' and 'dry as' started to float across Cressida's mind as he chewed quietly on another mouthful of terrine. Still, she was keen to find out more about his relationship with Selina and his time in Egypt, so made another attempt at drawing some information from him, as subtly as she could. Perhaps mentioning the person who introduced them would be a good place to start.

'Tell me, did you know Catherine well before meeting her in Egypt?' Cressida nodded across to where Miss Bly was explaining in great detail the agonies she'd been through to file an article for *The Express*.

Sebastian shook his head. 'It's all part of a diplomat's job to calm the histrionics of those who think they know best but of course have no idea of the wider cultural or governmental picture. What Miss Bly doesn't understand is the monumental amount of good the late Lord Carnarvon's dig is doing at both a macro and micro level, not just for our country and our museums but for Egypt too. Whether it's reported on by some chap at *The Times* or by every Tom, Dick and Harry from the regional presses really isn't a matter for the Foreign Office to get involved in.'

At last, thought Cressida, *more than just a few words uttered!* Though she couldn't help compare Sebastian Goodricke, once again, to the dry piece of Melba toast she was about to crunch down on.

'Sounds like she chewed your ear off, as she did to poor Randolph. Did you get letters too?'

Sebastian huffed. 'Know about those, do you? Well, no, luckily for me I wasn't party to her poison pen.'

'*Poison* pen...' Cressida thought out loud, and Sebastian turned to face her, placing his knife and fork together neatly in front of him.

'Speaking of poison, do you know what did it for Randolph yet?' He looked at her rather intently.

'No. Though I should hope DCI Andrews will have the results of the post-mortem tomorrow.'

'Hemlock's my guess.' Sebastian sat back in his chair as a footman leaned between them and collected his plate.

'Hemlock?' Cressida's interest was piqued. Suddenly, Sebastian had gone from dry as old toast to a sizzling grill of interest.

'Apt for a man like Randolph, who, as I'm sure you can guess, was as obsessed with the classical world as I am.'

'Why would that be? I thought asps had the monopoly on classical murders?' Cressida couldn't credit her schooling for much that occupied her brain, but she did remember once learning how Cleopatra had met her fate.

'Asps are relatively modern; Cleopatra was killed centuries after Socrates greeted his maker by drinking a libation made from hemlock.'

'Who killed him? Why was he poisoned?' Cressida was rapt by the suddenly much more interesting Sebastian.

'A death sentence, passed by judge and jury in Athens.'

'Crikey.' Cressida sat back to allow her plate to be cleared by the polite footman too. 'I had no idea. I assumed Socrates would have wandered around philosophising until his beard touched his toes and his toga fell off or something, not be sentenced to death via poison.'

'Not a pleasant end at all for the old man. Apparently, Socrates was told to "walk around until his legs felt heavy and then lie down", though, of course, hemlock, in reality, isn't so civilised as that, as we witnessed last night.'

'Do you know the symptoms of hemlock poisoning then?' Cressida asked, casting her mind back to how Randolph Canterbury had looked and acted just before collapsing the night before.

'Depending on the patient, it can be anything from instant to a few hours later, but it tends to involve trembling, followed by a loss of speech, the muscles then spasm and relax... the usual poison things.'

Cressida looked at Sebastian. *The usual poison things...* how much did this man know? Cressida shivered but she decided to press him further.

'You said "patient", that's a rather odd turn of phrase, isn't it?'

'Not everyone takes hemlock to poison themselves. In smaller doses, it can be a herbal cure. I'm not sure what for, but there's old rustic recipes for tinctures and whatnot that include it.'

'A case of kill or cure?' Cressida mused, and Sebastian nodded as she continued quizzing him. 'But if hemlock killed Socrates, it's a Southern European plant then? Surely hard to come by around here?'

'Oh no, there's plenty. I saw what I think was some quite close by. It looks just like cow parsley, but stinks of rotten parsnips. It can make you quite ill just from smelling it, and, of course, you have to smell it to check you're not just making a brew of humble cow parsley, not that anyone would make a tea from cow parsley, of course, which is why hemlock poisoning is rare – it's not easily mistaken for anything edible.'

'You know rather a lot about it, don't you?'

'A pet subject of mine. I read Classics, of course, but the fun is in the details, isn't it? You know Socrates could have chosen exile as his punishment, but he chose to drink the poison. There's something quite stoic in that.'

Cressida was feeling increasingly suspicious about Sebastian. There was something going on between him and the deceased's fiancée, after all... and Cressida reminded herself it was this that she had wanted to find out more about, not Socrates.

'Is there anything stoic in carrying on an affair with a dead man's fiancée?' Cressida said the words quietly so that she couldn't be overheard by anyone other than Sebastian, but he heard her all right.

He paused, not answering as the footmen slid plates of salmon en croute in front of them.

'I don't know what you're talking about, Miss Fawcett.' His formality set Cressida's teeth on edge, and his lie gave her cause to wonder afresh to what length he might go to get what he wanted.

'I saw you in Pencarrick earlier. Kissing.' She all but hissed the last word.

'I see.' He put a forkful of pastry-clad salmon into his mouth. Cressida found, even after all the rushing around this afternoon, that she had lost her appetite. Sebastian chewed and swallowed and then very quietly continued. 'I didn't think we'd been spotted.'

'You were hardly discreet.' Cressida pushed some green beans around her plate. Salmon was never her favourite anyway and the parsley sauce reminded her a little too much of the recent talk of cow parsley and its more sinister cousin.

'Selina and I are old friends.'

'I have "old friends", Sebastian, and we don't shout at each other and then land a smacker on the lips.' Cressida laid down her fork and turned to face him. 'What's your relationship really?'

Sebastian closed his eyes and took a deep breath. Then he looked at Cressida, 'I love her. And I believe she loves me too. We had spoken of marriage, but my work was to take me to far-flung places. With her father so often away from her mother, she wasn't sure she wanted that for herself, so that was that. I stayed in Cairo and next thing I knew she was engaged to Lord Canterbury...'

'That must have made you quite angry?'

Sebastian placed his knife and fork down and picked up his wine glass. He took a measured sip and then placed it down again. 'Miss Fawcett, you're goading me and I don't like it.'

'I'm sorry, Sebastian. And please, call me Cressida. But you have to understand that I'm only trying to get to the bottom of what happened to Randolph.'

'*Randolph*, is it? No Lord Canterbury for you. You were close to him too then?' Sebastian flickered with interest.

Cressida decided to just nod, hoping Sebastian would return to talking about Selina. Instead he picked up his glass and Cressida felt utterly unnerved by the whole affair. Perhaps this was how he negotiated with foreign embassies, buying himself thinking time with every tick of the clock and sip of the wine.

Finally, he spoke again, low and deliberate. 'I didn't kill Lord Canterbury.'

'And if perhaps the post-mortem confirms that the poison is hemlock, why should I not suspect you? You know how to use it, where it's growing locally... exactly how it kills...'

'I was barely alone before the ball started. I arrived by train from London yesterday and was collected by the Trevelyan's chauffeur. I didn't realise it, but Miss Bly was on the same train, thankfully not in my carriage, along with your friend Lord Delafield. They and Berry, the chauffeur, can vouch for the fact that we arrived at about five o'clock. I was greeted by my hosts and retired to my room, where I refreshed myself and changed into my costume.'

'You were dressed as a Victorian, if I remember rightly,' Cressida interrupted him.

'That's right. Isambard Kingdom Brunel. Anyway, at the ball I was almost always surrounded by people. I couldn't have possibly whipped up a local poison and given it to Lord Canterbury without being seen.'

'You could have slipped something pre-manufactured into his drink, couldn't you?' Cressida knew she was clutching at the smallest of straws now as Sebastian had put forward a decent case, and he completed that suit with a final flourish.

'Absurd idea. As I said, hemlock smells of rancid parsnips. It's far too strong a poison to be hidden in simple drinks, and I notice Canterbury was a champagne man. You'd need bitter Negronis or spiced rum or something exceptionally aromatic to disguise the taste and smell.'

With that, he continued eating. Their conversation was over.

Cressida spent the rest of the meal talking to Monty Nangower, who didn't have much to say except how their house was costing them an arm and a leg to run these days and there was never a decent butler to be had for love nor money after the war.

After dinner, coffees were served, and Cressida found Ruby in the drawing room where she had been petrified into a corner by the majestic Siamese cat, so much so that she looked like a podgy, furry version of the bronze lustrous dogs on the drawing-room mantelpiece. She finished her coffee and accepted a nightcap from Alfred, who came and sat down next to her.

'Anything of interest from Sebastian?' he asked, and Cressida filled him in on how much the Foreign Office official knew about hemlock.

Alfred looked askance at Sebastian, who was finishing off his coffee and bidding goodnight to his hosts. He puffed out his cheeks and exhaled a long breath.

'Could be a coincidence. But I agree, it's all rather fishy, him knowing quite so much.'

'Fishy indeed. And his talk of an evil version of parsley put me right off my salmon en croute. Also, I saw Morwenna fighting with someone earlier, down by the cove.'

'Oh yes? Who?'

'I couldn't tell, but I can't quite shake the thought that perhaps that very same man, for it was a man in black tie, you see – well, I can't help but think he was most likely around the table with us tonight.'

'Most likely indeed. And not very sporting of him to pick on a maid.'

'A maid who I think must be intrinsically linked to Randolph's murder.'

Alfred paused to take in what Cressida was implying. 'You think someone here tonight was definitely the murderer, don't you?' His voice was hushed.

Cressida looked into his dark brown eyes and then took a sip of her liqueur nightcap before simply answering, 'Don't you?'

27

Cressida had slept fitfully; her dreams plagued with bowls of steaming and nauseating hemlock soup being served to her by almost everyone here at Penbeagle House. She sat up in bed when she awoke and pushed her silk eye mask up so that it ruffled her hair as she blinked into the daylight. Ruby snorted herself awake next to Cressida and stood up on her skinny little legs, before she yawned, stretched and curled back up into a lightly snuffling ball. A maid had obviously been in and opened her curtains and left her a steaming cup of tea, which Cressida sniffed tentatively, her dream still resonating in her mind.

'You didn't see who brought this in, did you, Rubes? No?'

The small pup was no help at all, and Cressida sniffed the tea again. What had Sebastian said last night? Rotten parsnips? Fortunately, this pretty teacup contained nothing more suspicious than what smelt like lapsang souchong, and Cressida blew on it before taking a sip.

'I can see from your state of abject terror you were worried about me there,' she said sarcastically to her happily snoozing pooch. But still, she was glad to have this moment's peace before another day of sleuthing ahead of her. If only she'd been awake to see if it had been Morwenna who had brought this tea into her, as she was still keen as mustard to speak to the maid. 'I'm convinced she must know something,' she muttered to Ruby.

Before she could recount to herself too much of what she had found out the day before, she heard the familiar voice of DCI Andrews out on the terrace below. Cressida slipped out from under the eiderdown and padded over to the large sash window. She peered down and, sure enough, Andrews and Kirby were out there talking to Lord Trevelyan.

Cressida hurriedly put her cup down and then selected something sensible from her wardrobe. Tempted as she was to don her comfortable loose pirate blouse, she decided the striped trousers were too frivolous for the day's needs and opted instead for a smart tweed pencil skirt and a pale pink silk blouse. She may be on the hunt for a killer, but there was never an excuse not to look one's best.

Washed and dressed, she left Ruby snoozing on the bed, having found once again a thoughtful plate of chicken livers left outside her bedroom door for her pup's breakfast, and hurried downstairs.

'Andrews! Kirby!' she called over to the policemen as they entered the house from the terrace while she was halfway down the stairs. 'What ho there!'

'Good morning, Miss Fawcett,' Andrews greeted her. 'I trust you slept well?'

'Terribly, but that's by the by. You?'

Andrews looked like the sort of man who could sleep practically anywhere, probably snoring into his pillow before his eyes had even shut, and his reply confirmed it. 'Out like a light, Miss Fawcett. Sea air perhaps.'

'And hopefully a decent supper at the Bootlegger's Arms?' Cressida remembered her own lack of appetite last night and placed a hand on her stomach as it grumbled. 'Breakfast? I don't know about you, but I could murder a sausage. Oh. Bad choice of words.'

DCI Andrews smiled. 'A sensible man never turns down a sausage, Miss Fawcett. Lead on.'

'I've got quite a bit to tell you, Andrews. You'll be unsurprised to know that even since we last spoke I've been sleuthing somewhat.' Cressida raised an eyebrow at the moustachioed policeman, but his jolly demeanour had vanished.

'Miss Fawcett, I must urge you in the strongest terms not to interfere with my investigation.'

'If you're worried that I might accidentally stumble across the murderer, then please don't worry. I am sadly no further in my thoughts as to who could have done it, or why, though I have gathered some more information.' Cressida tried to sound businesslike as they entered the dining room, where luckily no one else was yet eating. 'Are we late or early? I can't imagine why no one else is here,' she added, business put aside as she headed straight for the buffet laid out with silver domes that when lifted revealed the creamiest of scrambled eggs, sausages piled high and crispy bacon. 'Early by the looks of it. How unlike me!'

When they had both filled their plates, with Sergeant Kirby shaking his head to decline, they seated themselves at the large dining table. Sergeant Kirby stood to attention behind his superior officer and Cressida started filling in Andrews on what she'd found out since she'd last seen him, finishing with Sebastian Goodricke's revelations about hemlock last night.

'So, you see, almost everyone here has a motive and Sebastian has even suggested the method. It's like we have all the bricks we could possibly need, but no idea what sort of house to build, don't you think?'

'I, well, I...' DCI Andrews, as had been the case several weeks ago, occasionally found Cressida's turns of phrase a little befuddling.

'I don't suppose you were able to find anything out before

you went back to the inn last night, were you? And have you contacted the coroner for the post-mortem results?' Cressida asked, before popping a piece of sausage in her mouth.

DCI Andrews raised an eyebrow at her. 'Do you also teach your grandmother to suck eggs?'

'Inspector?'

Andrews shook his head in resignation. 'What I mean is, I am perfectly capable of handling this investigation, Miss Fawcett, and would like to remind you that I really don't have to share any information pertaining to the death of Lord Canterbury with you at all.'

'Sorry, Andrews.' Cressida realised that her attitude had perhaps been a little too gung-ho this morning, and quickly thought how to make amends. 'You see, I'm dying to tell you what I've found out, and in return I would be so grateful if you could keep me informed.'

The policeman cleared his throat. 'I suppose I do have you to thank for getting me involved...' He sighed. 'But you must run all of your thoughts past me and not go gallivanting off trying to catch killers all by yourself.'

'Of course, Andrews. I shall be good as gold.' Cressida beamed at him, then popped a forkful of egg and bacon into her mouth.

'Happen that I did receive a very interesting telephone call once I was back at the Bootlegger's.' Andrews sat back in his chair and Kirby instinctively got his notebook out in case his boss needed any information to hand.

'Oh yes? Do tell.' Cressida put her knife and fork down and pushed her plate away, once more her appetite coming second to a juicy bit of news.

'The landlord called me to the telephone, you see there's one for the whole pub, and it being a busy Sunday night with a bunch of locals who'd played cricket all afternoon over in Petherick, the saloon bar was quite noisy, wasn't it, Sergeant?'

'Yes, sir.'

'... So it was hard to make out what the caller was saying, or even who it was—'

'Didn't they introduce themselves when you picked up the receiver? Didn't you ask?'

Andrews cocked an eyebrow at her again and Cressida mouthed a 'sorry' to him, letting him continue. 'No, they didn't, and yes, I did, but they didn't answer. *She* didn't answer, I should say, it was definitely a young woman. I could just about hear from her accent that she was a local girl.'

'And?' Cressida was keen to know more. Telephones were still relatively new and it would be quite notable for anyone to be using one, especially someone who wasn't necessarily of the landed classes.

'And she said she knew who the murderer was.' Andrews sat back in his chair and picked up his sausage from his plate with his fingers.

'I say!' Cressida was incredulous. 'That's a humdinger of a lead, Andrews. So, who is it?'

Andrews, still looking pleased with himself, swallowed his mouthful and then spoke. 'She said she couldn't say who over the line but wanted to meet me here at Penbeagle House this morning and she'd tell me everything.'

'Oh, how exciting, Andrews. And you better keep that note-book poised, Sergeant. This could all be wrapped up by elevenses.' Cressida followed Andrews's informal style and picked up an uneaten piece of bacon from her plate and popped it into her mouth, her appetite seemingly returned. 'I wonder who it was, who telephoned you?'

Almost as soon as she posed the question, a thought occurred to Cressida and the bacon, delicious but a few seconds ago, became intolerable and she swallowed it down with a choke and a cough.

'Are you all right, Miss Fawcett?' Andrews leaned forward.

Cressida righted herself. 'Yes, sorry about that. I've just had a thought, though. I wonder if—'

Before she could finish that thought, a flurry of voices could be heard coming from the hallway and Kirby, with a quick nod to Andrews, dashed out to see what the commotion was about. Cressida and Andrews stood up too and headed towards the door, only to find several of the household maids in tears.

'What is it, what's happening?' Cressida called across to one of the maids, who could only raise a trembling arm and point out towards the main front door that led to the terrace and from there down to the cove. Cressida's eyes followed her shaking finger. Andrews, who was standing with her, did the same and the sight that greeted them was enough to turn the most hardened of them to sorrow.

Roscoe was staggering up the lawn, his legs barely moving as he struggled under the weight of the sopping-wet girl he was carrying in his arms. She was soaked through and her head lolled down from where his arm was holding her, her long red hair nearly touching the grass as Roscoe cried out for help as he lurched on forward towards the house.

Cressida raised a hand to her mouth as Andrews, Kirby and a couple of footmen dashed forward to help the gardener. As they reached him, Roscoe collapsed to the ground. Cressida could see that he didn't want to let his precious girl go, though the men were offering all the help they could. But it was quite clear that there was nothing anyone could do to help her now. The soaking-wet girl he had been carrying from the cove was gone. Morwenna, the love of Roscoe's life, was dead.

28

'Oh Roscoe.' Cressida knelt beside him and, throwing all social mores to the wind, wrapped an arm around the weeping gardener. Morwenna's body had been gently taken from his arms and, as far as Cressida knew, Andrews and Kirby were alerting the doctor and coroner in order to make arrangements.

The noise of the discovery and Roscoe's tragic procession up the lawn from the cove had brought out some of the other guests who had just come down for breakfast and Cressida noticed a distraught Dotty being comforted by George Parish, while Catherine Bly, dry-eyed and firm of stance, looked on, her hands on her hips, before stalking off to go and talk to the Trevelyans, who, in turn, were comforting their maids, who were sobbing on the terrace.

Cressida could feel the wet dew of the early-morning grass seep through her tweed skirt, but she didn't spare it a thought as she turned her attention back to the grieving gardener. 'Oh Roscoe, I'm so sorry. Poor, dear Morwenna. Where did you find her? What happened?'

'I... I don't know, Miss Fawcett.' Roscoe, his voice cracking with tears, was still on his knees, in exactly the same position he'd been in when the footmen and Andrews, with Kirby's help, had wrestled the body of Morwenna from his arms. Cressida wished she had a handkerchief that she could give Roscoe, but as she thought it, he wiped his running nose and wet eyes with the sleeve of his linen shirt. One more sniff and he continued. 'We liked to meet down by the cove in the early mornings before she was due up at the house. It's beautiful down there first thing, you see, with just the sound of the water and the bells in the boat rigging.' He shuddered with emotion. 'I went to meet her, but there was no sign of her. I called out her name and looked about a bit and... and that's when I saw her... behind one of the rocks. Lying on the sand, she was, close to the water's edge, her hair all wet through like bladderwrack, but she hadn't drowned.'

'She hadn't?' Cressida blanched to think of it, but remembered the sodden skirts that had dragged as Roscoe had fallen to his knees, not to mention the poor girl's long wet hair.

'No, I mean, she was wet with water all right, the tide going out as it is, but I don't think it was the water that did for her.' He paused, his eyes brimming with tears. 'On account of the... the rope that was around her neck.'

Cressida reeled back and Roscoe wept into his hands again. Cressida did all she could not to weep alongside him, for his loss and in empathy for Morwenna's ghastly end. She girded herself, though; that rope meant only one thing, this tragic death hadn't been an accident. And the only thing they could do for Morwenna now was help find her killer.

'Roscoe, the rope... I'm sorry, but the police will need to know about it.'

'I'll tell them. I'll show them... I... Oh Morwenna.' His voice choked as tears ran down his face.

Cressida rubbed the poor man's back and tried to soothe

him. They stayed like that for what seemed like hours, though it was more likely only a few minutes. A shadow fell across them and when Cressida looked up she could see Andrews standing over them both, his face sombre, as one always is when faced with death. Sergeant Kirby was standing behind him, and Cressida fancied she saw a sheen under one of his eyes left by a hastily wiped-away tear. She urged the grieving gardener into a more upright position and beckoned for Andrews to come down to their level. He tugged at the fabric of his trousers as he squatted down in front of Roscoe.

'Mr Pearmain, I'm Detective Chief Inspector Andrews of Scotland Yard, and this is Sergeant Kirby.' His tone was firm but friendly. 'I'm sorry for your loss. And forgive me for asking, but do you have any idea who might have done this to Morwenna?'

Cressida replied before Roscoe could, her voice all but an anguished whisper, saving Roscoe from saying it himself. 'He found her with a rope around her neck, Andrews.'

Andrews nodded in thanks.

Then Roscoe took a deep breath and replied, 'I don't know... I just don't know.' He shook his head. 'Everyone loves... loved Morwenna.' He shuddered. 'She'd grown up here in the village, helped everyone she could with what her grandmother had taught her... there's not a person round these parts who doesn't know and love her, but—'

'But what, Mr Pearmain?' Andrews pushed him for an answer, while Cressida kept an arm around his back.

'Say what you can, Roscoe, please,' Cressida encouraged him, and he gulped down a sob before carrying on.

'You said yesterday that you'd seen her at Pencarrick Pottery? I asked her about it later and she denied it, though she looked upset too. Really upset.'

'I'm sorry,' Cressida whispered, hating the fact that her sleuthing had brought discord between the two lovers just hours before Morwenna's death.

'No, no. It's not your fault, miss. She'd been up to something for a few days, not turning up for her shifts and making excuses rather than meet me.' He rubbed his eyes with the heel of his hand.

'Really? I thought... Well, I spoke to cook yesterday and I thought, and I think cook thought, that she was spending more time with you. I was worried you'd both get into trouble if Morwenna missed any more shifts.'

Andrews let Cressida and Roscoe talk, subtly jotting down a few things as they spoke.

'No, it wasn't me she was skiving off with. Where was she then?' Roscoe looked up at Cressida and Andrews, with a look of pure pleading in his eyes.

'I saw her down by the cove last night, arguing with a man,' said Cressida slowly.

Roscoe and Andrews both turned to Cressida and simultaneously asked, 'Who?'

'I don't know.' She looked from Roscoe to Andrews. 'And I don't know what was said between them, but it looked like an argument. Whoever it was pushed her, but she held her ground. I tried to ask her about it before supper, but all she said was that she "had it in hand" and was going to fix it, saying it wasn't what I thought it was, though she hadn't let me get a word in. I couldn't keep pestering her while she had a job to do, but I saw her again on the terrace as we had cocktails. I wanted to ask her all about it... it seems foolish now, but I was sure that something about that argument down by the cove might have had something to do with Lord Canterbury's death.'

Roscoe was silent. Gradually, he moved and pushed himself up from his kneeling position. Andrews stood up too and offered a hand to Cressida. Once they were all upright, Roscoe spoke again.

'Inspector Andrews, Miss Fawcett, I very much doubt she had anything to do with that man's death. I know you think one of us here had some beef with him, and I'm sorry for his death, I truly am. But, like I said to you, I had made my peace with what happened between him and my father and, if I didn't have cause to hurt him, why would my Morwenna have been involved with anything?'

'We're not suggesting that young Morwenna was involved in anything untoward.' Andrews said diplomatically. 'But we'll need to ask you some more questions,' Andrews concluded, and Roscoe nodded along, promising to let him know if he thought of anything else.

Cressida placed a hand on the gardener's arm. 'I'm so sorry, again, for your loss.'

A frown passed across Roscoe's forehead as she spoke, and he shook his head. 'I don't think she had anything to do with Canterbury's death, miss, but you are right in that she certainly had something going on that she wouldn't tell me. Those absences from work, heading off to Pencarrick, fainting in the meadow. She'd been doing things I had no idea about. Things that might have got her killed.'

Despite the warmth of the morning sunshine, Cressida shivered, her arms turning to gooseflesh.

Andrews closed his notebook. 'In your own time, Mr Pearmain.' He gestured for Roscoe to follow him.

'More questions?' Roscoe pulled himself together. 'I'll answer whatever I can, Inspector, if it helps find who did this to her.'

Cressida clasped a hand to her chest, almost overcome with emotion at Roscoe's courage in the face of his grief.

'You'll be in good hands with Andrews,' she called after him, and accepted the nod from Kirby as they guided him back towards the house. When they had left, Cressida walked back to where Dotty and George were on the terrace. Despite her sadness she could feel the hairs on her arms stand on end. It was clear that Roscoe had had no idea what his sweetheart had been up to. But something Morwenna had done recently, something secret and possibly to do with that mysterious man in black tie last night, had led to the young woman's murder. Had Randolph's murderer struck again? Cressida shivered, despite the morning sunlight. *Or am I looking for two murderers in our midst?*

29

'Cressy!' Dotty looked up and waved as Ruby trotted away from where she'd been sitting with Dotty and George and toddled up to meet her. When Cressida was close enough for her to speak without raising her voice, she continued. 'Cressy, is it true? Is Morwenna dead?' Her voice shook, and Cressida sat down in a chair next to her and, with Ruby pulled onto her lap, placed a hand on her friend's.

'That's right. Except it's far from being *right*, but you're correct in thinking that it's happened.' Cressida chewed the inside of her lip, thinking about the poor maid found on the damp sand.

'Drowned?' asked George.

'No.' Cressida sighed and pulled her hand away from Dotty, sitting up straighter as the shock of it all wore off a little. She let Ruby down and watched as the pup sauntered into the drawing room. 'Strangled by a rope apparently. Roscoe Pearmain, who is her fiancé and the head gardener, found her.'

'Oh, that's so horrid.' Dotty shook her head. 'The poor things.'

'Do you think he...?' George's voice wavered as he asked the question.

'No. No I don't,' Cressida replied quite firmly. 'Though I know it can often be the husband or lover in these cases. But I'm convinced it wasn't him. Oh Dot, I can't bear to think of how he's grieving. He loved her so much.' Cressida squeezed Dotty's hand. 'And I just can't see him strangling her and leaving her on the shore to be washed away... then carrying her all the way back up to the house.'

'No, of course. That makes sense,' George replied apologetically.

'Also, he didn't know what she'd been doing at Pencarrick Pottery and said he wasn't the cause for her absences Cook told me about last night,' Cressida continued.

'Absences?' Dotty asked.

'Morwenna frequently turned up late for her shifts, it seems. Saturday in particular. Mrs Dawkins mentioned she'd fainted, so perhaps she was unwell and seeking treatment.'

'Was she, you know... in the family way?' George asked, reddening slightly around his shirt collar.

'Oh, gosh. I hadn't thought of that. I don't think so. Roscoe certainly didn't allude to it.'

'Perhaps he didn't know,' Dotty whispered.

'Perhaps. She was obviously keeping a few things from—' Cressida was interrupted by a resounding smashing sound from inside the drawing room, and all three of them leapt out of their chairs as the Siamese cat flew out of the open French windows, followed not nearly so quickly or elegantly by Ruby. 'Oh Ruby! What have you done?' Cressida scooped up the pup, who had sheepishly come to hide between Cressida's legs, before excusing herself to her friends so she could go and look in the drawing room. When she entered the grand room she could see a maid, horror on her face, staring at the remains of one of the large ornamental vases that stood either side of the fireplace. A thousand shards of blue and white porcelain lay on the floor. Cressida thought she could just about detect a wobble from the remaining vase, so she picked her way quickly and prudently over the shards towards it, as if she were playing hopscotch.

'It wasn't me, miss,' the maid said, a look of worry across her brow.

'I'm quite certain it wasn't,' Cressida said, holding tight to Ruby in one arm and the other making sure the remaining vase didn't tip over too. 'I'm just sorry that it's a whole pile of mess for you to clear up.'

'I'll go and fetch Amy, miss, she'll help me.' The maid bobbed a curtsy and left, leaving Cressida looking at the myriad pieces of porcelain on the floor. It reminded her of the pile of smashed and broken pottery at Pencarrick, except there the pieces looked like they came not only from vases but also tea sets, lustreware and various other things. She glanced around to check that nothing else was broken and adjusted one of the golden Foo dogs, which looked slightly askew on the mantelpiece.

'I'm going to hazard this was all your feline friend's fault.' She was about to take Ruby back out to the terrace when DCI Andrews appeared at the door.

'Did I just hear... Ah,' he said as he saw the devastation on the floor.

'Yes. The poor Trevelyans. This is the last thing they need.' Cressida walked over to him. 'I don't think Ruby is solely to blame, but I'll apologise to Lord and Lady Trevelyan in a moment. And tell me, how is Roscoe doing? Did he say anything else of any interest?' Cressida looked earnestly at DCI Andrews.

'Sadly, yes. The rope, it seems, is much like others stored in the boathouse. He said the boathouse is sometimes locked, but more often than not isn't. And, locked or not, if you had a boat, you could always access it from the waterside.'

'So anyone might know the rope was there and could have got hold of it.'

'Exactly.' The detective sighed. 'I've left Kirby with him. He's not holding together too well, but I thought I better have someone watch over him in case it's an act. But the poor lad, it looks genuine enough.'

'I believe him to be, for what it's worth,' Cressida concurred. 'And I was wondering, do you think it was Morwenna who telephoned you last night at the Bootlegger's Arms?'

DCI Andrews nodded slowly. 'I fear it may have been. Yes.'

'Do you think someone overheard her speaking to you?' Cressida asked, squeezing Ruby just a little tighter in her arms as she spoke.

'Perhaps, yes. Or she told someone of her intention to telephone. That may have been enough.'

'The man in black tie...' Cressida murmured, cursing herself again for not trying harder to talk to Morwenna last night and find out what the fight had been about.

'Who?' DCI Andrews pulled his notebook out and opened it up.

Cressida sighed. 'I told you about him earlier, Andrews, when we were with Roscoe. He's the one I saw Morwenna having an argument with yesterday evening before dinner. Someone in black tie, but that's all I could make out at that distance.'

'But you could tell it was Morwenna?'

'Her hair is... was, so striking. I was sure it was her. But all I could see was that the man was dressed in evening wear. A flock of gulls got in the way just as I was getting my eye in, I'm afraid.'

'I see. And no other features?' Andrews pressed her.

Cressida nodded thoughtfully. 'He had dark hair, I could see that much.' She sighed. 'Oh, I don't know, Andrews... I'm sorry I can't tell you more.'

'It's frustrating that you couldn't get a better look at him,

Miss Fawcett, but it's useful to know all the same.' He looked back a page in his notebook. 'I spoke to Lord Trevelyan just now. He didn't have much to say except the usual platitudes and making sure her family received her last wage. All very sombre, but not terribly upset by it. I think his mind is more taken up with a ship arriving at Falmouth today; he and Her Ladyship need to go and greet it. You'd think having the body of one of your employees found on your own private cove, not least barely twenty-four hours after your future son-in-law was killed, would shake someone up a bit more, but he was very businesslike, though, to his credit, fair as well.'

'He didn't mention by any chance that they were related?'

'His Lordship and the maid? Good grief no.' Andrews looked shocked.

'I couldn't say for sure, but Celia Nangower made a snide comment about it last night. Something about Trevelyans breeding like rabbits and that some burrows ran lower than others. She glanced over to Morwenna when she said it. It seems a perfectly vile thing to say, since, as far as I could see, Morwenna was twice the woman that Celia is.'

'You're not sure, though? About them being related, I mean,' DCI Andrews pressed Cressida.

'Well, no... but I'm sure I can find out. And if she is family, however distantly related, don't you think it's a bit suspicious that Lord Trevelyan didn't mention it?'

'Perhaps. I suppose it depends how distant. We're all related to Alfred the Great or some such, aren't we?' DCI Andrews asked rhetorically. 'Anyway, he did tell me some other interesting things.'

'Oh yes?' Cressida wasn't about to let the family connection between the Lord and maid go but also wanted to hear what Andrews had to say.

'I asked him about Lord Canterbury, of course, and he certainly had his answers ready. He said he had a very good working and social relationship with Lord Canterbury, what with him not only joining the business in an official capacity as,' he flipped the page of his notebook, 'acquisitions ambassador, but, of course, also because he was joining the family with his marriage to the Honourable Miss Trevelyan.'

'Who was carrying on some sort of affair with Sebastian Goodricke, it seemed.'

Andrews nodded, closed his notebook and put it away. 'Whatever Miss Trevelyan was doing, and I'll make sure I have a word with her, for now I think we can both agree that Lord Trevelyan had no motive to kill Lord Canterbury.'

Cressida sighed. 'You're right of course. And perhaps Morwenna really was killed because she knew something about what happened to Randolph. But I can't help but think there might be something in the fact that both Randolph and Morwenna were in some way linked to the Trevelyan family, he by business and soon-to-be marriage and Morwenna as a cousin... not just to Lord Trevelyan, but' – she released a hand from under Ruby and started counting on her fingers – 'to Patrick, Selina, Jago Trengrouse and Catherine Bly too...'

Cressida stopped short, a prickle going down her back. 'What if that's what's linking these deaths, Andrews? Someone picking off distant relatives to the Trevelyans?'

Andrews frowned, his pencil poised above his notebook. Cressida stepped gingerly over the sharp shards of vase that covered the Persian carpet until she was next to him.

'Andrews...' her voice was barely louder than a whisper, 'what if that means the murderer hasn't finished? What if another member of the family will be next?'

30

DCI Andrews sucked on his teeth and then nodded. 'I can see what you're driving at, Miss Fawcett, but it's all supposition for now. Was Morwenna the one who telephoned me? Was she related to the Trevelyans? If so, why would anyone want her dead? Did she have anything to do with Lord Canterbury's murder? These are all good questions, but we simply don't have answers.'

'Yet,' Cressida added, taking a few steps away from him and towards the window. She turned back to face him. 'And there's another mystery to add to the mix too, Andrews. Regarding something that definitely gets added to a mix, or a *mixer*, on a regular basis, namely ginger beer or possibly—'

'What are you talking about, Miss Fawcett?' DCI Andrews scratched his head as he looked at her, utterly perplexed.

'Rum, of course. And smuggled rum at that.' Cressida explained how Dotty and George had discovered the stash of illegal liquor in the boathouse along with the ledger.

'Lordy be.' Andrews shook his head. 'Murder, smuggling. And I thought the East End of London was bad.' He exhaled a long breath and got his notepad out again and wrote something down in it. 'Well, I'll certainly look into it, Miss Fawcett.'

'Thank you, Andrews.'

'And what about you, Miss Fawcett? What's your plan for the rest of the day?' He looked at her inquisitively.

Cressida narrowed an eye at him. 'Why do I have the feeling that that was a trick question, Andrews?'

He merely raised an eyebrow at her, and Cressida, with a wriggling Ruby now in her arms, tutted and made her apologies.

'I promise I'll be careful, Andrews. Don't you worry about me!'

Ruby was keen to be let down and Cressida only just made it out onto the terrace, safely away from the sharp and dangerous shards of porcelain, before she wriggled free completely.

'No more potentially expensive adventures please, Rubes,' she chastised the pup as she watched her loll onto the stone of the terrace and, like a grotesque little ballerina, cock a leg up and lick her tummy. Cressida was grateful no one else had to witness this acrobatic display as she was quite alone now on the sun-drenched terrace. Dotty and George must have decided to go for a walk to shake off the tragedy of this morning's gruesome discovery, and she couldn't blame them. Seagulls cawed and called as they circled overhead, and Cressida paused to wonder what she did have planned for the rest of the day. She hated being idle, and needed distraction more now than ever. She was about to walk down to the boathouse, though the thought of the deadly ropes within it caused her arm hair to flicker up again, so instead she sat down on the terrace's balustrade and stared at Ruby's gymnastics a moment longer.

Looking at her little pup reminded her of all the broken china in the drawing room and her mind drifted... It was a weekday now, Monday morning in fact, and she was determined to go and see if the pottery at Pencarrick was open and if anyone there could help her understand Morwenna's connection with the place.

'Come on, Rubes, I have a plan,' she said to the small dog, who had obviously scratched the right itch and happily trotted along next to her as she headed along the terrace and through the gate towards the driveway and garages. As she walked around the side of the house, Cressida spied Dotty.

'Dot!' She waved and walked towards her. Dotty was with George Parish and Cressida could see that he was standing quite close to her, his arm tenderly resting on Dotty's back. Cressida upped her pace and was by her friend's side in mere moments. 'Dot, what's wrong?'

It was obvious Dotty had been crying and she looked quite distressed as she wiped her eyes, nudging her lace-edged handkerchief under her glasses. She sniffled, then replied, 'Don't mind me, Cressy. It was just a bit of a shock.'

'What was? What's happened, Dot?'

George answered for her as she blew her nose. 'Coroner's just taken that maid's body away. We happened to be walking past and the sheet slipped as we were passing. Grisly sight.'

'How horrid.' Cressida reached out and touched her friend's arm, then, doing what she so often did in times of Dotty upset, picked up Ruby and passed her to her so she could bury her head in the pup's voluptuous and furry rolls of squidge. After a moment, she asked, 'Did you see anything of any interest? From a clue point of view?'

'No more than we saw earlier when Roscoe brought her up the lawn. She was...' George's countenance faltered slightly. 'Well, we didn't see much.'

A voice from Ruby's neck piped up. 'We did see Celia Nangower hanging around the ambulance, though.' Dotty emerged from Ruby's soft neck and, with a grateful smile, passed her back to Cressida, who took her and cradled her in the crook of her arm.

'Celia Nangower? What would she have been doing loitering around the ambulance?'

'Or here at all, indeed?' George said, and Cressida nodded at him.

'Keeping an eye on what the police are doing in her precious part of the world?' Dotty suggested.

'Or returning to the scene of the crime,' Cressida added. 'In any case, I feel like I should go and pay her a call. Then I'm off to that pottery again. There's got to be something there, what with both Randolph and Morwenna paying it a visit, both the day before they died.'

'Shall we come too, Cressy?' Dotty asked, pushing her glasses back up the bridge of her nose.

'No, I'll be all right, chum,' Cressida reassured her. 'I'm going to have to go full charm offensive on Celia Nangower and Ruby can be my wing dog. Wish me luck, though.'

'Good luck, Cressy.' Dotty looked at her, consternation written across her face. 'And, for heaven's sake, be careful!'

31

Peacehaven Gables was only a mile or two down the high-hedgerowed lanes from Penbeagle House. Built a hundred years after its great neoclassical neighbour, Peacehaven Gables was far less imposing, and far less well kept. There was no grand facade or towering columns, instead the wide, white-painted front door sat under a colonnaded semi-circular porch that led straight from the gravelled driveway. Either side of the porch were two large round bays, each with windows on the ground and first floors. From them, the house spread width-wise into the wings, and around it overgrown herbaceous borders merged into lawns and terraces. There was no view of the sea; instead it looked over farmland and small clumps of trees that no doubt formed part of its own parkland. The whole house was rendered in a gesso the colour of Cornish clotted cream, blotched in places where the severe West Country winds had blown guttering awry and damp had formed. In some ways, Cressida, who had pulled up to the front of it in her Bugatti, preferred it to the pomp and circumstance of Penbeagle House, though she yearned to give it a thorough spit and polish. She only wished its owners could behave in the same moderated style of pretension, but wishing these things often got one nowhere.

Still, the noise of her motor or the tyres on the gravel must have alerted the owners to their visitor, so it was as Cressida was getting out of her car that Celia Nangower appeared from the front door and greeted her.

'Miss Fawcett. What an unexpected pleasure. I suppose you young London types thrive on spontaneity. Oh, your dog has come too. How charming,' Celia Nangower greeted her, her voice dripping with sarcasm.

'I'm sorry not to have waited for an invitation, but I was told Peacehaven Gables was a fine example of late Georgian architecture, and as a devotee of the style I just had to come by.' Cressida knew flattery could usually get one anywhere, and she was correct as Celia's face softened and she looked as though she were the cat that got the entire house-worth of that clotted cream.

'You are kind,' she simpered. 'Come, do take a morning coffee with us on the terrace. Monty is reading his newspaper, I'm afraid, but we can talk. It seems it was quite the morning up at Penbeagle today.' Celia indicated that Cressida should follow her into the house, which was dark and cool compared to the summer sunshine outside. They passed through a gracious hallway with a beautifully curved staircase within it, the whole aspect only marred by a faint, but pervading, smell of damp. Celia led her through and they emerged out at the rear of the house through French doors that opened onto a terrace. Monty Nangower was sitting at a table, his newspaper flicked up taut in front of his face.

'I heard you were at the house just now?' Cressida asked.

'Please, sit down, Miss Fawcett,' Celia invited. Then she turned to the maid, who looked neat as a pin, but with dark rims under her eyes and a pallor that made her look even paler than her fair skin suggested. 'Paula, hurry, girl. Coffee for our guest.'

'Thank you, Mrs Nangower. And please, call me Cressida.'

Celia nodded but made no suggestion for Cressida to do likewise.

Paula, the maid, brought out a shining bright silver coffee pot and an equally perfectly polished milk jug and sugar bowl. Fine china cups clattered as she placed the tray down and Cressida watched as Celia Nangower carefully selected one with a slight chip in the rim for herself.

'So, as I was saying, you were at Penbeagle House earlier, Mrs Nangower?'

'Yes.' She waved Paula away, who bobbed a curtsy and disappeared back into the gloom of the house. 'I had just returned before you arrived. I thought there was a lot of fuss made over the death of a maid.' Celia said it so matter-of-factly that Cressida hardly knew how to react. Instead she watched as her hostess poured out the steaming coffee and topped up her cup with a splash of milk. 'Sugar?' she offered, and Cressida shook her head, still struck dumb by her companion's crassness. Celia Nangower sat down and sipped from her own cup before carrying on. 'It's one thing after another up there at the moment. Though we are but a modest residence, we do at least steer clear of the dramas that seem to surround the dear Trevelyans at Penbeagle. Lord Canterbury the night of the ball, Selina getting herself into all sorts of mischief, now a maid dead in the cove.'

Cressida finally found her tongue. 'Murdered, Mrs Nangower. Morwenna, for that was her name, was murdered. As was Lord Canterbury.'

This seemed to bring Celia up short somewhat and Cressida watched as she sipped her coffee, her nose wrinkling as if the expensive luxury was as foul as a witches' brew. Then, in a complete change of subject, she said, 'It was nice to see Catherine yesterday. We sailed out for lunch in one of the other coves.'

One of the other less murderous ones, Cressida thought to herself as Celia continued.

'Catherine really is very astute about many things, you know. I do admire her.'

I'm not surprised... Cressida thought, comparing the spikiness of the two women in her mind and finding them both equally as caustic. She cocked her head to one side, inviting Celia to continue.

'She's got a first-class mind, that one, and I don't need to tell you, Cressida, that those are hard to come by in our sex.' Celia put her cup and saucer down. Cressida copied her and settled in to the hard wrought-iron chair, her eternal struggle between her excellent manners and her natural forthrightness battling on.

'She obviously does have a talent,' Cressida conceded, as much to mollify Celia, 'but do you know she wrote some beastly letters to Lord Canterbury, some of them just before he died, I hear.'

Celia pinched her lips together, the wrinkles looking not altogether dissimilar to Ruby's bottom, which was on display as the small dog snortled in the overgrown flowerbed. 'Well, I hear he was a man being attacked from all sides, as it were.'

'All sides?' Cressida asked, glad her salvo had initiated a retaliation. A retaliation with some interesting information in it.

'There were those who wanted an awful lot from him. More perhaps than he was able to provide.' Celia took up her cup and sipped her coffee. 'Hoist by one's own petard, you could say.'

'I'm sorry?' Cressida was confused.

'His reputation had preceded, and perhaps exceeded, him. I can't name names, of course, but perhaps he should have been more careful before signing contracts with a large company that would require a huge number of pieces of antiquity from him. Catherine had put two and two together, you see, using that first-class mind of hers, and realised, after she'd done some digging of her own, that there might not be the appetite from the Egyptian authorities to sell as many pieces to Britain as a certain importer was hoping for.'

'Without naming names, of course,' Cressida kept the artifice up, 'would you say that Lord Canterbury was in danger of not fulfilling his side of the contract?'

Celia arched an eyebrow at her. 'All I'm saying is that he was a brave man to promise the ancient world to a thoroughly modern businessman.'

'I see.' Cressida assumed Celia was talking about Lord Trevelyan, or perhaps Jago Trengrouse, who had admitted earlier to arguing with Randolph about the finer points of a contract. Jago or Lord Trevelyan... cousins in business... and cousins to Catherine Bly too. 'Mrs Nangower, did Catherine, with her first-rate mind, as you say, ever think of joining the Far East Company?'

'Oh,' Celia laughed conceitedly. 'There's those modern ideas of yours again. A woman in business. How funny.' She shook her head, then cocked it to one side as she thought about something. 'Still, now you mention it, there are other cousins on the Bly side and the Blys and Trevelyans have always been close, which is why it's odd that...' Celia paused.

'Yes?' Cressida was all ears.

'Just that it's odd Edgar is favouring the Trengrouse side of the family so much more. I heard him telling dear Catherine to "put up or shut up", and I can only think he heard such a vulgar phrase on the dockside somewhere, but anyway, he told Catherine that if she wanted to be invited to Penbeagle again, she would have to refrain from writing to Lord Canterbury about that scoop she wanted and generally stop sticking her oar in.'

Cressida's mind raced. Catherine obviously hated Randolph, but did she hate him enough to risk angering Lord Trevelyan? If her poison-pen letters were enough to get her cousin to ban her from Penbeagle, and therefore society, would actual poison have been on her agenda? And what could she possibly have against Morwenna, except she was a distant cousin too, and clearly not one being over-promoted in anyone's eyes?

'And why is it odd for the Trengrouses, or at least Jago, to be favoured more than the Blys? Jago seems to have an aptitude for the business,' queried Cressida.

'The Trengrouses, though respectable enough, have fallen far from the family tree in terms of wealth and privilege,' Celia responded sharply.

'Jago seems very gentlemanly.' Cressida thought of the handsome young man and how he had blended in so seamlessly with the upper classes out on the terrace last night, even acting more superior to his cousin Patrick and putting him in his place.

'He *seems* gentlemanly indeed. Schooling paid for by Edgar and Allegra. But there's not a bean on his side of the family. His cousin on his mother's side is a fisherman in Falmouth, for heaven's sake!' Celia amused herself so much with her revelation, she rattled her coffee cup in its saucer and had to recover herself. 'So, you have to ask yourself, who *are* his people really? Are they Trevelyans, or are they trash?'

'I don't believe anyone to be trash,' Cressida said, politely but firmly. 'And I think it's a wonderful notion of Lord Trevelyan to elevate his less well-off cousin. That is a truly gentlemanly thing to do, and wise no doubt too, as Mr Trengrouse seems to have excellent business acumen and has done awfully well for the company.'

Celia straightened her shoulders and became more guarded again. 'He has done well for Edgar, that's true. But he's descended from Edgar's uncle, who was very wild. Barely ever in the country, and when he was, he was a libertine, by all accounts.'

'Lord Trevelyan's uncle, so this must have been in the last century?'

'Yes. Edgar was fond of him, enjoyed his stories of a life of adventuring, in and out of China long after the Opium Wars. I think that's why Edgar now favours the Trengrouses over the Blys, who have been nothing but respectable all these generations.'

'He feels Jago shares his grandfather's sense of adventure, I see. And what about Morwenna? I got the impression last night that you think she's related in some way to the family?'

Celia Nangower arched an eyebrow again, but put down her coffee cup with a certain finality. 'As I say, Edgar's uncle was very wild.'

Cressida nodded and sat back and listened as Celia went off on a tangent about other local families and more generic gossip. Frustratingly, the topic of the Trevelyans and the Trengrouses seemed to be closed. But what she had gleaned had been interesting indeed. Jago was brought up by his richer relatives and favoured over the other side of the family. Morwenna *was* more than likely related too, though possibly conceived the wrong side of the bed sheets... And if Celia was talking about who Cressida thought she was talking about earlier, then Jago might have been putting a lot of pressure on Randolph to deliver. Pressure that might have made Randolph make some very dangerous enemies.

32

Celia had definitely given Cressida food for thought, if not much in the way of actual food, and Cressida was pleased she'd helped herself to a hearty portion of eggs and bacon at breakfast. Her stomach rumbled as she drove off away from Peacehaven Gables, and images of a delicious Bootlegger's Arms' pasty kept interrupting her train of thought regarding what Celia had said about Jago Trengrouse. Would he really kill someone who had joined the company he was helping to lead, and not just the company, but who was about to join the family too? Let alone kill a young woman who was a cousin of his?

Cressida drummed her fingers on the steering wheel as she flung the Bugatti around the high-sided lanes of this perfect little patch of Cornwall. Glimpses of sapphire-blue sea appeared between hedges, and the sun was high in the sky, glinting off the smart chrome work on her car. Ruby bounced around on the seat next to her like an India rubber ball, happily snorting and trying to catch the occasional fly that darted in over the windscreen.

'Sorry there were no crumbs for you under that table. Sadly, no crumbs for me either, but there were whole slices of information.' Pasties would have to remain a wistful dream, as while she was in the car she was still determined to visit Pencarrick Pottery. Despite the sun's warmth, she shivered as she remembered how both Morwenna and Randolph had visited there on the days before they died. 'Am I being mad in thinking that place has something to do with their murders?' Cressida asked Ruby, who was now standing on her back legs, her puny front ones perched up on the door of the car, her tongue lolling out in the rushing breeze. 'Good idea, pup, get some fresh air and those brain cells working.'

Cressida drove on and before too long pulled into the dusty courtyard of the pottery. There was definite life to the place today, with the doors and windows of the single-storey sheds open and voices wafting out of them. A tractor was pulling a trailer through a gap between the buildings and it thundered past her as it drove off in the direction from which Cressida had just come. She coughed out some of the dust that got caught in her throat as she brought her motorcar to a stop, parking it next to another, smaller and older tractor.

Cressida got out swiftly and smoothed down her skirt. 'I'm glad we went to stiff old Celia's before we came here,' she said to Ruby as she bent down and looked in her wing mirror. 'Though Peacehaven Gables wasn't as spruce and spry as she would have one believe from her snobbish demeanour and three-string pearls...' She murmured as she wiped a few smuts and smudges off her face. Satisfied, she picked up Ruby from the passenger seat and decided that it mattered not a jot how she looked in this place of hard work and industry.

'What matters,' she whispered into her dog's ear, 'is finding someone to talk to, someone who might know what was going on with Randolph and Morwenna.'

. . .

Cressida, sadly, wasn't in much luck. Although the many voices she'd heard had all belonged to diligent workers, they had all, to a man or woman, shaken their heads when she'd asked if anyone knew anything about a gentleman called Randolph Canterbury. A couple of them knew Morwenna but couldn't tell her much, save that she grew up locally and had family down Falmouth way. A sandy-haired chap was dipping vases into glazes, and Cressida noted the lustrous bronze and gold they turned after firing as another fellow removed a load from a kiln. She'd let a struggling Ruby down as she'd spoken to a woman who was painting details on a delicately patterned plate, but all she could tell her was that management was away on a meeting with some folks in Falmouth and no one round here knew much about the accounts and such. Cressida thanked her for her time anyway and followed Ruby out to the courtyard.

'Ruby!' she called, worried that another tractor might come out of nowhere and the driver not notice the small pup from his elevated seat. She needn't have worried, though, as she noticed her pup's pig-like tail wiggling at her as the curious dog disappeared through a broken panel in one of the hut's doors. 'Oh Rubes,' Cressida cursed but, recognising the hut as the one that had been locked up like the Tower of London the day before, trotted across the way to see if the door was still locked.

Luckily for both of them, it wasn't, and it swung open easily as Cressida turned the handle. Ruby was sitting panting, looking pleased with herself for finding what looked like a dead bat on the floor.

'Oh Ruby, trust you to find the one grim thing round here.'

Cressida bent down and picked up the poor departed creature of the night and dropped it in a wastepaper bin by one of the workbenches. In so doing, a few things on the workbench itself caught her eye and she looked closer at the designs being drawn for an intricate, very Eastern-inspired pot. Next to it was a mould and Cressida narrowed her eyes until the recognition came to her; it was a Foo dog like the ones on the mantelpiece at Penbeagle House.

'Interesting...' Cressida ran her fingers along the bench until she came across another Eastern-inspired piece, a curious teapot in the shape of a laughing Buddha but with holes just above and below the handle. 'What a curiosity,' she murmured. Posters on the wall gave ingredients for glazes, and more moulds in eastern designs lined the shelves. 'It's not very Cornish, all this,' Cressida whispered to Ruby, who was looking longingly at the bin. 'I was expecting slipware and chunky, rustic bowls and jugs, not Buddhas and Foo dogs!'

Ruby snorted in agreement and, with only a moment's hesitation after one last wistful look at the bin, followed her mistress back out into the midday sunshine. Cressida picked her up again, worried about thundering tractors, and carried her back towards her car.

'We might have to call on them again, once management is back from Falmouth,' Cressida told Ruby, popping her back into the passenger seat of the Bugatti.

Before she walked around the car to her own door, she glanced into the trailer attached to the small tractor parked next to her. Wooden crates were packed into it, and one of them didn't have its lid nailed down. After a quick glance over her shoulder to check she wasn't being watched, Cressida cautiously lifted the lid and peered in.

'Hmm,' she said. Having found so many Eastern-inspired designs on her clandestine visit to what she thought of as the 'dead bat' workshop, she was surprised to find plain ceramic bottles in the crates. Plain as day...

Cressida lowered the lid and walked back to her car. As she started up the engine and drove off in the direction of Penbeagle House, she couldn't help but wonder if those ceramic bottles had anything to do with the similar-looking stash Dotty and George had found in the boathouse. Had Randolph perhaps stumbled across a ring of rum smugglers while he'd been visiting the pottery and accosting them had got him killed? But then why was he there in the first place? Advising on designs for the Eastern-inspired pots? Inspired, or would a better word be 'faked'?

33

Lunch, however deliciously tempting it smelled coming from the dining room of Penbeagle House, would have to wait. An idea had occurred to Cressida as she'd driven down the cow parsley-lined lanes back to the scene of the two crimes. Her friend Maurice Sauvage, who worked in the fabric and uphol-stery department at Liberty of London, was not only a dab hand at sourcing fabulous fabrics, but he also kept an ear to the ground on all the comings and goings and uppings and down-ings of objets d'art and decorative pieces throughout London. If Staffordshire Spaniels were in, he'd know about it; or if button-back upholstery was having a heyday, he'd be buying in velvet buttons... and, in this case, if there was a sudden demand for English-made versions of Eastern designs he'd know, with Liberty possibly being one of the main suppliers of said pieces to the professional classes and gentry.

Cressida let Ruby run off to terrorise some dust motes in the hallway as she found the telephone, which had been conve-niently installed in a cubbyhole in the passage on the way to the orangery. Although it may have once been a proper cupboard, it would be easy enough to overhear what a caller was saying and it occurred to Cressida that Morwenna may well have been the last person to use this handset when she'd called DCI Andrews the night before she was murdered. With this in mind, she whipped out her handkerchief from her pocket and carefully lifted the receiver while trying not to remove any fingerprints.

'Hello, operator, Liberty of London, fabrics and upholstery please. Yes, I'll hold.' Cressida spoke down the line and waited to be connected.

'Good afternoon, Liberty of London, how may I help you?' Maurice's familiar voice came across clearly, despite the odd crackle in the background.

'Maurice? It is you, isn't it? Marvellous. Cressida Fawcett here.'

'Ah, Good day, Miss Fawcett. The operator said the call was from Cornwall. I take it the fancy-dress ball was a success?' Maurice asked.

'For Ruby, who was belle of the ball in that parrot costume you designed, yes; but for the rest of us, sadly not.' She filled Maurice in on the murder of Lord Canterbury and the subsequent discovery of Morwenna's body too.

'They've been lucky to keep it out of the papers.' Maurice paused and the line crackled. Then he spoke again. 'I will offer any help I can, of course, but, Miss Fawcett, please do be careful. Are Lady Dorothy and Lord Delafield still with you?'

'Yes, and both as cautionary as you are, Maurice. Detective Chief Inspector Andrews is here too, so please don't worry about me. In fact, it's with Andrews and his investigation in mind that I thought of you and wondered if you could help. There's something fishy going on concerning ceramics from the Far East Company. Have you heard of them?'

'Yes, indeed I have.' This was good news for Cressida, and she carefully adjusted the telephone receiver closer to her ear as Maurice carried on. 'We sell their wares here at Liberty, in fact.'

'Bingo. I'd rather hoped as much. What sort of pieces is Liberty taking?'

'Well, old Sir Arthur Liberty himself was a keen collector of Far Eastern-inspired decorative objects and, although he's no longer with us, God rest his soul, it's still an important department at Liberty and the Far East Company is one of our most prestigious suppliers. There's vases and ornaments, those big plates one hangs on a wall, tea sets, of course, both English and Chinese style, oh and silks and ready-made kimonos and that sort of thing.'

As Maurice was listing them, Cressida was mentally ticking off each and every one against the moulds, glazed vases and even the odd little teapot design she'd found at Pencarrick Pottery. It couldn't be just a coincidence, could it?

'Maurice, would you do me the most wonderful favour?'

'Anything for my favourite client, Miss Fawcett.'

'Could you get your hands on the complete list, or a catalogue if such a thing exists, of what the Far East Company brings into the country? Especially if it's labelled genuine antique or of Far Eastern origin. I'd be awfully grateful. Not just what Liberty take either, but everything if possible.'

Maurice agreed, and, without much more ado, except for swapping a few tidbits of gossip about the most recent newspaper headlines, Cressida rang off.

'Toodle-ooh, Maurice, and don't worry, I will take care. But, you know me, I do have to poke my—'

'Aristocratic nose...'

'Yes, my noble old nose into everything. Toodle-ooh again.'

Cressida was just replacing the earpiece to the candlestick-style telephone, carefully removing her handkerchief in the process, when a cough behind her made her jump. She turned and was relieved when she saw that it was only DCI Andrews clearing his throat in the passageway behind her.

'Miss Fawcett,' he said, standing back so she could exit the small cubbyhole where the telephone was situated. 'I hope I wasn't interrupting you?'

'No, not at all. The contraption's all yours, Andrews.'

He nodded but instead of moving into the cubby, he hovered. 'Miss Fawcett, I'm sorry to have overheard your last few words to your caller, but did I hear you promising not to get yourself into trouble? You know my feelings on you putting yourself in danger.'

Cressida looked at Andrews' furrowed brow. It was only a few weeks ago that she'd believed him capable of sabotaging her efforts in order to promote his own views on a case, but in the end she'd realised that there was no one more on her side than DCI Andrews.

'I'll be careful, Andrews, I promise. But I *have* found out some more information today.'

She filled him in on the objets d'art that sounded increasingly like matches for items brought into the country by the Far East Company.

'So, you see, Andrews, I was just consulting with Maurice Sauvage. You remember him, don't you? He's going to send a list down to us and I'm going to check it over and see if anything goes ping in my head.'

'That's an interesting avenue, Miss Fawcett.' Andrews scratched his beard. 'You will keep me informed of your pinging head, yes?'

'Yes, Andrews.' Cressida rolled her eyes at him.

'But you might be on to something. I'll have Kirby quiz Lord Trevelyan when he's back from Falmouth, see if he knows anything about this Pencarrick Pottery operation and if it's above board.'

Cressida beamed at Andrews, happy that, despite his ribbing, he was taking her lead into consideration. She held the receiver up to him, still delicately grasped between her thumb and forefinger with her handkerchief over it. 'I had a thought that Morwenna might have used this telephone to call you last night. Hence the handkerchief to protect her prints.'

DCI Andrews carefully took the receiver from her and then handed back her handkerchief. 'Already in hand, Miss Fawcett. Kirby took the prints first thing this morning and we're comparing them to the young lady's body – the post-mortem is happening today.' He looked sombre. 'Such a young one.' He shook his head.

'Celia Nangower definitely believes she was related to the Trevelyans, you know. Something else to check with Lord T, don't you think? It might be nothing but spurious and spiteful gossip, especially knowing the source, but I think we should look into it.'

'I'll ask Kirby to make a note. Thank you for your information. In return, I have some news for you. The post-mortem has been conducted on Lord Canterbury.'

'Oh.' The hairs on her arms stood on end as she shivered. She still couldn't think of poor Randolph, so used to the heat of Cairo, now dead on a cold slab in the mortuary. 'Anything to report?'

Andrews took a deep inhale and then sighed. He looked at Cressida and said what he'd heard from the coroner. 'Death by poison. Hemlock, to be more exact.'

'Oh.' Cressida leaned against the wall as a support. 'So Sebastian was correct.'

'Sebastian Goodricke? The Foreign Office chap?' Andrews asked.

'And an expert on hemlock, so it seems. He told me with some certainty it was that, from the symptoms he observed as poor Randolph lay dying.'

'Sounds to me like Mr Goodricke might be a very good person to interview next.'

'He definitely has one of the strongest motives too, if his love for Selina is anything to go by,' Cressida said, and Andrews nodded. 'Speaking of motives, I had a rather awkward convo with George Parish, but the upshot is that he has no motive if we can prove that Randolph contacted the London museum that's cataloguing the finds shipped back from their dig. If he did request that George be credited, then we know George's story checks out. There's some paperwork in his room that relates to it all too, I think.' Andrews noted down the queries and looked up at her. Cressida carried on. 'Any thoughts on the cache of rum we found in the boathouse?'

'That's why I'm here waiting for the telephone, Miss Fawcett. Putting in a call to Customs and Excise. This sort of thing is their jurisdiction, but I'll ask them to work closely with us.'

'I saw similar ceramic bottles at Pencarrick Pottery today,' Cressida told him. 'And that's the same pottery that both Randolph and Morwenna went to the days preceding their deaths. Smuggling or not, there's definitely something rum about that!'

34

'What ho, Cressy!' Dotty called across to her, waving from the terrace as Cressida poked her head out of the orangery. It was the quickest route from the telephone cabinet to the terrace, though it had been strange entering the room where Randolph had collapsed and died just two nights ago. She'd tried to avoid looking at the exact spot as she'd crossed the marble floor of the glasshouse-like room, its tropical plants and lush green leaves so verdant, so alive. *Unlike poor Randolph...*

Cressida shook the thought from her head and walked over to where Dotty was sitting, much to Cressida's relief, with a plate of food in front of her.

'Hello, Dot.'

'Luncheon is served, Cressy, do go and help yourself. It's buffet style again – I think Lady Trevelyan has had to allow some of the kitchen staff time off to talk to the police and of course grieve. How horrid for them, to lose a friend like that.'

Cressida raised her eyebrows. 'I think I know how they feel. Randolph and I weren't close, of course, but he did propose to me.'

'Oh Cressy, yes of course.' Dotty put her knife and fork

down and looked up at her friend. 'I'm so sorry.'

Cressida shrugged. 'No need for you to apologise, Dot. As I said, we weren't very close. I'll get lunch and join you in two ticks. Come on, Rubes, you can help choose exactly which pieces will accidentally fall on the floor while I'm eating...'

A few minutes later and Cressida was seated next to her friend at one of the pretty wrought-iron tables on the terrace, with Ruby contentedly wolfing down tidbits under her chair.

'Dot, tell me, are sparks flying between you and George?'

Dotty blushed to her eyebrows, but finished chewing her mouthful and replied, 'George is... I mean I... Oh I don't know, Cressy. It's complicated.'

'Why, chum?' Cressida was intrigued. She thought Dotty and George had hit it off, but Dotty seemed hesitant.

'Well, it's so soon after Basil. Decorum aside—'

'Decorum can go hang. I don't think decorum is bothering Basil too much, not now he's packing up for South Africa.' Cressida referenced the affair Dotty's ex-betrothed had been having with a South African diamond heiress.

'I know you're not one for following convention, Cressy, like that time you donned a fake moustache and slipped into the Athenaeum with Brewster and—'

'I know, I know,' Cressida cut her friend off. 'But what I mean is that I wouldn't let any old-fashioned sense of decorum stop you from getting to know George a little better.'

'I think that's why it's complicated. We simply don't know George. He's been away in Egypt while we had our debutante season and my parents don't know his people at all. At least Alfred's been getting to know him, I feel better about that. They've taken some lobster pots down to the jetty and are trying to snag some. I think Alfred wants to impress you by catching your favourite supper.'

Dotty's eyes twinkled as she spoke and Cressida avoided having to answer by popping a new potato smothered in rich Cornish butter into her mouth.

Dotty chortled and then continued. 'We do have fun together, though. Despite everything that's going on here at Penbeagle. Even discovering the rum in the boathouse was a wheeze. Oh, we went to go and see Lord Trevelyan this morning before he left for the docks and told him all about it.'

'Oooh,' Cressida finished chewing and swallowed her spud so she could ask more questions. 'What did he say? Did he know about it?'

'Not a clue!' Dotty was smiling, obviously enjoying herself. 'He didn't believe us at first and thought we were pranking him, which is a little insulting as now is hardly the time for pranks.' Dotty pushed her wayward glasses up her nose.

'Quite. Did he know about the secret floor under the rotten boards?'

'He says not, but he did have to pause a bit before he answered, which reminded me terribly of Pooky Marchpaine at school who always bought herself time with an enigmatic pause when she was lying to Madame Mirabelle about not doing her French verbs.'

'I remember her. Didn't she run off to the court of the Aga Khan? Anyway, so Lord Trevelyan *might* have known about the secret stashing place, though, of course, he says he doesn't. Did he go down there with you and see for himself?' Cressida was all ears.

'Yes, and you should have seen his face when he saw crates and crates of... what did George call it? Moonshine, that's it. Honestly, Cressy, when Lord T saw quite how much illicit booze there was in his boathouse, with Scotland Yard detectives just yards away...'

Something in what Dotty said caused a flicker of recognition in Cressida's mind and she made a mental note to try to tease that thread out later.

'... So he said he'll have to turn them all into the authorities,' continued Dotty.

'And so he did. That must be why I've just bumped into Andrews making that very call to the Customs chaps. And, Dotty, do you think I'm barmy in thinking the smuggled rum has to be linked to the murders? You see, I've just seen some of those ceramic bottles at Pencarrick.'

'I don't think that makes you barmy, Cressy. But it could all be a coincidence.' Dotty put down her cutlery and pushed her plate away, making sure that a small piece of leftover ham found its way under the table to her friend's panting pooch. 'Did you manage to speak to anyone at the pottery?'

'No one of much use, but I did find a lot of interesting things. Pieces exactly like those brought in by the Far East Company – vases and lustreware and tea sets and the like. But no one knew of Randolph and if they knew Morwenna they'd never seen her at the pottery, though the manager wasn't there to ask. If it hadn't been for Ruby sniffing out an unfortunate dead bat in one of the huts, I wouldn't have found any of the Eastern-inspired designs or whatnot.'

'A dead bat? How grim.' Dotty wrinkled her nose at the thought.

'Yes, but thanks to her snubby-yet-sensitive nose and deprived delectation in dead things, she did find the most amazing collection of not-very-Cornish pottery.' Cressida reached down and patted her pet, slipping her a small piece of roast beef as she did.

'That nose of hers sniffed out Mama's diamonds,' Dotty reminded her. 'Perhaps she's just sniffed out something important here too.'

'And not just a dead bat.' Cressida agreed.

Dotty nodded. 'Quite. Something much more interesting.'

35

Cressida and Dotty were just finishing their lunch when DCI Andrews appeared on the terrace.

'Andrews!' Cressida called over to him, pulling her napkin off her lap, and he walked over to where they were sitting.

'Miss Fawcett, Lady Dorothy.' He nodded a greeting to them both, but Cressida waved away the formality, pulled out one of the chairs next to her and gestured for him to sit down.

'Andrews, how did your call to Customs and Excise go? Were they terribly thrilled at Dotty's find?' she asked with a certain amount of relish, but then noticed that Andrews, far from settling in to tell all, looked pensive and thoughtful. He perched himself on the edge of the chair, and leaned forward in thought. Cressida changed tone and asked quite plainly, 'What is it, Andrews? What did they say?' She glanced over to Dotty, who was now looking more seriously at the policeman.

Andrews sucked his teeth, then replied. 'They were less than thrilled, but only because I was telephoning in to tell them that rum had been found.'

'I thought the smuggling of it was rife around here. That's

what Lady Trevelyan and Selina had said.' Cressida leaned back and folded her arms across her chest.

'And they may be right, and the officers will be down to deal with it pretty promptly, but they were hoping I was calling with information on something far less salubrious. Drugs.'

'Drugs?' Cressida and Dotty said in unison, and Cressida found herself wondering if Selina really had been getting her dope from somewhere quite close to home.

'There's an illegal drugs ring that we've all been working on together, across departments throughout London and the country. Some of my colleagues in the Yard have tinkered around the edges, arresting petty dealers and busting up some opium dens—'

'I've read my fair share of Sherlock Holmes, but I thought opium dens were all in the past, or over-egged by Conan-Doyle for atmosphere. Do they really still operate?'

'More than you'd think. Since it was all made illegal in 1920, it's driven it to the back rooms of clubs and gambling houses. Not nice places.' As if to emphasise this, he sat back in his chair and looked up at the grand facade of Penbeagle House.

'So your Excise chaps were hoping you might have found drugs? But why here?' Cressida asked, wondering if Lord and Lady Trevelyan had any inkling at all about their daughter's addiction. *Still, Jago had said the Far East Company had nothing to do with bringing in the opium she was using...*

'Whenever they catch one of these petty dealers, the only thing they get out of them is that there's a "Head Shepherd" down here in the West Country.'

'That sounds more like something *Country Life* would report on rather than a name that would crop up in a police report,' Dotty said, just as a very cross-looking Jago stormed out of the house. He looked over to where they were sitting and then across the rest of the terrace and strode off in the other direction.

Cressida raised a finger to her companions and quietly got up from her chair and, as stealthily as possible, snuck into the house to see what Jago had been thundering away from. Inside, she saw one of the maids looking a little flushed in the hallway, about to disappear behind the green baize door.

'Hello there! Amy, is it?' Cressida called out to her, and the maid bobbed a curtsy and nodded.

'Yes, miss, can I help you, miss?'

'I just saw Mr Trengrouse dash out of here in an awful bother. Do you know why?'

Much to Cressida's horror, the maid burst into tears.

'Oh, I am sorry, I didn't mean to upset you, here...' Cressida offered her a hanky from her pocket and the maid took it gratefully.

'I'm awful sorry, miss, but he's just been hellishly cross with me.' She gulped in air as she tried to speak through her sobs.

Cressida rubbed her shoulder and comforted her until the poor girl had calmed down enough to speak again. All the while, though, she was wondering what could have set the charming Jago off. It wasn't done to shout at servants, everyone knew that.

'Tell me what happened, Amy, what did he say?'

'I was cleaning up the broken vase, miss. I had meant to do it earlier, miss, but the policemen wanted us to tell them all about Morwenna, miss, so I had to leave it, having picked up the main shards and that. I had just got back to it now when Mr Trengrouse saw me finishing off my sweeping and hollered at me, so he did. Said we had to be more careful with the antiques and that some of these pieces were irreplaceable. Said how costly those horrid-looking lions on the mantelpiece are and that we should never touch them. Never ever. Not even for dusting.'

Cressida bit her lip. She felt terribly guilty that it had been Ruby, or more likely the cat with Ruby in hot pursuit, who had been responsible for the vase breaking and told the maid as much before adding, 'I'm sure he's just under a lot of pressure. We all are after Lord Canterbury and your friend Morwenna were killed. I'm sorry, though. And after all that lovely beef you found for Ruby the other day. Never does a good deed go unpunished, eh.'

The maid seemed cheered up a bit by this and Cressida left her to go back through the green baize door and she returned out to the terrace, where Dotty and Andrews were waiting expectantly for her.

'Well?'

'Cross about the vase being broken.' She glared at Ruby, who was nonchalantly staring out across the lawn, not a care in the world.

'Oh dear,' Dotty said. 'Bit of an overreaction. Those aren't even his vases?'

'That's what I thought. All very peculiar. I'll have to ask him about it at dinner tonight. In the meantime, I'm afraid I'm going to have to love you and leave you. I promised Lady T that I'd look in on Selina and I haven't had a chance to yet today. I just hope she's not in the middle of all of this.' Cressida shook her head. 'Will you excuse me?'

Dotty nodded and Andrews gave her a mock salute. Just before Cressida left them, she had one more question for the detective.

'I'd be interested to know more about how you get on with Sebastian Goodricke when you get a chance to collar him, Andrews, if you wouldn't mind sharing. He knew too much about hemlock for my liking and with his passion for Selina, he's got to be one of the main suspects, hasn't he? He rather clammed up on me last night when I pushed him too far.'

'Very well, I'll let you know what he says,' DCI Andrews replied, getting up from his seat. 'But I'll beg the same favour of you and be grateful if you could let me know if Miss Trevelyan has anything of interest to say.'

'Of course, Andrews. There's something brewing in this house, I can feel it. Without knowing why the murderer, or murderers, struck, I'm not entirely confident that they won't kill again. But one thing I do know is that there's safety in numbers, so let's stick together.' With that, Cressida nodded a farewell to them both and went back into the grand facade of Penbeagle House.

36

Cressida knocked softly on Selina's bedroom door and let herself in. The room was dark, the curtains drawn against the bright summer light and the air within it felt stale and smelt vaguely aromatic.

'Selina?' Cressida said softly, and heard a low, sleepy moan from the bed. Cressida thought of leaving the poor thing to sleep, but she knew that sometimes being left on your own to mope and sleep didn't help, especially if your world had just been turned upside down. So, instead of leaving, Cressida closed the bedroom door behind her and stepped lightly over to where the heavy interlined curtains were blocking out the sunlight. One firm tug and dust motes swished around her as the light streamed in.

'You there,' a sleepy voice called over from the bed. 'Close those, won't you.'

Cressida ignored her and instead swung back the catch then pushed up and opened the large sash window. A breeze greeted her and Cressida took a deep breath, thankful for clean air.

Rustling came from the bed behind her and Cressida turned around.

'Selina, it's me. Cressy.'

'Oh. Hello.' Selina pushed herself up and blinked a bit as her eyes adjusted to the sunlight.

'How are you feeling? Still woozy from the sedatives?' It was tempting to go further and suggest self-administered ones, but Cressida held off and instead walked around to the edge of the bed and perched down by Selina's feet.

Selina pulled the bedclothes up around her and lay back against her plumped-up pillows. 'It's all been so ghastly. Dr May was a dear and gave me a stupendous amount of sleeping powder, but I can't... I can't just sleep forever, can I?' Selina started to sniffle, and Cressida regretted giving her handkerchief away to the maid earlier. She looked around and spied one on the dressing table, so fetched it for Selina before sitting back down again.

'I'm sorry, Selina. As horrid as this weekend was for us, it must have been one hundred times worse for you.' Her gentle words caused a fresh wave of tears in Selina and Cressida started to worry that she might be having an odd effect on people today. Selina's tears were no simple matter of a maid being shouted at by Jago Trengrouse. She had watched her fiancé die in front of her, yet, not twenty-four hours later, been kissed in public by another man. She had to ask her about it. 'Selina, I hate to upset you more, but what's going on between you and Sebastian Goodricke?'

Selina sat up from her tearful slouch at the sound of his name and murmured, 'Sebastian...' before crying again.

'I spoke to him,' Cressida continued, 'since I saw you yesterday in Pencarrick. You looked upset.' She decided not to go straight in with the accusation of their affair. She may not have been a romantic sort, but Cressida did have a heart.

Selina sniffed a bit and wiped her eyes.

'What did he say?' she all but whispered.

'That he loved you. And that he wished it was him that you

were marrying.' Cressida decided to leave out the bit about how much he also knew about hemlock and its effects and concentrate for now on his relationship with Selina.

'I did want to marry him. Very much.' Selina sniffled. 'But Mother and Father said he was a nobody. Just a clerk in the Foreign Office.'

'Did you tell him that?' Cressida remembered Sebastian's version of the story and wondered if Selina's would tally.

'Of course not, I'm not a monster. I told him that I couldn't possibly have a marriage like that of my parents, with Mother always at home and Father overseas. I said I wanted to stay here in England and wanted a man who would be here with me.' This seemed to start off another set of sobs, but Cressida at least had her answer: the stories matched. And Cressida could start to see where the upset might really lie, too.

'I think I see what you were arguing about now. Sebastian couldn't understand why you'd agree to marry Lord Canterbury, as surely the same principles would apply to him.'

'Exactly.' Selina nodded. 'Sebastian had bought my lie about not wanting to marry him due to his job, despite me simply loving our time in Cairo... but he couldn't understand when my engagement was announced to Lord Canterbury. Of course, you, Dotty, all of our friends would know exactly what had happened. Mama and Papa, him especially, thought Canterbury a far superior match, never mind what I thought. Or how I felt. After that little adventure I had in the cloakroom at The Savoy, they thought I needed someone of impeccable breeding to bring me back into society. But I was still pining for Sebastian, you see, and I... well, I tried to numb out the pain with poppy.'

'Poppy... opium,' Cressida said matter-of-factly. As Selina's tale of a broken heart came out, Cressida understood why she needed to rely on the drug so much to get her through her days.

'Randolph was a good match, I understand why my parents

insisted on it. And there would have been a cachet to being Lady Canterbury. I was very fond of him, you know. I just didn't love him.' She wept a little more. 'And it's not that I'm not upset about his death. It was gruesome, and I wasn't in a fit state this weekend to deal with it, what with the announcement coming up and the vile arguments Randolph had been having with almost everyone.'

'You included?' Cressida asked her, hoping it wouldn't set her off crying again.

Selina twisted the handkerchief in her hands as she spoke. 'Yes. I think he knew I wasn't happy and he didn't like me using the poppy pipe as much as I did. I was embarrassed about it all, too. I hate the fact that I'm not happy. Do you understand, Cressy? Everything we're taught to aspire to as girls – a good marriage, a nice man, a title even! – I had them all coming, but I wasn't happy and it made me feel so empty inside, I had to numb it sometimes.'

Cressida thought about her own views on marriage and how trapped someone like Selina must have felt. Money, stability, a title; these were all outside signs of success in their society, but how many of their friends were truly happy with men they loved?

'I understand, Selina. I do, really. It's why I tend to shy away from it all together. It would have to be someone incredibly special to trump my holy triumvirate of Ruby, my motorcar and my independence.' She coaxed a smile out of Selina.

'Your mother must be more understanding than mine then.' Selina folded her arms, but Cressida was pleased to see the tears had stopped.

'Oh, I don't know, I've had every eligible man from here to John O'Groats suggested to me. I think at this stage Mother would even be pleased with a rushed elopement, but then she grew up in a different age, where any husband was better than none.'

The two young women thought about this for a while, before Selina, lip trembling again, asked Cressida a question. 'Do the police think I did it? Do they think that I killed Randolph, so I wouldn't have to marry him?'

Cressida perhaps paused too long, like Pooky Marchpaine in Lower Remove French, and Selina welled up again.

'I didn't, I didn't, I swear! That's what I was so cross with Sebastian about yesterday. He tried to kiss me, did he tell you that? I pushed him away, saying it was the most terribly silly thing to do as someone would see us and think we'd orchestrated Randolph's death together.'

Cressida couldn't help but think about how much Sebastian knew about hemlock... Selina continued, 'But we didn't. I swear it. I swear it!'

Cressida looked into the red-rimmed eyes of her friend. Could Selina and Sebastian have concocted a plan to kill Lord Canterbury to save her from an unhappy marriage? 'For what it's worth, I believe you, Selly.' Cressida rested her hand on the bedclothes above Selina's leg. 'Personally, I think that if you were planning on killing Randolph this weekend, you would have dispensed with the poppy pipe and had all your wits about you.'

'Thank you, Cressy,' Selina whispered. 'Sebastian didn't do it either, I promise you.'

Cressida nodded. 'He knows a lot about hemlock... but I'll wager you know him and his character much better than I do. In fact, Selly, why don't you put the case to your parents again for marrying him? I'm no romantic, but I can see that not having him in your life is tearing you apart.'

'I don't know, Cressy, they're so upset about Randolph...'

'We all are. But just think on it. Better to be plain old Mrs Goodricke but happy, than Lady So-and-so and addicted to opiates the rest of your life.'

Selina nodded and cast her eyes over to the sunlight coming in through the window. 'Perhaps it is time for a new start.'

'That's the spirit.' Cressida patted Selina's leg. 'Oh, there's another mystery to solve too.'

'Morwenna...' Selina said softly.

'Yes, of course, Morwenna.' Cressida had in fact been thinking of the rum smuggling, but took this opportunity to quiz her. 'Was she a cousin of yours?'

'I think so, but barely. Some distant cousin. I am sorry for her, though.'

'I know, we all are.' Cressida paused. 'So she was a more distant cousin than Jago then? Who your father paid to educate and has all but handed the Far East Company to on a silver platter?'

'I suppose so, yes. She was maybe *his* cousin, but all from the same grandfather who was our grandfather's brother. Very low-born, though, daughter of a fisherman in Falmouth and some say *his* family were very... how does one put it... *of the land*... natural remedies and superstitious and all that. I think Morwenna grew up with her grandmother who was one of those wise women you hear about – you know, the sort you go to for love potions and tinctures and the like.'

Cressida remembered Celia Nangower speaking of Jago's people... *a fisherman in Falmouth*... A thought came to her...

'Selina, what was Morwenna's surname?'

Selina looked up as if this was the easiest thing she'd had to find an answer for all day. 'Why, she was Morwenna Tren-grouse, of course.'

'She was Jago's first cousin?' Cressida stood up and paced across the room. Did this change things at all? A maid and a gentleman, related and all but living under the same roof? It was very strange. And now one of them was dead... did this make Jago the prime suspect? *Or perhaps*... the hairs prickled up Cressida's neck once more... *the killer's next victim?*

37

Cressida pulled the door closed behind her as she left Selina dressing, her thoughts regarding the Trengrouse and Trevelyan families swimming around her head.

'She was a maid and he's a gentleman, but they were cut from the same cloth,' Cressida muttered to herself as she went back downstairs to where Dotty, Alfred and George Parish were sitting on the terrace.

'Cressy,' Dotty called her over and Ruby leapt off her lap and waddled over to her mistress, steering clear of the lobsters clicking their claws together in the basket traps next to the table. 'DCI Andrews said to let you know Kirby had the prints back from the telephone, he said you'd know what he meant.'

'Yes, I do. And...?'

'Morwenna's were on there,' Dotty said, pushing her glasses up the bridge of her nose in earnestness.

'That's that then, she must have been the one to telephone him at the Bootlegger's and be about to reveal who the murderer was. She knew who it was and was killed for it. At least that clears up *why* she was done for. But who was it? And why and how did she know?'

The others shook their heads, and Cressida sighed.

'I've just been speaking to Selina. She and Sebastian are very much in love and she was only marrying Randolph because her parents decreed it a better match,' Cressida explained as she scooped up Ruby and sat down with them at the table.

'Making Sebastian Goodricke the top spot on the list of suspects?' asked George.

'A *crime passionel*?' Alfred suggested.

'I hope not as I've just encouraged Selina to follow her heart.' Cressida glanced at Alfred. 'Did you just catch those?' She pointed at the lobsters.

'Ah, yes. Used a bit of bacon from the kitchens, much to Mrs Dawkins' displeasure. She runs that kitchen with a rod of iron. Thought these might be good for supper tonight. Dawkins said she hasn't had any decent crustaceans in for weeks.'

'Slathered in Cornish butter and wild garlic, hopefully.' Cressida thought momentarily of her stomach, and how thoughtful Alfred had been, but her train of thought was interrupted by Patrick Trevelyan and Sir Jolyon wandering onto the terrace. They were smartly followed by a maid bringing out a tray of teacups, another following suit with a teapot, water pot and plates teaming with baked treats from the kitchen.

'Ham sandwiches, delicious.' The portly baronet sat down at the table, took a small plate and loaded it high.

Catherine Bly joined them too, having come in the direction of the boathouse, and Jago, obviously attracted by the sound of crockery and conversation, appeared from the house.

'Good afternoon, ladies,' he greeted Cressida and Dotty, ignoring his cousin Catherine, who just raised her eyebrows and filled up a plate with some plain bread and butter.

There was something not right, thought Cressida, as she surveyed the assembled family and guests around the table. Catherine standing awkwardly, Jago charming everyone in sight, Patrick taking the largest slice of cake, Sir Jolyon tucking into the sandwiches... She was trying to work out what it was that was troubling her, while surreptitiously slipping a cream horn under the table to Ruby, when Selina made an entrance onto the terrace, Sebastian Goodricke by her side.

The chatter of the guests abruptly stopped as the pair emerged from the French doors and headed towards the table where the rest of the party sat, with teacups half raised to mouths and knives half cut through cakes.

Selina folded her arms. 'No need to act like that, everyone.' She let Sebastian pull one of the wrought-iron chairs out for her and sat herself down.

Cressida nodded as she caught her eye, realising that her advice had been acted on, albeit quicker than she'd thought it might be. Still, the change in Selina was clear to see. Her eyes were still red from the tears, but she'd put her hair up and applied enough make-up so that you'd really have to do a double take to know how depressed she'd been recently. She was dressed smartly, too, in a silk blouse and red tweed skirt. Sebastian looked different as well. Pleased as punch, with a grin spread across his face, which he was trying to contain and flatten, but it kept creeping back.

'Sister?' Patrick clattered his cake plate down on the metal table. 'What's all this?'

'I have an announcement to make. Well, we do. Sebastian and I are engaged to be married.'

Teacups rattled down onto saucers and quite audible gasps escaped from lips that would no doubt be gossiping about this for the few next days, weeks and months to come in all the society circles.

'I say, Selina, don't you think that's a bit soon.' Patrick put his teacup down. He looked about him, and his frown told Cressida that he was not happy at all that there was an audience for this family conversation, but he cleared his throat and carried on regardless. 'It's not seemly to announce this sort of thing like this. Have you spoken to Father? And Mother?'

'No, I haven't,' Selina replied, her folded arms looking like a show of strength compared to the loosely hanging ones of her brother.

'And have you asked Father's permission, Sebastian?' Patrick demanded.

Before he could answer, Selina did so for him. 'He doesn't need to. I'm not some chattel to be given in marriage to whoever it suits Father to chum up with. Sebastian and I have been in love since Cairo.'

Sebastian found his voice. 'It's true. We have.' He reached over and as Selina unfolded her arms, he took her hand. 'And I will do things properly and ask for Lord Trevelyan's blessing, but, as Selina says, she's her own woman and can decide for herself who she wants to marry.'

'Lucky for her Lord Canterbury's dead and not here to hear this,' a snarky voice from the other side of the tea table said. 'He might have had something to say about his fiancée marrying another man.'

Everyone turned to face the speaker, Catherine Bly.

Before Selina could retaliate, a slow clap sounded and, as one, the faces all turned to see who it was.

Jago stopped after the fifth or sixth clap. 'Congratulations, cousin. And Sebastian. You've just earned yourselves front-row seats for the gallows, by the looks of it. So close in fact, you might be the starring roles.'

Cressida defused the tension that was obviously starting to boil up. 'I don't think that's called for, Jago.' She looked at him and saw that his handsome face was quite changed by the snarl across his lip. She carried on. 'There's been too much sorrow this weekend here at Penbeagle and I for one am happy for you both.'

'Hear, hear.' Sir Jolyon knocked his knuckles on the table.

'There's been too much talk of death these last few days, it's good to have some happy news.'

'Happy news? My sister incriminating herself?' Patrick strode off to the other end of the table and sat down on the balustrade at the edge of the terrace. 'Wonderful!' he exclaimed again.

'Thank you, Pat, you've made your point.' Selina took her hand back from Sebastian and crossed her arms again. 'Anyone else want to say anything? Cousin Catherine? Any comment? At least you didn't send nasty letters to this one. That should make Christmasses slightly less awkward.'

Catherine blushed and opened her mouth in shock. 'Selina!' she snapped. Then she composed herself and retaliated. 'I just hope Mr Goodricke knows what he's getting himself into, marrying a drug addict.'

There were a few audible gasps around the table.

Sebastian leapt to his lover's defence. 'Come on now, Miss Bly, that's below the belt. Selina is—'

'Is giving up,' Selina interrupted him. 'I'm resolved to never touch opiates again.' She unfolded her arms and reached over to hold Sebastian's hand. 'I don't need them anymore. Once Mama and Papa realise why I started self-medicating, where I get the opium from and how being with Sebastian will mean I won't need them from now on, I'm sure they'll understand.' She looked over at Cressida, who smiled at her, nodding her own blessing.

38

Dotty slipped her arm into Cressida's as they walked down to the cove. Selina and Sebastian's revelations had broken up the party somewhat, with guests breaking off into smaller groups, none of which contained the new couple.

'What are you thinking, Cressy?' Dotty asked her. 'You always have Thoughts, with a capital T.'

'I am having capital-T Thoughts, it's true. But I can't quite pull the right thread to make sense of them yet. Talk to me about something else, anything, it might trigger something and help!' Cressida laughed, and Ruby, who was obediently trotting along at their heels, snorted in unison with her.

'You've put me on the spot there!' laughed Dotty. 'My mind is as full of the case, and of course the guests. But here's a thing you might be interested to know.'

'I'm all ears, chum, what is it?' Cressida asked.

'George said to me – and this is strictly entre nous – that he's going to approach Jago about taking over Randolph Canterbury's job. He doesn't want it to be widely known, or much discussed, as obviously it would look dubious at best, but he did see the opportunity and was asking my opinion of it.'

Cressida looked at her friend, who was glowing with pride that George was asking her opinion on these sorts of things. 'And what did you say?'

'Well...' Dotty started, and squeezed Cressida's arm tighter, '... I hope you'll not be cross with me, but I advised him to do it. Poor Randolph is dead, and I hope that we've established that George had nothing to do with it—'

'I think so, yes,' Cressida said, though the conviction wasn't there in her voice. She liked George immensely, but she was glad that Andrews was checking his story out.

'I believe so,' Dotty said more firmly. 'And I think he could do worse than try to fill his mentor's shoes. He might even gain a knighthood if he works very hard.'

Cressida smiled at her friend. Lady Chatterton, her mother, wouldn't have been doing her job properly if Dotty hadn't been able to sniff out a man with potential for a title at fifty paces.

The pair of them had made it down to the edge of the lawn, where rougher grasses and a fence held the sand and tide at bay. Ruby toddled under the fence and sought out her new favourite pastime of seaweed appreciation. Cressida turned back to Dotty.

'Why did George mention Jago rather than Lord Trevelyan? You'd have thought it was Lord T who was calling the shots, employment opportunities-wise.'

'That's a good point. I didn't ask him. Maybe because Jago is seen as the next generation and the future of the business, and, of course, they're the same sort of age, so perhaps George thought it best to approach him first.'

Cressida nodded. Sir Jolyon would not be pleased if another young buck beat him to the Far East Company job, and she hoped George hadn't just put himself in the older man's crosshairs. Something told her, however, that the recrimination for such a thing would be a cold-shoulder at the Mutton Pie Club rather than death, and her arm hairs remained unprickled.

She looked back up the lawn towards the house and saw Alfred, George and Jago talking, George gesturing with his hands as if he were explaining some grand idea and Jago deep in thought, tapping a finger on the wrought-iron filigree surface of the table. 'It looks like they might be talking about it now.'

Dotty looked up towards the house and a blush rose in her cheeks again.

'I'm so glad you've found some happiness these last few days, Dot.' Cressida squeezed her arm tight.

'Me and Selina, it seems.' Dotty pointed to where Selina and Sebastian could be seen walking down the lawn towards the shoreline too, hand in hand.

The two friends leant over the wooden fence rail in silence for a few moments before Cressida blurted out her frustrations over the case again. 'I just wish I could see through this haze of motives and possibilities to work out who killed Randolph and Morwenna. It's like trying to piece together the rose window at Westminster Abbey, if it had fallen out and smashed to the ground.'

'Come on, Cressy, let's go and look in the boathouse. You always have good ideas when you're thinking about decorating things.' Dotty pulled her sleeve and they walked along the edge of the beach to the old wooden building. 'Key's in the door, we're in luck.'

'You'd think with all that rum being public knowledge now they'd have locked it away,' Cressida remarked as she turned the handle and walked in. The smell of alcohol fused with damp and seawater assaulted her nose and she wrinkled it. 'Gosh, this place will really benefit from a lick of paint.'

'Horrid to think that the rope that killed Morwenna was stored here. Some things just look so harmless in one context, don't they, and then in another quite deadly.'

Cressida shivered in the cool of the boathouse, and looked around. A large oar rested on brackets on the wall, and a metal hook hung sharp and low from a beam, tar-covered rope was coiled tightly on the floor. All innocuous and perfectly normal in a boathouse, but all deadly if used with malice, as Dotty had pointed out.

'It was going to be hard enough to jazz this place up, but now we also have to contend with the connotations it will always have with the death of Morwenna.' Cressida tapped the tightly coiled rope with the tip of her shoe.

'And the illegal smuggling.' Dotty peered in around the shattered boards that had given way under George the night before.

'I'll have to reframe it, change how the family look at it.'

'But you'll have to get rid of all the nasty bits.' Dotty pushed her glasses back up her nose, having let them slip as she'd peered into the depths below.

'Or come up with some way of changing how we view them. Coiled rope tables or oar lampstands. It's amazing how you can forget how dangerous something can be when you view it completely differently. And plenty of storage for the useful stuff, of course, just hidden away a bit more. Take inspiration from the smugglers, what?' Cressida had a glint in her eye.

'Oh bravo. Excellent idea, Cressy. And speaking of decorating,' Dotty raised a finger, 'I quite forgot to tell you. George, when he was asking my advice about talking to Jago, mentioned that he'd heard the Far East Company was taking a new direction. He's been looking into it, you see, and, of course, talking business with Jago, and apparently his plan is to reproduce versions of the antiquities here in Cornwall.'

'Versions of? That sounds like fakes to me.' Cressida furrowed her brow, thinking of the designs she'd seen in the pottery.

'Perhaps there's a thin line, I don't really know.' Dotty sounded a little unsure of herself. 'I suppose it's how it's sold to you, isn't it, as a customer, I mean. If it's never sold as anything other than a replica and at a sensible price, then it's not a fake.'

'You're quite right, of course, Dot. Did he say why they were doing it?'

'I think *I* can answer that.' George Parish popped his head around the door of the boathouse.

'Oh George, you quite frightened the life out of us,' Cressida exclaimed, though Dotty, once over the initial shock, was grinning like a lunatic at him. 'Go on then, explain what Jago said about the Cornish-made non-antiquities.'

'I can see his point of view, of course,' George said. 'He believes that once the Far East Company start importing proper antiquities, it'll spike the market and everyone will want some. Say you can't afford the Ming dynasty vase that's in the catalogue, then, no fear, there's a replica for a fraction of the price made here in Cornwall. Sphinx all the rage? Have your own ceramic one for the mantelpiece. He thinks it'll be a big new arm for the company, hugely profitable and all that.'

'But maybe Randolph didn't like it? Didn't like the thought that his real antiquities would get lost in the noise,' mused Cressida. 'Perhaps that was why he was so intent on going to the pottery, but why would Morwenna go too? Oh and, George, did you know Morwenna was Jago's first cousin?'

'No, but does it matter?'

'I don't know.' Cressida twisted her lip as she nibbled the inside of her cheek. 'I just don't know.'

A few minutes later, George suggested a walk down on the beach to Dotty. Cressida waved them off and was curious to discover that she felt a slight pang of jealousy. She shook the thought out of her head and was relieved when she saw DCI Andrews heading across the lawn towards her.

'What ho, Andrews,' she called over, and he waved as he

came close. 'How are you getting on?'

'I see Mr Goodricke wasted no time, having spoken to us.' He pointed down to where Selina and Sebastian were playing on the Cornish lugger together.

'No. And quite the entrance they made back out onto the terrace. Apparently, when Lord and Lady Trevelyan come back this evening, they'll tell them, and Selina will admit to her drug misuse and hope they see that Sebastian is her only way out of her funk.'

'He certainly knows about drugs all right.' Andrews flipped open his notepad. 'It could just be a coincidence that he knows an awful lot about hemlock, but if you ask me, it's not looking good for him.'

'But when would he have administered it to Lord Canterbury? He made that point himself to me. I wonder... no...'

'What is it?' Andrews asked, intrigued.

'I wonder if someone knew his passion for classical poisons and used it against him? Tried to frame him?'

'I'll make a note of the possibility.' Andrews licked his pencil and made a jotting. 'There was something else that Kirby turned up. Morwenna was—'

'A Trengrouse? Selina has just told me. Jago's first cousin.'

'And related to Catherine Bly, and the Trevelyans. All of them. And also Kirby found evidence of hemlock in the area, so not only is it a drug known to one, or more, of our suspects, but it's very much here roundabouts.'

'Andrews, I think I've just had an idea. I need to talk to Mrs Dawkins the cook and then do some measure twicing, you know, going over the case again. Will you come?'

'Of course, Miss Fawcett, I can't have you getting yourself into danger. What would your father say?'

'Probably something along the lines of "if you can't be good, be careful", but don't worry, Andrews, I'm going to be damn careful.'

39

'Mrs Dawkins!' Cressida called through the kitchen door and the harried cook scurried over to her and waited, wide-eyed, for what was coming next. She grew more confused when Cressida asked her about Morwenna's fainting fit but answered her all the same. Cressida turned to DCI Andrews. 'Was that the same place that Kirby had said there was hemlock locally?'

'Yes, Miss Fawcett. Spot on.' Andrews scratched his head.

'We'd wondered if she'd been ill, or even in the family way, what with the fainting and being late to work, perhaps due to fatigue, but it sounds to me as if the poison might have something to do with it,' Cressida remarked.

'Mr Goodricke said hemlock was such nasty stuff that...' Andrews flicked back through his pad. 'It can cause nausea and fainting even just by being smelt, especially the sticky sap that emerges from the stems when it's cut or picked.'

'Did you say hemlock, dear?' Mrs Dawkins, who'd been hovering by the door to the kitchen, piped up.

'Yes, it's how Lord Canterbury was killed.' Cressida turned back to face her.

'Nasty stuff indeed.' She wiped her hands on her apron.

'But a medicine too if used in the right way. For chesty coughs and the like. A local woman used to brew some up for young master Patrick when he was young.'

Cressida frowned. 'Hmm.' Then, after a moment, 'Mrs Dawkins, do you know what happened to the tea set that was used on Saturday, for the Chinese tea ceremony?'

'Morwenna must have cleared it away, God rest her soul. I ain't seen sign of it, if I'm honest with you. Funny little pot they use, shaped like one of them bald, pot-bellied gods of theirs. Never know which hole to hold, you know, pouring it and the like. Funny old thing.' Mrs Dawkins shook her head and excused herself, and Cressida let the cook get back to her busy kitchen.

Andrews interrupted her thoughts. 'Come, let's go back to the drawing room. The light in these servants halls is never so good as you'd like.'

Andrews ushered Cressida back into the main part of the house and into the drawing room, where the afternoon light was gloriously and goldenly illuminating the wonderful decor; the lone vase shone in the sunbeams and the Foo dogs on the mantelpiece glowed their deep, deep bronze lustrously. Cressida looked at them. They had been one of the designs that she'd seen at Pencarrick Pottery. But what else had she seen?

She looked over to Andrews. 'If I gave you a lead, would you follow it?'

Andrews narrowed his eyes as he looked at her. 'Go on,' he said non-committally.

'I've asked Maurice Sauvage to send me a list of all the Far East Company pieces that Liberty import. I think there might be something on it that could really help us – you, I mean.'

'What in particular?'

'I don't know. But you know, the old mind-pinging thing.'

Andrews raised an eyebrow, but nodded all the same. 'I'll see if Kirby can call and take a dictation from your Mr Sauvage.'

Andrews left the room in search of his sergeant and Cressida wandered over to the window. She gazed out across the lawn and thought about Morwenna, killed with her whole life ahead of her, perhaps by someone covering their tracks. Perhaps by someone who had asked her to brew a poison, but when it had worked all too well, she'd realised her wrongdoing and wanted to admit all to the police.

'But, Rubes,' for the little dog had patiently been listening to them speak all this time, 'no one else who drank that tea was ill. It just doesn't make sense. Unless...'

Cressida stared out of the window and saw Selina frolicking on the Cornish lugger with the love of her life. Randolph had been a good man, but she hadn't loved him and she'd turned to drugs to cope with the unhappiness. Randolph had hated her using drugs, and indeed it was the only thing they'd fought about, to the extent that she'd threatened him with the fact she would "do anything" so that her parents wouldn't find out. But here she was now, mere moments away from revealing all to her parents. What if it wasn't herself that she had been protecting as she'd tussled with Randolph? What if she had been protecting someone else? Her supplier, perhaps?

Andrews entered the room again. 'Kirby's making a call to Mr Sauvage now. Let's hope your lead is a good one, as I need him to be carrying out interviews with the household staff too.'

'I hope so too. And, Andrews, I was just thinking about what you said about the Excise men not being terribly excited about the rum Dotty found. They're interested in drug smuggling, aren't they?'

'Primarily, yes. Though, as I say, the blighter in charge hides behind this "Head Shepherd" moniker.'

'But you think this Shepherd chap is from Cornwall?'

'We believe so. The West Country in any case, but that could mean as far north-east as Bristol.' He looked at Cressida, his head tilted to one side. 'Tell you what, I'll telephone Higgins at the Yard and get as much information on the blaggard as I can.'

Cressida smiled at him. 'I'm sure you and Kirby have your processes and interviews to carry out, but would you indulge me by listening to my thoughts?'

Andrews looked at his watch. 'It'll give Kirby time to speak to Mr Sauvage, so go on then.' He hitched up his trouser knees and sat himself down.

'We have one man murdered who had people round here all practically baying for his blood.'

Andrews tutted. 'Exaggeration will get you nowhere, Miss Fawcett, you would be wise to remember that and stick to the facts.'

'Fine, well, almost every guest here had a motive, and as the thought of there being two murderers in our midst is just too awful to contemplate, not to mention highly unlikely, I think whoever killed Randolph went on to kill Morwenna.'

'Morwenna, who, according to Mrs Dawkins, had been seen in the same location as where we now know hemlock is known to grow,' Andrews added.

'Yes. And let's assume she harvested some, because of the fainting fit she had in that patch of meadow. Who was she harvesting it for?' Cressida sat herself down opposite Andrews, Ruby following her and settling down at her feet.

'Do you mean who was she wanting to kill, or who was she abetting?' Andrews helped to try to clarify Cressida's thoughts.

Cressida chewed the inside of her cheek. 'Apart from fighting Roscoe's corner for him, she didn't have much motive to kill Randolph. So it makes more sense that she was working for someone else—'

'Who in turn killed her when she threatened to out them to me,' Andrews postured.

'Precisely.' Cressida clapped her hands on her knees, which

quite startled Ruby. 'But then how was the poison administered?'

'Through some sort of food,' Andrews reminded her. 'That's what Lady Trevelyan heard him say, his last words as it were.'

'But he only had lunch with George—'

'We looked into it, his story checks out. Lord Canterbury had contacted the museum and Mr Parish was to get the credit he deserved on his finds.'

'Oh good. That's a relief.' Cressida puffed out her cheeks and let out a breath. 'Then he had tea with Lord Trevelyan, Jago and Patrick, but no one else who drank from it got ill – and oh yes, some sandwiches with Jago.'

'Ones that could disguise the taste of poison?'

'Yes. Crab paste, according to Patrick... though when I asked Jago, he couldn't remember there being any sandwiches.' She looked up at Andrews, who nodded sagely.

'Sounds like Jago—'

'Who Patrick said was having a row with Randolph...'

'Might need to come in for further questioning.' Andrews was about to call for his sergeant when Kirby, with great efficiency, entered the room holding a piece of paper.

'Your list from Mr Sauvage, Miss Fawcett.' He handed over a neatly handwritten list to her. 'He also says to not go getting yourself into any mischief, miss.' Kirby blushed as he relayed the message.

'Thank you, Kirby.' Cressida looked up at him and spared him a smile. As she took the list from him, she glanced at the mantelpiece and saw the glowing bronze of the Foo dog sitting there. Then she turned her head and gazed out of the window, and then back to the Foo dog. 'You know in some lights those dogs... Oh, oh gosh. I wonder... Yes, it's when he...' Cressida got up and walked over to the window. 'Selina has nothing to do with the pottery,' she muttered. 'But everything to do with the deaths...'

Andrews and Kirby looked at each other.

'Miss Fawcett, what are you thinking?' Andrews asked. Cressida turned to him, the colour drained from her face, the list tightly scrunched in her hand.

'It's the Shepherd.' Cressida said. 'Andrews, Kirby. We've got to find Selina and quickly.' She looked up at the mantelpiece and the ormolu clock between the bronze dogs. '... Before Lord and Lady Trevelyan return. If we don't, I think Selina Trevelyan could be in danger. Indeed, I think the murderer is going to strike again, and I believe Selina will be next!'

40

Cressida, with DCI Andrews and Sergeant Kirby by her side, and Ruby scooped up and lodged under her arm, ran out of the drawing room and through the glazed doors out to the terrace.

'Miss Fawcett, will you explain?' Andrews managed between drawing breaths as they ran.

'No time, Andrews! But hurry!' Even with Ruby under her arm, Cressida was a few steps ahead of the two policemen and was covering the ground between the house and the shoreline as quickly as she could. She made it down to the jetty, where the Cornish lugger with its traditional red sail was still moored, but there was no sign of Sebastian or Selina.

Cressida drew herself to a stop, letting Ruby down as she bent over, panting. Life as an aristocrat was all very well, but it had been a fair few years since she'd been forced to run anywhere, and she had to admit that her lifestyle of cocktails and late nights and nothing more sporting than a vigorous dance party or a stealthily played game of croquet had done no favours to her now burning lungs and aching legs. DCI Andrews didn't seem in much better shape and passed his handkerchief over his brow as he gulped for breath too. Cressida was pleased to see that Kirby had taken the brief sprint much more in his stride and was the first to ask, 'What next?'

'Where would he have taken her?' Cressida scanned the scene around them. The cove where Morwenna's body had been found was off to their right, the stone and wood jetty where the lugger was moored was right by them and the old boathouse was to their left. Cressida waved at Dotty and George, who were standing noticeably close together on the shoreline of the cove, relieved to see that they were there and not wrapped up in anything except perhaps themselves. Still, there was no sign of Selina or Sebastian, and Cressida reached the same conclusion as Andrews as they both said in unison: 'The boathouse!'

The three of them, with an excitable Ruby at their heels, dashed towards the decrepit old building and Kirby, who this time had the head start, reached the door and started tugging at it.

'It's locked, miss,' he called back to them, but then just as he tried it one more time with his shoulder firm against the peeling paintwork of the door, it opened and he all but fell in.

'Good work, Kirby.' Cressida thanked him and passed through the door as he gained his balance and stood upright again.

The smell of damp wood and rotting timbers, along with the brackish salt of the creek water, filled her nostrils once more. As Cressida's eyes adjusted to the dark, she noticed a slumped figure where the floorboards formed a jetty around the mooring space.

'Andrews, look.' She pointed to the figure that lay deadly still up against an old coil of rope, the oar that had been on its wall brackets lying awkwardly next to him. Over the sound of her own breathing, and the blood pounding in her ears, she could hear a soft moaning coming from the man on the floor and in moments both she and Andrews were next to him, falling to their knees to see what they could do.

'Sebastian Goodricke,' Cressida said to Andrews before calling out the man's name to him several times while trying to rouse him.

'Out cold.' Andrews gave his opinion and pointed to the oar, where a sticky wet patch of blood was visible on the blade.

'But alive?' Cressida asked, almost not wanting to know the answer. She breathed a sigh of relief when Andrews nodded as he took the young man's pulse.

'He's alive. Kirby,' he called over to his sergeant. 'Fetch a doctor, this man needs help.'

Kirby nodded and Andrews took his handkerchief and held it tight to where Sebastian's strawberry blond hair was darker and matted with blood.

'But where's Selina?' Cressida didn't want to panic, but finding Sebastian, who had no doubt been hurt trying to protect Selina, left for dead on the floor, wasn't filling her with hope for the young heiress. She pushed herself up from her knees and looked around the boathouse again. Nothing was different, except... except – 'The boat's gone, Andrews!' Cressida called out and stepped the few paces to the very edge of the board-walk, where she could lean over the rail and see out to the creek.

Sure enough, cutting through the water was the wooden rowing boat that had always been tied up in the gap between the U-shaped floor of the boathouse. She could make out Selina's blonde hair as she gripped the sides of the boat. And pulling the oars, rowing the boat out further and further into the wide mouth of the creek was a man, his dark wavy hair blowing in the breeze and his handsome face snarled up in a grimace. Jago Trengrouse.

Cressida turned back to see how Andrews was getting on. He was still pressing the handkerchief to the temple of the unresponsive Sebastian. 'Andrews, we need to get out on the water. Quickly.'

'I can't leave this man like this,' Andrews asserted. 'He needs help.'

Cressida nodded and was mightily relieved when Alfred poked his head around the door.

'What ho— Oooh, Crikey, what's happening here?' he asked, quickly moving to Cressida's side.

'No time to explain, Alfred, but would you stay with Sebastian and try to get him conscious? Please.' She looked at his kind chestnut eyes and was relieved when he nodded and gave her arm a gentle squeeze. He knelt down by the stricken Foreign Office clerk and Andrews stood up, nodded at Cressida and headed out of the boathouse.

Cressida felt a hundred things at once, but brushed them away at the thought of Selina, and with a smile to Alfred she ran past him, following Andrews out into the sunlight.

'Ruby, time to get those little legs of yours in motion.' Cressida patted her thigh as she started to run after Andrews. She was held up from going anywhere fast, however, by Dotty and George appearing from the boathouse end of the sandy cove.

'Cressy, what's happening? Why's Andrews trying to get into that old boat?' Dotty asked, having reached out a hand to stop Cressida in her tracks.

Cressida was about to answer her friend when she noticed something shining on the ground, Ruby pawing at it. Torn between wanting to dash after Andrews and board the lugger too and finding out what her small pup had found, Cressida stammered and was grateful that it was Dotty who bent down and picked up the worn old key. She passed it to Cressida, who pocketed it and thanked her. 'Come on, there's definitely something rum happening between Selina and Jago... we need to help her!'

. . .

While George and Andrews busied themselves with the rigging of the Cornish lugger, Dotty and Cressida hung over the bow and desperately tried to see what was happening in the rowing boat. Jago had stopped rowing and appeared to be moving over to where Selina was shrinking away from him.

'Who knows how many opiates and sedatives she might still have in her system. If he throws her in, she might drown.' Cressida thumped her hand on the wood of the boat. 'We have to get out there and stop him.'

'Look!' Dotty pulled at her sleeve and pointed towards where another boat was cutting across the water towards the rowing boat. It was under sail and making up ground far faster than Jago had managed with his oars.

Cressida and Dotty started waving and shouting at the boat, screaming for help and pointing madly towards the rowing boat, hoping to attract the sailor's attention and get them to intervene.

'It's working, look,' Dotty exclaimed, and they both stared as the sailboat tacked across the creek and headed straight for where Jago was now pulling Selina up into a standing position, both of them shouting and tugging and pushing each other.

'Who is it?' Cressida strained to see, her hand shielding her eyes from the sun that had started its descent to the west straight in front of them. She was glad when Dotty tapped her on the shoulder and passed a pair of binoculars over.

'Here, George just found these. See who it is.'

Cressida raised the binoculars to her eyes and adjusted the focus until she could see quite clearly who was on board the sailing boat. Monty and Celia Nangower, with a surprise extra passenger, Catherine Bly.

'By Jove.' Cressida lowered the binoculars and looked excitedly at Dotty. She turned her attention back to the boats a moment later and kept up a running commentary. 'Celia looks like thunder. She's shouting at Monty, but he's ignoring her. Oh cripes! They've just rammed Jago and he's lost his balance.

Ouch! Ooh that must have hurt, poor Selina's just collapsed back into the boat. But Jago's up again now and... Oh Monty, good on you! Monty's just leaned over and socked him in the jaw with a rather good right hook. Well done him. He's helping Selina into their boat now. Thank heavens for that.' Cressida lowered the binoculars again and let out a relieved sigh. 'I didn't think I'd say this, Dot, but I think the Nangowers have just saved the day.'

41

'What on earth's happening?' Lady Trevelyan asked as she appeared at the scene by the jetty, where a proud Monty Nangower was manhandling a woozy Jago Trengrouse off their sailing boat, while Celia and Catherine were seeing that a shivering and shocked Selina alighted safely too. 'Can someone explain this all please? Why's Selina been out with the Nangowers?'

'Jago?' Lord Trevelyan was at her side. 'Monty, what have you done?'

'Whether he realises it or not, he's just given a shiner to the Head Shepherd,' Cressida said under her breath.

'The who?' Lord Trevelyan asked the question that everyone else was thinking. 'Who on earth is that?'

DCI Andrews shot Cressida a look before answering. 'Actually, My Lord, I'm about to arrest Mr Trengrouse here for the murder of Lord Randolph Canterbury and Miss Morwenna Trengrouse.'

Cressida looked at the detective and at his sergeant, who was cuffing the heir to the Far East Company. Heirs... Cressida glanced back at the boathouse and thought about the rope, the oar, the hook... things that are harmless, overlooked, innocuous in one context but deadly in another. 'Andrews, can I beg a favour?' She realised that all eyes were on her. 'Can you give me five minutes and I'll meet you all back up on the terrace?'

Among the baffled head-shaking and tutting, she saw Andrews nod and Dotty smile at her.

Cressida raised an eyebrow and headed back into the boathouse, shouting 'just five minutes' to the crowd on the jetty.

Back in the boathouse, she found Alfred, just getting up and passing over the stricken figure of Sebastian to Dr May and a couple of maids.

'How is he?' Cressida asked, grateful of Alfred's brief and spontaneous hug.

'He'll live, we think. But, more importantly, did you do what you needed to? I heard all sorts of commotion outside.' He looked at her intently and Cressida shook her head and tutted.

'No, not quite. Alfred, it just doesn't make sense. Andrews has just arrested Jago Trengrouse for the murder of Randolph and Morwenna. And he's a wrong 'un, I'll give you that, but I'm not convinced he's the murderer. There was something someone said, and I need to find him to make sure I'm not going mad, but it's been niggling me like a loose thread ever since.'

'Can I help?' Alfred held her shoulders and she could see his offer was genuine.

'Yes, please.' Cressida, who normally hated relying on other people and prided herself on her independence, whispered the name of someone who she wanted Alfred to find. 'It will look less suspicious if you ask him to meet us all on the terrace. Everyone's heading up there now. Oh, and that... yes, I'll need that...' Cressida moved away from Alfred and knelt down at the edge of the jagged hole where the rum was stashed. She pulled out the leather-bound ledger and held it up. 'Might as well at least solve one crime for sure. Five minutes. On the terrace. Thank you, Alfred.'

As she watched him go, she glanced down at the poorly Sebastian and then again at the chandlery items in the boathouse. It would make a wonderful summerhouse, full of beautiful imports from the East once the oars, rope and lobster traps were cleared away...

Lobster... that was kind of Alfred to catch them earlier. Randolph would have never... Oh. Oh. 'Oh Alfred...' She looked up through the door with its splintered frame where Kirby had shouldered it open. 'It was locked and Ruby found the key... outside...'

With a final glance to Dr May and his patient, who sadly looked too out of it on morphine and blows to the head to confirm her suspicions, Cressida strode out of the boathouse and up to the terrace, where she hoped Randolph's and Morwenna's killer was finally about to be unmasked.

As the sun began to set over the cove, the Trevelyan family and their guests, at Cressida's invitation, gathered on the terrace of Penbeagle House. It had been barely seventy-two hours since she'd arrived at this grand Cornish stately home, dressed as a pirate, complete with a dog-shaped parrot. That night, the house had been alive with jazz music, chatter and laughter, a hundred people or more enjoying the party, lights strewn across the glass ceiling of the orangery and lighting the way down paths towards the moon-shimmering cove. Now, however, after two murders and several more attempted, a handcuffed Jago Trengrouse was sitting on one of the white wrought-iron chairs, with Kirby's strong hand on his shoulder.

Selina Trevelyan, still in shock, sat quietly next to her mother, who had a look of resignation about her. Cressida wondered if she perhaps had an inkling of her daughter's wishes to marry the injured clerk who was now being stretchered from the boathouse up the lawn. Lord Trevelyan had a face like thunder and it didn't help that Patrick, his wet fish of a son, could barely contain his pleasure at the sight of his cousin in cuffs. Alfred, having done exactly as asked, sat next to him, with Dotty and George nearby. The Nangowers looked as if they'd rather be anywhere else, yet Cressida was pleased they were there, and even more so that Roscoe and Mrs Dawkins had also come to see what all the fuss was about. Sir Jolyon Westmoreland, who had barely moved from the table since tea, lowered his newspaper and looked aghast that he'd been joined by so many people, and Catherine Bly pulled her cardigan tight around her as Andrews cleared his throat.

'Lord and Lady Trevelyan, ladies and gentlemen, please may I have your attention. The local constabulary will be here soon to escort Mr Trengrouse to the station, where he will be charged with the murders of Lord Canterbury and his cousin, Morwenna Trengrouse. I hope you won't mind, but the Honourable Cressida Fawcett says she has a few words she'd like to say.'

'That rascal will go to trial, won't he?' Patrick asked almost gleefully.

'So he's the one who killed my Morwenna? Rascal's not the word for it.' Roscoe seethed at the man who was sitting shackled on the terrace, his hair in a mad tousle, tension clamped in his jaw. In a few strides Roscoe was almost upon the arrested man, but luckily Kirby had been paying attention and caught up with Roscoe before he could lunge a punch at Jago.

'Please, sir, stay calm and let Miss Fawcett speak. I think she'll have something interesting to say.'

'He killed Morwenna, my Morwenna...' Roscoe burst into sobs and all but collapsed into Kirby's arms.

'I think you better hurry up, Miss Fawcett,' Andrews urged her.

'Thank you, Andrews. And thank you, everyone, for being here.' Cressida realised that everyone was looking at her, and not everyone looked that friendly.

'What is going on here?' Lord Trevelyan asked.

'I'll explain everything,' Cressida reassured him. 'But I think it'll help us all understand if I work through it from the beginning.'

'From when dear Randolph died?' Lady Trevelyan asked, squeezing her daughter's hand.

'Exactly. And how he died.' Cressida looked serious. 'And who had the greatest motive for killing him.'

There was a murmuring from the guests and Andrews hushed them all down. 'Let her speak, please, everyone.'

'Thank you, Andrews.' Cressida rested her bottom on the stone balustrade of the terrace, from where she could see everyone clearly. She took a deep inhale and then started. 'Seeing Lord Canterbury, or Randolph as I knew him, collapse and die on Saturday night was a horrible thing to witness. But what was almost worse were the vile things some people around here started saying about him. So many of you had motives to kill him it seemed!' She glared at Catherine Bly, who shifted uneasily in her seat, pulling her thin cardigan around her. 'You, for example, Catherine, hated the fact that he barred you from his dig in the Valley of the Kings and gave exclusive reporting rights to an old chum of his. Your career was stalling as you couldn't get those scoops, and I don't mean to be rude, but unlike your wealthy cousins, you need the money you make from your writing.'

'Don't you think I might have been more subtle if I had intended to kill him?' Catherine snapped, pulling the worn cuffs of her cardigan down over her pale hands.

'You're not the one in handcuffs, so best not say too much, old thing,' Monty Nangower said, followed by an 'ahem' as his wife elbowed him in the ribs.

'He's right. You're not the killer, Catherine, though I did wonder if your motive was two-fold; namely, you could have either wanted Randolph dead due to him quashing your career, or because you were jealous of your younger, prettier and, perhaps most importantly, *richer* cousin, Selina.'

'That's a bit much.' Catherine furrowed her brow and crossed her arms tighter. 'I had no such feelings towards Cousin Selina or her husband-to-be.'

Cressida ignored her and turned to Sir Jolyon. 'You had a motive too, Sir Jolyon, and although you didn't say anything horrible about Randolph after he died, you were trying to convince Lord Trevelyan on Saturday night to choose you as his antiquities advisor, rather than Randolph.'

'As I told you, young lady, we had a gentleman's agreement in place, and—'

'And... it didn't stop you from trying to stab him in the back.' Cressida raised her palms to the group, 'Metaphorically, of course. Though with him out of the way and not about to marry into the family either, well, then all the antiquities dealings that the Far East Company were about to embark on could have come to you, Sir Jolyon. And a nice sum it would have made you, too.'

Cressida noticed Dotty shoot a look across to George Parish, but let it be.

'This is all moot, young lady, as I didn't—'

'I know, Sir Jolyon, you didn't kill Randolph. Your motive isn't the strongest and you're one of the only people who didn't sit down to eat or drink with him at all, or have an argument with him on the day of his death. Unlike you, Roscoe.'

The beleaguered gardener looked up from the chair that Kirby had escorted him to.

'I didn't kill him, Miss Fawcett, we spoke about this. I'm in love...' He dropped his head into his hands.

Cressida walked over to him and laid a gentle hand on his

shoulder. 'I'm so sorry, Roscoe, and you're right. Even though Randolph acted appallingly towards your father and was the catalyst to his business failing, and perhaps even his premature death, you didn't kill him. As you said to me, a happy man is not a killer. And Morwenna made you happy.' She squeezed his shoulder and moved back to her spot on the balustrade. 'Morwenna is really important here. That poor girl, a cousin of the Trevelyans and a first cousin to you, Jago, was killed by the same person who murdered Randolph.'

'But why?' Lady Trevelyan asked. 'Why would Jago kill Randolph and then Morwenna?'

'I didn't!' Jago blurted out. 'You all have to believe me, I didn't!'

'I'll come to that, Lady Trevelyan,' Cressida said over Jago's outburst and waited until Andrews had restrained the prisoner before carrying on.

'Morwenna's and Randolph's deaths are linked by one simple fact. She was working for the man who killed Randolph. But after Randolph died, she didn't want anything else to do with it. She said to me, the morning after the fancy-dress ball, that it had "all got a bit much" and, thanks to a fresh set of fingerprints and a bit of deduction, we know it was her who telephoned Andrews at the Bootlegger's Arms the evening before she was murdered and said she knew who the killer was.'

'Our enquiries of the household staff showed that no one else had used the telephone that evening,' Andrews said, adding quietly, 'And she promised to tell me everything the next morning.'

'But the killer overheard her and killed her that night,' Cressida continued.

The gathered guests stayed quiet until Jago, rattling his cuffs with his wrists, burst out again: 'It wasn't me. I didn't kill either of them.'

'And neither did you, George, luckily.' Cressida looked over to where Dotty was sitting rather close to the young archaeologist. 'Your museum paperwork checked out. Unlike most things you work with in Egypt, Randolph was worth a lot more to you alive than dead, if you'll excuse my crassness.'

'Excused.' George rubbed his hands on his thighs and looked mightily relieved as he exchanged a happy smile with Dotty.

'I don't understand, Miss Fawcett,' Andrews had started to look worried. 'I have arrested the right man, haven't I?'

'No, no...' Jago rattled his cuffs again. 'I'm not the killer.'

'Don't worry, Andrews, you've definitely got a criminal in those cuffs.' Cressida hopped off the balustrade once more and watched who noticed her leave the leather-bound ledger on the stone top, saving that little piece of information for later. 'Everyone hold that thought.' She raised a finger. 'I'll be back in a jiffy!'

Cressida headed into the house and emerged a moment or two later with one of the bronze lustrous Foo dogs from the mantelpiece.

'What's that then?' Andrews asked, and Cressida watched as Jago slumped even further into his chair.

Lord Trevelyan spoke up, his voice not as sure as usual and hesitant, to say the least. 'It's a seventeenth-century Chinese Foo dog statuette. Along with its partner, they form a priceless pair of late Ming dynasty tongshi, or bronze lions. It's one of those Western inaccuracies to call them dogs, they're...' He stopped talking as Cressida, deliberately and with quite some force, threw the Foo dog she'd been holding down onto the stone slabs of the terrace, causing it to splinter and shatter into a thousand white and bronze pieces.

42

'What the—!'

'By Jove!'

'She's mad!'

The voices of the Penbeagle House guests shouted and exclaimed as they either stood in shock or clasped their hands over their mouths. Only Jago, and not just because Andrews stood behind him with a firm hand on his shoulder, didn't react. Cressida noticed this as she tiptoed her way across the ceramic shards and picked up the small brown-paper-covered parcel that had obviously been hiding inside the Foo dog. As everyone's voices diminished, she held it up and then put it on the table.

'One slab of top-grade opium. And one, not very antique and now smashed Foo dog. I'm sorry if I gave you a heart attack, Lord Trevelyan, but I've been noticing how these Foo dogs change colour every so often in the drawing room, and when I thought about it, I realised that it coincided with when Jago came to visit.'

'But the sunlight in that room's extraordinary – how did you know it wasn't just the sunset causing it to look different?' Dotty asked, familiar with how much Cressida always loved the way the light changed colours in her decorating schemes.

'Because they looked different in the same light. Some days they looked bronze, and some days they looked a lot more golden. And it helped that I saw the same lustreware glaze being used at Pencarrick Pottery, and designs for ornaments that looked just like this. Talk of the Far East Company reproducing copies of antique objets d'art cemented it all in my mind.'

'But how did that opium get in there?' Lady Trevelyan asked, her hand clasped to her neck in shock.

Cressida looked at Selina, who was still pale with the shock of being all but kidnapped by her cousin. Selina met her eyes with a pleading look. Perhaps now was not the time for her to admit all to her parents, not without the support of Sebastian. Cressida nodded at her, and picked up the story.

'Jago.' Cressida said his name to gasps from the other guests. 'Despite going out of his way to tell me that the Far East Company had nothing to do with smuggling in opiates,' she glanced at Selina, 'I believe he's been at the heart if it.'

Lord Trevelyan glared at Jago.

'Drugs! Smuggled in via my ships?' He stood up and thumped his fist on the wrought-iron table that sent reverberations across it.

Cressida turned to Jago. 'Smuggled into Falmouth, and then you brought them here and Morwenna took them to Pencarrick Pottery, where they were smashed to reveal their contents, while locally made replacements stood on the mantelpiece.'

Jago looked stony-faced, giving nothing away, so Cressida turned to Dotty.

'Dot, that book you found of old Cornish. Could you fetch it?'

'Of course, Cressy.' Dotty slipped out of her seat and disappeared into the house, only to return a few agonising minutes later with the book from the library. 'Here's the chapter we were looking at, Old Cornish Names.'

'Thanks, Dot.' Cressida took the book from her friend, found the paragraph she wanted and looked back up at the guests. 'Andrews, you were telling us about how the Metropolitan Police are struggling to find the Head Shepherd. Well, here he is.' She pointed to Jago. 'Pen, meaning headland, or big, as you said in your speech the other night, Lord Trevelyan. But beagle doesn't just mean dog, it can come from the old Cornish for shepherd too.'

Those gathered, who had only just got over the shock of discovering Jago was a drug smuggler, gasped again.

She carried on. 'Jago used Penbeagle House as his supply chain, and his coded name.'

'And they come from our warehouse in Falmouth.' Lord Trevelyan repeated, processing the betrayal.

'Yes,' piped up Selina, finding her voice at last. 'And Cressida is right. Jago would have the Chinese ones smashed open and sell on the opium. Then he'd...' She paused and her mother reached a comforting hand over to rest on those of her daughter. An almost imperceptible shake of Lady Trevelyan's head in her daughter's direction confirmed to Cressida what she had suspected. Lady Trevelyan had had an inkling about her daughter's drug use. But maybe now wasn't the time for yet more dirty laundry to be aired in public. Andrews, unaware of these subtleties, was still looking at the package of drugs.

'Top-grade opium, and sold at top prices, I should imagine.' Andrews held the opium in front of him.

'Enough to restore someone's family fortunes, even,' Cressida said, looking at Jago. 'Someone whose side of the family had lost out to their richer cousins over the years. You, and your cousin Morwenna, hatched a plan I think to rebalance the family finances, not just by you joining your cousin's company and doing rather well, but by making a pretty penny dealing in drugs too. Sadly, Randolph had discovered your scheme, hence his trips to Pencarrick Pottery. He saw the smashed lustreware much like I did. He always did have a very good eye for detail.'

'Randolph knew...' Lord Trevelyan seemed unable to process it all. 'But why here, why bring them through Penbeagle?' He asked, his voice shaky, no doubt worried about how this would play out for his business.

Cressida sighed. 'Because no one would ever suspect anything here. This bastion of class and propriety. Penbeagle House was used as a sort of patsy, a safe house for the drugs to stay while the Head Shepherd found buyers and organised routes up to London, no doubt via more pottery that was soon to be making its way to Liberty and other fine establishments.'

Jago glared at Cressida as she continued. 'So, yes, there's a very good case to make that Jago Trengrouse, scared of being outed to the Trevelyans about his drug smuggling, killed Randolph.'

'Where would I have got the poison from?' Jago argued, his frustration palpable. 'I have no idea what hemlock looks like.'

'But your cousin Morwenna did.' Cressida looked at him. 'She grew up with her "wise woman" of a grandmother, and thanks to Andrews' investigation, we know that there's a patch of wild hemlock growing locally.'

'And she fainted there,' Mrs Dawkins chimed in. 'Though she'd often harvested it before.'

'Exactly, Mrs Dawkins.' Cressida smiled at the cook. 'So, Jago has the motive and his cousin Morwenna knew how to brew a deadly poison. So when we found Sebastian just now in the boathouse, walloped over the head with an oar, and we saw Jago rowing off with Selina... well, we put two and two together and—'

'Arrested our killer.' Andrews crossed his arms.

'Sorry, Andrews, but no, we put two and two together and got twenty-two, not four.'

'What *are* you on about?' Patrick asked, and even DCI Andrews looked at her inquisitively.

Cressida continued, 'Kirby, when you got to the boathouse, the door was locked, wasn't it?'

'Yes, miss,' the sergeant replied, nodding. 'I had to barge it open with my shoulder, miss, and I'm afraid to say, Your Ladyship,' he looked at Lady Trevelyan, 'that I quite took the lock off the jamb. I am sorry.'

Lady Trevelyan, who looked thoroughly exhausted, just waved a hand in forgiveness to the appreciative sergeant.

'So the door was locked, we can all agree. And Jago it seemed had clunked poor Sebastian over the head and made off with his cousin in a boat, having locked the door to hinder anyone following him.'

'But he didn't...' Selina sighed as Cressida rummaged in her pocket and pulled out the key that Ruby had found.

'No, he couldn't have done. I found this key to the boathouse on the path outside *after* we had burst our way in.' She held the key up and then passed it to DCI Andrews.

'You mean, the person who locked the door, did so from the outside?' he asked.

'Exactly, and that's rather hard to do if both of your hands are on oars, and you're on a boat in the middle of the creek.'

'By Jove, that's a point.' DCI Andrews held the key out in front of him and rubbed his bearded chin with his other hand.

Cressida turned to the cuffed man, who, for the first time since he was arrested, looked a little more hopeful of his situation. 'Jago, did you hit Sebastian over the head with an oar?'

'No, no, I didn't. Sebastian caught us up just as I was pushing off in the boat. I had to talk to Selina somewhere where she couldn't go off in a huff and I thought the boat would be the best place.'

'Selina, is this true?' Cressida turned to her.

'Yes. Jago found me while Sebastian was playing with the

lugger's rigging, and he was quite insistent.' She rubbed her wrist.

'It seems you have quite the explosive temper on you, Jago,' Cressida admonished him.

'I'm sorry we fought, Selly,' Jago sounded desperate, 'but I had to make you listen to me. Pointless now it's all out in the open, but I'd just heard you declare to the world that you'd tell your parents about your, well, you know, *poppy*. But of the murder charges, I'm innocent, I didn't kill your fiancé or Morwenna.'

'Then who did?' Lord Trevelyan asked, sitting forward in his seat. A murmur of 'yes, who?' followed from the others.

'Someone who had an even greater motive for killing one of us here than Jago. Jago did not want to be found out as a drug dealer, but he had no real motive to kill Randolph. With another illustrious fellow in the Far East Company, it was a chance for Jago to further increase his wealth. If he killed Randolph, he would have killed the golden egg from which all his replica golden eggs were to follow.'

'You mean, as with me, Lord Canterbury was worth more to him alive?' George asked.

'Yes, exactly that. He didn't need to kill Randolph to keep him quiet, he could have charmed him, or bribed him, or convinced Selina to stop... There was much more recourse to solve his problem than kill him. But, sadly, Randolph thought it *was* Jago, and in his last dying moments said the word Foo... not food, as we thought. And he was right. On the day he was killed, he'd argued with Selina about her drug dependency. Worried about her, he'd found the pottery where the fake Foo dogs were being made and had been to Falmouth to suss out where the originals were coming in on Far East Company ships. He'd pieced it together and discovered Jago's smuggling ring. And then, after a blowout of an argument with Jago, he realised he'd been poisoned and said "Foo...." to alert us. But the real murderer made use of the fact that we all thought he'd said, or meant, "food". And told me, that he'd seen Jago fighting with Randolph as they'd eaten crab sandwiches.' She paused for breath and looked around at the faces all rapt with what she was saying. Except one, who looked as cross as a cancelled Christmas. 'But it wasn't the crab sarnies that were poisoned with hemlock. In fact, the crab sandwiches never existed. Alfred, what did you tell me when you caught those lobsters earlier?'

Alfred smartened to attention. 'Right, yes, I said that Mrs Dawkins would be pleased as she hadn't had any decent crustaceans in for a while.'

'That's true, those were fine lobsters thank you, my lord,' Mrs Dawkins chipped in.

'So, no crab sandwiches existed, and even if they had, it bugged me when I heard them mentioned. Randolph hated lobster... and crab. Hated, because he was allergic to it. He would never have sat down to eat a plate of crab sandwiches. So, the person who told me about those was fibbing. No poisoned sandwiches ever existed as no sandwiches ever existed. So that leaves only one place left the poison could possibly have been; the tea served as part of the tea ceremony.'

'But we all drank that too, Jago, Patrick and I,' Lord Trevelyan pointed out. 'And we were fine. It couldn't have been poisoned.' He looked upset, confused, and shook his head as he spoke.

'Yours wasn't, Lord Trevelyan. And neither was Jago's... although the poisoner meant for it to be.'

'The poisoner?' Lord Trevelyan looked troubled. 'You mean Morwenna?'

'Morwenna created the poison, it's true. But not for Jago to use. She'd been making a tincture for her other cousin, perhaps for a few coins too, but not as a poison, she thought it was a cure.'

'What do you mean?'

'Hemlock, collected and processed in the right way, has been a centuries-old medicine for bad chests. Mrs Dawkins, you told us that.' The cook nodded, and Cressida carried on. 'Those with weak lungs can use it to help them breathe... or put the whole dose into a teapot to kill their cousin.'

'No...' Lord Trevelyan shook his head. 'This can't be.'

'But why didn't we get ill?' Jago asked.

'Only you were meant to, Jago.' Cressida reached into her pocket and pulled out the rather scrunched-up list that Kirby had taken by dictation from Maurice and smoothed out the creases. 'Aha...' Cressida ran her finger down the list. 'Buddha-shaped teapot with holes in the handle. I believe it's what's called an assassin's teapot. And it's what you used to try to kill Jago, wasn't it, Patrick?'

43

'What rot!' Patrick stood up, pushing his chair back with such force that it clattered to the ground and almost everyone gave a little jump, including him.

'Mrs Dawkins said there was no sign of the tea set, having assumed Morwenna cleared it up. Is not that strange? I wonder if Morwenna was taking the Buddha-shaped teapot back to the pottery to smash it on Sunday when I saw her there?'

'Patrick, is this true?' Lord Trevelyan asked his son, his face almost as pale as the white wrought-iron table.

All of a sudden, Patrick, who was shivering now and looking terribly exposed as he stood among his family and friends, bolted for the boathouse.

Kirby's whistle filled the air and, although Patrick had a head start, the athletic young sergeant easily caught up with him and wrestled him to the ground.

'Patrick!' Lady Trevelyan wailed. 'Why oh why, there must be some mistake. Cressida, how could you do this?'

'I'm sorry, Lady Trevelyan, I truly am. I know you invited me here to decorate your boathouse, not accuse your son of murder, but it was the boathouse and its key that gave it all away. And seeing its contents, those ropes and hooks and oars – so easy to overlook, yet so deadly in the wrong hands. Patrick felt like that too – he said so to me yesterday. He was being side-lined by his business-minded cousin, and his own father, and had to fight back.'

'It's always the quiet ones,' mumbled Sir Jolyon from behind his newspaper.

'But...' Dotty looked confused. 'How did he do it? Even though he got it wrong, how did he not kill everyone?'

'I assume it was a slip as he poured the tea. You see the teapot is designed to have two chambers within it. And there's a hole above and below the handle, as it's described in this cata-logue Kirby so beautifully transcribed for me. When you place your thumb over one hole, it creates a vacuum seal and the other chamber's liquid is poured. It means a poisonous drink can be poured from the same teapot as a non-poisonous one, and no one suspects a thing.'

'Except the smell of the poison?' Alfred chipped in.

'Disguised by the strong aromas of the green tea.' Cressida saw Dotty pull a face from the corner of her eye. She carried on, 'As soon as Patrick realised that Randolph had received the poison, which took an hour or so to do its gruesome thing, he had to work out how to cover his tracks.'

Jago, who'd been following with much interest, exhaled, then acknowledged, 'I gifted him that one, I suppose. He must have seen me arguing with Morwenna.'

'I certainly did.' Cressida looked at him. 'Carry on.'

'She said it wasn't the worth the money anymore, the smug-gling,' Jago replied. 'With Randolph dead, which, of course, I didn't know she'd had anything to do with, I think she wanted out. A fresh start away from all of it with Roscoe. I let my temper get the better of me.' Jago hung his head in shame.

'And it really put you in the soup, too. Seeing her fight with you meant that Patrick could frame you, Jago, for the murders –

Randolph's, and Morwenna's yet to come. If his own poison hadn't worked, then the hangman's noose was a close second.'

'Why did Patrick need to murder Morwenna?' Dotty asked.

There was silence as Patrick was escorted back to the terrace by Sergeant Kirby. Every guest turned to face him. Lady Trevelyan mouthed what looked like a prayer as she grasped her daughter's hand, her knuckles almost white with tension. Lord Trevelyan was ashen-faced, but he stood and faced his son.

'Did you murder Morwenna, Patrick?'

Patrick hung his head.

'Why, Pat, why did you do it?' Selina whispered, barely able to get the words out.

Patrick looked at his family, then at Cressida and DCI Andrews.

'I overheard her on the telephone to you.' He wiped his eyes with his cuffed hands. 'She said she'd reveal the murderer and I couldn't let her, not when it was all coming together.'

'She'd been helping you for years, hadn't she?' Cressida asked him, her tone more gentle than you might think a murderer deserved.

'His chest...' Lady Trevelyan murmured.

Patrick sniffed, his eyes more watery than ever. 'Yes, Morwenna had been making me a hemlock tincture for years. It's why I thought that, even if I made a mistake with that dratted teapot, I'd probably survive as I've built up a tolerance for the stuff.'

'You did get it wrong, though, didn't you?' Cressida coaxed the confession out of him.

Patrick nodded slowly. 'I didn't want Canterbury to die. Then, Selly, you started talking about marrying Sebastian and I didn't want you to get into trouble and the police try to hang it on you.' He looked from his sister to Jago, a real rage showing now in a flare of his nostrils. 'Not when Cousin Jago should hang, hang for taking my family business away from me, smarming his way into Father's affections. What next? The house! I could have done it, Father, I could have run the company and the estate like you do...'

'Come on now.' Kirby led Patrick away as he ranted, his mother and father pushing back their chairs and following him out to where the local constables had arrived with a police van to take him away.

'So am I free to go?' Jago asked DCI Andrews rather hopefully.

'Not on your life,' Andrews replied, keeping a firm hand on his shoulder. 'You'll be charged with drug smuggling and whatever else the Excise men want to try for.'

'He's not the only one they'll be interested in.' Cressida reached behind her for the leather-bound ledger on the balustrade.

'Oh, the rum,' Dotty exclaimed. 'I'd quite forgotten all about that.'

'I think Mr and Mrs Nangower rather hoped we all had.' Cressida turned to them.

'I say,' Catherine Bly blustered, 'you can't go accusing upstanding members of the community of smuggling rum.'

'Upstanding members of the community who happened to be sailing down the creek hours before the Excise men were due to take the stash away? Who have a cocktail named after them in the Bootlegger's Arms? Whose ancestors lost their wealth to huge fines in the 1700s and never regained it? Whose house is falling apart and teacups are chipped?'

'Steady on, old girl.' Monty Nangower looked affronted. 'Nothing wrong with those teacups. Been in the family for generations.'

'Just like smuggling has?' Cressida held the ledger up and then opened up the first page. 'PH Vol VI. What could that mean?'

'Public houses?' Dotty asked. 'There's a few listed in there receiving the contraband.'

'Penbeagle House?' George said, looking at Jago. 'Another code for the old pile?'

'No, Peacehaven. As in Peacehaven Gables, the Nangowers' crumbling family seat.'

'Crumbling's a bit much,' Monty Nangower grumbled.

'Still, the money from the smuggled rum helps keep the wolf from the door. And I can't say I blame you. It was good stuff!' Cressida looked at Dotty, who giggled.

'Still, contraband is contraband.' Andrews asserted as more constables and members of the Coast Guard arrived to assist in the arrest. 'Mr and Mrs Nangower, I'm afraid you're under arrest, too.'

'And what about me?' Catherine Bly bustled forward.

'Shh, Catherine.' Celia rested a hand on her friend's arm. 'We need you to look after Peacehaven for us.'

Andrews looked at the spindly journalist, her threadbare cardigan unravelling at the cuffs. 'Miss Bly, if I were you, I'd keep your mouth shut. And maybe get your typewriter out. This could be the scoop of the century.'

44

'Poor Lord and Lady Trevelyan,' Dotty said as she sipped from a steaming cup of coffee the next morning on the terrace. 'Their only son a murderer and their favourite nephew or cousin, or whatever Jago is, a drug dealer.'

'Not to mention their daughter now marrying a lowly Foreign Office clerk,' Cressida said, hoping that Dotty would pick up on her sarcasm. She did, and threw a well-aimed piece of toast crust at Cressida's head. Once it had rebounded off her forehead, it found itself devoured on the ground by Ruby, who had already had a plate of perfectly cooked chicken livers this morning.

'Poor Selina then too,' Dotty said and stuck her tongue out at her friend. 'And poor, poor Lord Canterbury. I'm sorry he had to die so that Selina could marry the man she loves.'

'What about you, Dot? I thought you and George were hitting it off splendidly?' Cressida asked, and Dotty blushed behind her coffee cup. She took a sip before answering.

'George is a dream. I do like him, Cressy, though I'm determined to take this one slowly and not feel rushed into anything, unlike with Basil.'

'Good idea, Dot. And I'm sorry that his idea about replacing Randolph at the Far East Company never came to anything after Jago was led off in cuffs. Or at least I assume that meant his opportunity was lost?'

'We'll see. He wants to let Lord Trevelyan cope with Patrick and Jago's trials in peace before he starts pestering for a job, but I think noises were made last night which have given him cause for hope.'

'Fingers crossed, Dot. When Andrews checked over his paperwork, the letter of recommendation from Randolph to the museum, apparently it said all sorts of nice things about George. And don't forget that rich uncle.' If Cressida believed winking ever had a place in decent society, she would have added one as a little garnish to her words.

'I'm sorry you didn't find anyone to catch your eye, Cressy. There was a very handsome grizzly bear at the fancy-dress ball, but I suppose things did all get a bit murdery that night, which puts one off somewhat.'

'Plus, you know my views on marriage, Dot. There's nothing I need in this world more than my little motorcar, my pug, my independence—'

'And me as a close fourth. I know.' Dotty sipped her coffee. 'Did you know Alfred got pinched by one of those lobsters?'

'No? Oh poor Alfred.' Cressida laughed.

'George told me that he said he'd withstand multiple pinches from the most powerful of claws if it meant getting you some lobster.' Dotty peered at Cressida over the top of her coffee cup.

'Dotty...' Cressida warned her friend, but the thought that Alfred had suffered in his mission to bring her one of her favourite treats did make her smile. 'Turns out it was a very important lobster.'

'A crime-solving one, no less.' Dotty laughed. Cressida

chuckled too. 'So,' Dotty continued, 'I'm just going to leave it there and say Alfred got you a lobster.'

'Yes.' Cressida smiled at her friend. 'I know.'

They sat in silence for a little while, listening to the birds in the trees and the distant slap of waves on the rocks down in the cove. The lugger and some other fishing boats gently clanked and splashed down by the jetty the other end of the lawn and, by and by, maids came out and cleared away breakfast and refreshed the coffee cups.

'It's a shame Lady Trevelyan can't go through with her plans for the boathouse, but what with it being a crime scene and them having more important things on their mind, I can't blame her for deciding to leave it for now,' Cressida said matter-of-factly.

'And I can't blame her for asking us to toddle off at our earliest convenience either,' Dotty added.

'Yes, she doesn't want us hanging around like limpets on a lugger. I suppose that's to be expected as I did just accuse her son of being a murderer. We'd better say our goodbyes and start the drive back up to London, Dotty,' Cressida said, pushing her chair back and picking up Ruby.

'Oh.' Dotty paled slightly. 'Yes. The drive back to London...' She rolled her eyes and managed a little 'good-o'.

Cressida ignored her sarcasm. 'Come now, chum, it won't be that bad and I promise I won't take my eyes off the road or my hands off the wheel for a moment, not for a minute of all those glorious speedy straights and twisty turns.'

Dotty gulped.

'And just think, Dot. We have that marvellous invitation to the Highlands in the diary for next month... a whole 450 miles of motoring. Fancy a lift?'

A LETTER FROM FLISS

Dear reader,

I want to say a huge thank you for choosing to read *Death by a Cornish Cove*. If you did enjoy it, and want to keep up to date with all my latest releases, just sign up at the following link. Your email address will never be shared and you can unsubscribe at any time.

www.bookouture.com/fliss-chester

I hope you loved *Death by a Cornish Cove*, the second in the Hon. Cressida Fawcett series. If you did, I would be very grateful if you could write a review. I'd love to hear what you think – did you feel transported down to the West Country and on the hunt for a killer, too? Reviews from readers like you can make such a difference helping new readers, who will hopefully love the cosy crime setting of 1920s English country houses, discover my books for the first time.

I love hearing from my readers – you can get in touch on my Facebook page, through Twitter, Instagram or my website.

Thanks,

Fliss Chester

KEEP IN TOUCH WITH FLISS

www.flisschester.co.uk

 facebook.com/flisschester
twitter.com/socialwhirlgirl

ACKNOWLEDGEMENTS

Many hands make light(er) work... and I couldn't have written this book without the help and guidance from my fabulous editorial team at Bookouture. My editor, Rhianna Louise, has definitely improved this book tenfold with her amazing advice and wise words, and without the eye for detail that my copyeditor Jade Craddock and proofreader Anne O'Brien have, I'm sure it would be littered with typos! Sarah Hardy and Jess Readett in the publicity department deserve buckets of thanks for really getting this book out there and blogged about and reviewed – you both do a marvellous job.

Thanks also to my agent Emily Sweet, who is also always on hand with words of advice – and a very useful knowledge on the history of food, saving me from 'ploughing' into a big mistake in this book!

I have a brilliant bunch of author friends who not only act as a 'hive mind' for random questions and queries, but offer unswerving support and WhatsApp high-fives on a daily basis. So thank you, my fellow criminally-minded authors, and especially Tim Kinsey, who read the first of these Cressida Fawcett books and gave it a big cosy crime thumbs up, as well as designing all sorts of wonderful graphics for me to ping out on social media. Thank you, Tim.

Ideas for books come from all sorts of places, but I have to thank my niece Izzy Culty for giving me the idea of using the assassin's teapot. Who would have thought that a family lunch (luckily a non-poisonous one!) would have ended with Izzy showing me YouTube videos of how these teapots work – and the idea for a very useful way to kill someone!

Speaking of family, mine are, as always, amazingly supportive of the time I spend glued to my keyboard and screen; my wonderful husband Rupert especially. And hopefully my mum, who also plants iron bedsteads in herbaceous borders, will agree that I'm living up to her credo of being 'anything but dull, darling!'

CPSIA information can be obtained
at www.ICGtesting.com
Printed in the USA
BVHW030033030223
657809BV00002B/12